"You are looking very pleased with yourself," said a deep voice to her left.

Her heart skipped a beat and her lips involuntarily curved upward. She didn't need to turn to know who had ridden up beside her. Erik's blue-eyed gaze was never without an amused twinkle. Every afternoon he would ride next to her and keep her company. She loved how he always made her laugh, and she admitted to herself, that these interludes were the favorite parts of the day.

"That's because I am very pleased with myself," she replied lightly. "Only five days ago I didn't know how to ride a horse."

"And here I was thinking you'd obviously had a full knight's training you ride so well."

Laughter gurgled out of her. This was what all their exchanges were like—he teased her and she played along. Even though everything between them was light and relaxed, her heart still raced whenever they spoke.

Author Note

Linota Leofric is one of my favourite heroines and I've loved writing her story. Her beloved father was executed when she was only a child, and she's lived in almost complete seclusion since then.

The story begins just as she is finding her way in the world for the first time, and I love that everything she comes across is new and exciting. She's feisty, young and courageous, and she looks at every adventure with optimism.

My hero, Erik Ward, has had everything thrown at him, but he always gets up and fights back. In a world that's dark and lonely, Linota is a burst of light who turns his life upside down and gives him a reason to hope.

These two characters were never meant to have their own book, but as I wrote about the other Leofric siblings, these two started talking to me and they really wanted to share their sides of the story. I hope you enjoy what they have to say!

This is the last title in my The House of Leofric series. I've really enjoyed spending time with the Leofric siblings and the people they come to love. I'm going to be sad not being with them every day, but I'm so pleased that I got to tell their stories.

I hope you enjoy!

ELLA MATTHEWS

The Warrior's Innocent Captive

ISBN-13: 978-1-335-50616-0

The Warrior's Innocent Captive

Harlequin Enterprises ULC
22 Adelaide St. West, 40th Floor
Toronto, Ontario M5H 4E3, Canada
www.Harlequin.com

Printed in U.S.A.

Ella Matthews lives and works in beautiful South Wales. When not thinking about handsome heroes, she can be found walking along the coast with her husband and their two children (probably still thinking about heroes, but at least pretending to be interested in everyone else).

Books by Ella Matthews

Harlequin Historical

The Warrior Knight and the Widow
Under the Warrior's Protection
The Warrior's Innocent Captive

Visit the Author Profile page
at Harlequin.com.

To Andrew

Chapter One

Ogmore's fortress—winter 1331

Candlelight flickered from sconces high up on the Great Hall's walls. The press of people watching the various entertainments kept the temperature from plummeting on the cold winter's evening.

Erik Ward stood still, his arms folded in front of his chest. In front of him, puppeteers performed a ribald comedy. Those around him laughed as something happened, but he missed the action. Opposite him, across the semi-circle of spectators, stood Linota Leofric. Her long, golden hair was tied back in an intricate braid and, unlike the other women around her, no ornament adorned the plait. The way she clapped her slender hands in delight at the sketch amused him far more than the comedy she was enjoying.

He wasn't the only one to notice her. Every so often a man would try to catch her eye. One or two had even struck up a conversation, but after a moment or two she would politely turn away, her interest once more caught by the entertainment. If he were the sort of man who could pay court to her, he would have thought up an original idea to capture and hold her attention. As it was, he was content to watch her enjoy herself.

Erik moved slightly as a man stepped in close behind him, the stranger's heavy wheezing too close for comfort.

Linota laughed out loud and Erik swallowed. He couldn't help but laugh at his reaction; he was acting like the kitchen boy he'd once been, mesmerised by the prettiest girl in the fortress.

He'd been this way since he'd first caught a glimpse of Linota over a month ago. He was glad he and his liege, Jarin Ashdown, the Earl of Borwyn, were away from home. It would do no good to the fearsome reputation he'd spent years cultivating, if Borwyn's men could see him mooning after a pretty young woman he'd not actually spoken to yet.

A heavy hand settled on his shoulder and he frowned. His notoriety normally preceded him and now that he and Borwyn had been guests at Ogmore's fortress for so long, everyone should know that reputation was not an exaggeration. He wasn't the sort of man you clapped on the shoulder. He was the man you stayed well clear of.

'I have news of Mary,' said a thick nasally voice below his left ear.

Ice flooded through Erik's veins. No one had spoken to him of his younger sister in years. Even when she'd lived in the same fortress as him, he'd worked hard to keep her hidden. After she'd left he'd searched for her, but he'd found no sign. It was as if she had been wiped out of existence.

'Meet me by the stables,' the voice commanded.

The hand disappeared from his shoulder. Erik whipped round to see who had been talking to him, but whoever it was had already melted into the crowds of people milling around the puppeteers.

He took one last look at Linota Leofric and glared at a pimply man who stepped near her. The man paled and reared back as if he'd been punched. Erik nodded, pleased his reputation had produced *some* results tonight.

The night was cloudless and a sharp wind bit through Erik's clothes as he kept to the shadows thrown by the towering walls of the keep. Laughter from a nearby group of guards had him flattening himself against the rough stone and he laughed to himself as he straightened. He was doing nothing wrong, so why was he acting like a criminal?

He would meet with this stranger, who would probably try to feed him some nonsense in return for Erik using his influence with Borwyn. Erik could dismiss the man and get back to the festivities…and to watching Linota.

He shook his head; he wasn't watching her, he was protecting her. Little did she know that a large dowry had recently been added to her name, and her sister's, by the hugely influential Earl of Ogmore. It made her an excellent choice of bride for Erik's liege, Borwyn, and Erik always guarded Borwyn's interests. Linota's wide, blue eyes and gentle curves made this assignment pleasanter than most.

Only Erik and Jarin knew how much Jarin needed the money and connections marrying Linota would bring. If the thought made Erik want to drive a fist through somebody's face, then he'd just have to ignore the sensation. If she didn't become Borywn's wife, she wouldn't become Erik's either. Linota was not a potential bride for a bastard-born steward, her huge dowry placing her so far out of his reach he might as well aim for the moon.

He came to a stop by the stables and waited. The wind whipped through his woollen clothes and he wished he'd had time to pull on his cloak, his tunic didn't provide enough warmth. He rubbed his hands together as the cold cut to his bones. He'd give the stranger a little longer and then he was returning to the delights of the Hall.

A shuffling to his left made him turn his head. A short, rotund man stood in the darkness.

'Well?' said Erik.

'Erik Ward,' said the man softly.

Erik groaned. This stranger clearly had the drama of a stage player with this lurking about in the dark and demands for secret meetings. Erik didn't want this encounter to last any longer than absolutely necessary. He had things to do. 'You said you have news of my sister.'

'I do.'

'And what do you want in exchange for the news?'

'Ah, straight to the heart of the matter. I like it that you are so ready to make an exchange.' Erik rolled his eyes. He was ready for no such thing, but he'd wait until this character had revealed his plans before letting on. He let the man continue. 'You're right, I do want something in return, but for now we'll settle for proof of my sincere intentions. Here, take this parcel. When you've had time to take a look at it I'll be in touch.'

'What's in here?' Erik took the proffered small package and tucked it into his belt. There was nothing the man could give him that would hold any interest.

'You'll see,' said the stranger, who turned and disappeared down the way he had come.

Erik sighed and strolled away from the shadows.

This wasn't the first time someone had tried to take advantage of his position and it wouldn't be the last. This latest one certainly had a flare for drama, though.

Linota stepped away from the puppet show. It was vastly entertaining but there were so many things to see and who knew when she'd get the opportunity to do so again. She'd not seen anything like this celebration in the first eighteen years of her life.

In the corner of the Hall a juggler tossed batons of fire through the air, catching and throwing them effortlessly. She watched, mesmerised, until her attention was caught by the conversation happening next to her.

'There he is again,' hissed a woman. 'What I wouldn't give for an evening with that.'

'I'd take a whole night. Look at the way his muscles move under his clothes. I hear he knows exactly how to please a woman. I imagine it would be hard and fast.' The two women giggled.

Linota looked in the direction the women were staring. She was unsurprised when she saw it was Erik Ward who had caught their attention. The man was standing just inside the entrance to the Hall, rubbing his large hands together vigorously, as if he'd been outside for some time. But hadn't she seen him watching the puppet show not that long ago? His tall, muscular frame was hard to miss as he towered over nearly everyone else in the Hall.

She'd felt his heavy gaze upon her more than once, but whenever she'd looked back at him he was frowning. She'd tried to dismiss it, but she couldn't help the strange flare of awareness that shot through her every time she realised his eyes were on her.

She tugged at her tight braid and wished she'd had the confidence to tell her sister she wanted to wear something looser.

'He's coming over,' said one of the women behind her.

Linota turned her attention back to the jugglers rather than watch Erik approach. She didn't want him to know how fascinated she was about the way he moved. With his thick, muscular body he should be cumbersome, but he carried himself with the grace of a cat stalking its prey. While other women, including her older sister, Katherine, sighed about Erik's liege, the Earl of Borwyn, Linota had watched his steward. Unlike Borwyn, Erik existed on the fringes, always watching, always an outsider. She'd never spoken to the man, but she had a feeling he was a bit like her, waiting for life to start happening, biding his time until he could break free.

'Mistress Leofric.' Linota jumped when a man standing next to her addressed her directly. She'd been so busy thinking about Erik Ward that she hadn't seen anyone approach. 'It is very good to see you and your sister out of your chambers. A beautiful little thing like you shouldn't be hidden in the dark.'

The hairs on the back of Linota's neck stood to attention at being called a 'thing', but Katherine had ingrained in her the need to be polite to everyone they met. The taint of treason had hung around their family like an unwanted stench for so long. Today their brother had married into the influential Ogmore family. The wedding and the celebration was the first time she and Katherine had left their chamber for this long in years. It was liberating and exciting, but Linota knew that it could all be over in an instant if she made the wrong move.

So she turned to smile politely at the speaker and then wished she hadn't. The man's thick lips were wet and there were flecks of food in his long beard. His gaze ran over her body and she shuddered.

Involuntarily, she stepped backwards and hit a wall. A wall that hadn't been there a moment ago. She glanced upwards and realised she'd hit the solid muscle of Erik Ward's chest.

'Leave the lady alone, Mabon.' Erik's deep voice rumbled through her.

Mabon paled and didn't wait to be told twice. He scuttled away, not even saying good evening as he departed quickly.

'Thank you kindly, sir.' She stepped away from him and turned to look up at him. Her gaze met his piercing blue eyes and her heart fluttered wildly in her chest.

'It was no bother,' he said, his eyes twinkling in the dim light of the room. 'Mabon is a foolish little toad. I enjoyed putting him in his place.' His lips curved into a half-smile and Linota couldn't help but smile back.

'I'm Erik Ward.'

'I know.'

He raised an eyebrow and heat spread across her cheeks. She didn't want him to think she had noticed him particularly, although she had. He was hard to miss. Most other men in the room were polished, but Erik was a little rough around the edges with his hair ruffled and worn long to his shoulders.

'The Earl of Borwyn has caused quite a stir by coming to Ogmore,' she floundered. 'Even though I've been sequestered in my rooms it is hard to miss the excitement of his arrival along with his entourage.'

Erik's lips quirked. 'Thank you for putting me in my place.'

Linota felt herself become even hotter. She was not experienced with talking to men. Was this a flirtation? From the way those women were talking, Erik was experienced in a way she was not. Not one of the men who had approached this evening had caused her stomach to turn over in the way it was doing now. She was hooked on Erik's piercing gaze and couldn't turn her head away.

'Um... I'm Linota Leofric,' she said.

'I know.'

She giggled; she couldn't help herself. Erik Ward had a reputation of being the Earl of Borwyn's muscle, the one who fought the Earl's battles, and with his broad shoulders she didn't doubt that the rumours were true. But now that she was talking to him she could see the tell-tale humour in his gaze which suggested there was more to him than just mindless thuggery.

'Are you going to ask how I know?' he asked.

She shrugged. 'Everyone knows who I am. I'm the

younger daughter of the infamous John Leofric, traitor to the Crown. One of the two daughters who hardly
ever come out of their chambers because their mother
has gone insane due to the upset of being thrown from
our castle when I was only a young child. My brother
is the one whose wedding celebrations we're attending
and, while not infamous, he is certainly well known due
to the hideous scarring on his face. I would guess that
there isn't a single person in here who doesn't know my
name or my family history.'

Erik raised both eyebrows. 'I wasn't going to put it
quite like that.'

'Oh?'

'I was going to say I know who you are because
you are by far and away the most beautiful woman in
the room.'

Linota's breath caught in her throat and her lips fell
open in shock.

She'd been told many times that she was pretty, but
that was by her sister. To be told so by this hulking
stranger was a very different experience. The strange
swooping sensation in her stomach began to spread
through her whole body, making her heart race faster
and the fine hairs on her forearms stand to attention.

Erik's gaze dropped to her open mouth and a look
she didn't understand crossed his face. The noise of the
crowd dropped away as if it was only the two of them
stood in the Great Hall.

For one long, heady moment she thought he was
going to kiss her, but then he smiled and said, 'But
I'm sure you hear comments on how beautiful you are

all the time. So tell me, are you enjoying the evening, Mistress Leofric?'

The sounds of the room rushed back in and Erik's eyes twinkled with amusement, as if the intense moment had never happened. Perhaps it hadn't. Maybe Erik went around telling all women they were beautiful.

Those women she'd overheard had been talking about spending the night with him and she wasn't so naive that she didn't know what that meant. It was best not to engage in a flirtation with this man. She couldn't give him the impression she was fascinated with him, even if that was the truth. Her family were depending on her marrying well and dallying with a steward wasn't a good idea. He wasn't high enough in importance even if he did fill out his tunic well. It wouldn't hurt to be polite though.

'I love everything about the evening,' she answered honestly.

'Have you tried any of the entertainments yourself?'

'No! I don't think juggling fire is a good idea.'

He smiled, a large warm grin that lit up his face and made him appear younger. 'I meant the skittles or the horseshoe throwing, the things put on for the guests to do rather than watch.'

The heat that had slowly been easing from her face flooded back. Of course he meant the games; she folded her hands into the fabric of her dress.

'No, I've not tried the skittles. I've never played and haven't the faintest idea what to do.'

'Ah, it's easy. Come on. Let's have a game.'

'Oh… I…' She really should try to find her sister. Or, if she couldn't, she should at least stay away from this man, but her body didn't seem to be listening to her head and she followed his broad shoulders through the crowd. Groups separated to allow him to pass, but nobody stopped to talk to them, eyeing them, instead, with slight disdain. She was used to such disparaging looks being directed at her, but she couldn't understand why they were aimed at Erik as well.

'It's simple,' said Erik as he picked up a small wooden ball. 'Throw this at the skittles over there and see how many you can knock over. The one who knocks over the most wins. I'll go first.'

Linota clapped her hands in delight as Erik's ball knocked down every last one of the skittles.

He grinned at her and made his way towards the fallen target. 'I'll set it up again and then you can have a go.'

He strode back and passed her the ball, his fingers brushing hers as he did so. Linota gasped at the shock of his touch, but he didn't seem to notice anything out of the ordinary. Her hand shook as she took her place. She tried to steady it as she lined the ball up, but her body betrayed her and the ball flew wide of the mark.

Erik smiled and handed her another ball without comment.

Her next three goes produced the same result. Her fourth attempt knocked down two skittles and she yelped in delight, clapping her hands with joy. Who would have thought that knocking things down could be so satisfying?

Erik grinned and bent down to pick up another ball. As he did so, a loose bundle of cloth fell from his belt. As it hit the floor the binding fell apart and a small object skittered towards her, coming to rest at her feet. She bent down and picked it up.

'Oh, this is pretty. Where did you get it from?' she said, admiring the miniature horse carved from wood. The detail was exquisite, making it look as if the animal was in fluid motion. A fine chain was threaded through a loop, making the object into a necklace, but it was the carving that held her attention. It was small, but so intricate. She tilted her hand to hold it up to the nearest candle, but before she could study it any more it was whisked from her fingers.

Linota inhaled sharply and looked across at Erik.

Gone was the laughing man of a few moments ago and in his place was the wild warrior she'd heard about. Erik's lips were stretched thin, his jaw clamped tight. His eyes were flashing with an emotion she couldn't read. His gaze snapped to hers and she took a step backwards, her fingers trembling.

Erik's eyes were filled with rage and they looked straight through her. His thick muscled arms were tensed as if they were ready to tear someone apart.

She opened her mouth to say something and then faltered. The slight movement snapped him out of his trance and his eyes cleared.

'I'm sorry, Mistress Leofric, I must go.'

He nodded briefly and then strode past her. She stood, watching him get swallowed up by the crowds, wondering what on earth had just happened. She touched her throat, her pulse beating wildly underneath her fingertips.

Already it felt as if the strange encounter hadn't happened.

Chapter Two

Erik passed a brush over his horse's already glistening coat. Cai didn't protest even as Erik went over the same area again and again.

That necklace! He hadn't seen it in years. Images, long buried, assailed him. Mary, his sweet little sister with brown eyes so huge in her thin face, had loved horses. Whenever he'd had a spare minute he'd tucked her tiny hand in his and taken her down to the stables—anything to see joy on her face during a childhood of hardship. The stable master hadn't minded the two quiet children and, if he wasn't busy, he would hold Mary up so that she could stroke a docile mare's nose. Those quiet, still moments were Erik's favourite memories from his early years. Hell, they were his only good memories of that time.

Erik had carved Mary the small wooden horse and had managed to scrape enough coins together to buy a thin chain. He'd presented it to her one Christmastide. From the time he'd given it to her until he'd last seen her she'd worn it around her neck. It had cost him almost nothing to make, but to her it was priceless.

He leaned his forehead against Cai's flank. He'd sworn to his sister that he would always protect her. He'd failed. Within a year after he'd given her the carved horse she'd been sold into a marriage with a much older man. She'd begged Erik to come and get her as soon as he could. He'd sworn that he would. It was a promise he'd not been able to fulfil. No matter how much he'd searched, he couldn't find her. His bastard of a father had made sure her location was hidden. He'd never wanted Erik to be happy. Now the man was dead so Erik couldn't beat the truth out of him no matter how much he wanted to.

'Here you are, Erik Ward. You're a hard man to find.'

Erik whirled round, pulling a dagger from his belt and pressing it into the throat of the stranger from last night.

'Where is my sister?' he growled.

A sleepless night had done nothing for his temper. He wanted to gut this man for playing games over something so important. As much as his arm shook with the desire to plunge his dagger into the stranger's thick neck, however, he didn't. He needed him alive for now.

There was no answer to his question. Only a slight thinning of the man's lips showed that Erik's words had registered at all, or perhaps it was the blade pressing into him that drew his attention.

'Where is she? And what have you done to her? She would never have parted from that necklace. Never!'

'You will not manhandle me into giving you any answers, Erik Ward.'

Erik counted to ten in his mind to stop himself from running the runt through. He shoved the man away from him before he could give into the temptation. 'Start speaking.'

'I'm Simon de Bevoir,' said the man, unnecessarily straightening his clothes, as if Erik and he had been fighting.

Erik's stomach plummeted. He'd heard that name before. Spies in Borwyn's enemy's castle had spoken of de Bevoir. He was rumoured to do all of Lord Garbodo's dirty work, much like Erik did for Jarin. The only difference was that Jarin was an honourable man and Garbodo was a piece of vermin.

'I should have known. You're the little toad who works for Garbodo, the greasy-haired sot who's after my liege's land.'

De Bevoir flinched, but held Erik's gaze, 'I don't think you're in the position to call me or Garbodo names, Erik Ward. We both know where you come from after all.'

Erik felt heat sweep up his neck at the reference to his unknown parentage, but he held his dagger steady. 'Whatever it is that you want, you can forget it. I will not work against the Earl of Borwyn. He has my complete loyalty.'

De Bevoir raised a bushy eyebrow. 'And what about Mary?'

Erik paused. Jarin did have his loyalty, but... His liege was a fully trained knight, fluent in the art of warfare and politics. Mary was alone in the world with only Erik to look after her. 'Tell me about her.'

'I'm afraid to say your sister is dead,' said de Bevoir.

Air rushed out of Erik's lungs. He dropped to his knees, his dagger clattering to the floor as a piercing pain spread through his body. He'd failed, failed to protect the one person he should have spent his life keeping safe. His existence was pointless. He should have been the one to die, not his sweet, vulnerable sister.

'I'm sorry to be so blunt, but our time is precious,' continued de Bevoir. 'Your sister had a daughter. Isabel turned six this past summer. Her father is also dead. She has no one in the world apart from you. As much as I'd love to hand her over to your guardianship my liege has certain…how can I put this?' De Bevoir paused dramatically, his hand pressed to his chest.

Erik had never hated someone so much. The loathing burned through his veins as if it were a living thing.

A faint smile crossed de Bevoir's lips, as if he was enjoying this very much. 'My liege has a simple requirement from you. It's a fair exchange, I think, for the life of your niece.'

Erik stood slowly, his gaze never leaving de Bevoir's face. He wanted to run his dagger through the man, but he held his breath and waited.

De Bevoir watched him warily, but when Erik said nothing he continued. 'I understand Borwyn and you are escorting the Mistresses Leofric to their new home with their brother and his new wife. It's a journey that will take about a week.'

Erik nodded slowly. It was a week to which he been looking forward. A week in which he'd been hoping to coax more smiles out of the delightful Linota. Although she was denied to him, that didn't mean he couldn't enjoy such innocent pleasures.

A lead weight settled in his stomach as he knew he wasn't worthy of even that simple enjoyment. How could he be when he had failed someone he had sworn to protect?

De Bevoir continued. 'You are to ensure that journey isn't shortened in any way. It must take a week, longer if possible.'

Erik closed his eyes. That was a simple enough demand. It was likely they wouldn't return to Borwyn in that many days anyway and the journey would be longer if Jarin decided he did want to marry one of the Leofric sisters. The request was obviously hiding some bigger plot. Garbodo had to be planning some sort of attack during that week, an attack that could potentially destroy his friend and liege. Was it worth betraying the man he'd known most of his life for a child he'd never met?

He swallowed. He had to know the truth. 'What else do you want?'

De Bevoir fiddled with the end of his sleeves. 'I'd also like the names of some of Borwyn's men who might be open to a bit of bribery. That's it.'

Erik inhaled sharply. This was it. This was what the whole exchange had been leading up to. Unable to stay still, he paced down the length of the stable and back, stopping directly in front of de Bevoir. 'You want me to betray Borwyn, my liege and closest companion, for a girl I have no evidence actually exists.'

'I'm not asking for much from you.' De Bevoir ran his hands down the length of his straggly beard and smiled. 'I could have lied to you and told you Mary was still alive, but I didn't. Isabel does exist. I asked her if she knew about her mother's brother. She has heard of you. Her mama always said you'd come for them, that you were going to buy them somewhere to live, somewhere away from where you both grew up. It seems you let her mama down. Surely you don't want to let the little girl down, too?'

Erik stilled. He had talked about such a place with Mary, a sanctuary where they could both live. Even though none of his searches for her had been successful, he had bought them a place as soon as he'd been able to. It was only a simple peasant's cottage with some farmable land surrounding it. It wasn't a luxurious dwelling, although he'd furnished it well, but it would be safe, far away from the place where they had spent their miserable childhoods. It was his secret. Nobody knew about it, not even Jarin.

He returned his dagger to his belt and leaned his shoulder against Cai, the animal's solid bulk grounded him.

'You'll be leaving for Castle Swein soon,' said de Bevoir. 'I need an answer and, just to make things perfectly clear between us, if your answer is "no", then Garbodo will keep custody of Isabel.' He paused. 'She's going to be pretty, like her mother. I'm sure there'll be plenty of low-born men keen to take a young wife.'

Impotent rage flooded through Erik. He'd failed to keep Mary from such a fate—could he allow the same thing to happen to her daughter?

If he betrayed Jarin now there was one way he could make it up to him. He could promote the match between his liege and one of the Leofric sisters. The dowry and alliance a match would bring would more than make up for any plot Garbodo was planning. Garbodo didn't have half the wealth and influence of Ogmore. Erik's heart tightened. He could hope and pray that Jarin would prefer to wed Katherine, but he knew that Linota was the more obvious choice. Not only was Linota beautiful, she was also much younger, with many more childbearing years ahead of her. Jarin was the last of the legitimate Borwyn line and needed to ensure he secured his succession.

Was there any other choice?

Erik could ignore de Bevoir and pretend Isabel didn't exist. He could carry on with his life as if nothing had happened this morning. He closed his eyes tightly. If he did nothing, he would be failing Mary for a second time.

But there was another option. Now that he knew of Isabel's existence he could go and find her for himself.

'I know what you're thinking.'

Erik met de Bevoir's amused gaze.

'You're thinking you could go and get her yourself.'

Erik pressed his lips together.

'It wouldn't work. I'm not as foolish as to keep Isabel anywhere obvious. And let's say you ventured into Garbodo's land to look for her. Imagine if you got caught.'

Erik could imagine it only too well. There would be nothing Jarin could do to help him.

'At best, you would be hung without trial. At worst…'

Erik didn't need de Bevoir to go on. If he were caught in Garbodo's land, it would be assumed he was spying for Jarin and it could spark a battle between the two men. If the King sided with Garbodo, Jarin would be sunk.

The rage that swept over him must have shown on

his face because de Bevoir stumbled backwards. Good. He wanted de Bevoir to be frightened.

De Bevoir tugged on his beard. 'I swear to you that what I have planned will not harm Borwyn physically. At worst, he will be mildly inconvenienced.'

Erik didn't believe that for a moment, but for now he would agree. If there was a way around the problem, he would find it. He took a step towards de Bevoir. 'If you cross me in any way I will hunt you down and gut you like a pig.'

De Bevoir paled, but didn't falter. A grudging amount of respect nudged Erik's conscience. De Bevoir was like Erik in a way. Both of them were at the mercy of powerful men, both willing to fight dirty for their liege, which was good because de Bevoir would know, without any doubt, that Erik would follow through on his threat. Unfortunately, Erik knew that Garbodo would make good on his threat, too.

De Bevoir nodded. 'I will deliver Isabel to you if you do these two things for me. I swear it to you.'

Erik took a deep breath, his heart stilling as he betrayed his friend for the first time. 'John Parkins and Melwyn Cookson would forsake their oath to Borwyn for a handful of coins.'

Sweat dripped down his neck. There was no going back now. He had made a deal with the devil and he would have to suffer the consequences.

Linota inhaled deeply and smiled as the crisp morning air filled her lungs. She'd only been riding for five days, but already they counted as the best of her life.

She was riding to her new home. A home with her

brother and sister-in-law, a home where her violent and oppressive mother was not welcome. For the first time in eight years she was free of the constraints that had kept her largely in her chamber for so long.

Before this journey she had never ridden a horse. She'd assumed she would find the large beasts terrifying, they'd looked so fearsome from her chamber window, but she'd been wrong. Unlike her poor sister, who looked miserable on horseback, Linota found she was born to be in the saddle.

She trotted in the middle of the male outriders, enjoying the sensation of the wind against her skin as they raced along.

She threw a guilty glance towards the back of the pack. Far in the distance behind her, Katherine plodded along, her posture slumped. Behind her, the Earl of Borwyn frowned as he watched Katherine's tortuous riding. It was difficult to tell whether he was annoyed at her lack of progress or life in general. He was a difficult man to read.

Another wave of guilt assailed her and she twisted back in her saddle to face forward. She'd started out riding with Katherine this morning, but after they'd stopped for a break she'd been pleased to join the rest of the riders up front. It wasn't just that Katherine was slow, it was also the guilt Linota felt at not wanting to engage the Earl of Borwyn in conversation. Borwyn always rode at the back and conversation between the three of them was painful and stilted.

Before leaving for the trip Katherine had been keen for Linota to make a match with the eminent Earl. Even before they'd met him, Katherine had wanted to somehow throw Linota into Borwyn's path, believing he would be instantly smitten with Linota's beauty. Even when Linota argued that she didn't believe she was all that pretty and that she didn't really understand all the fuss about the Earl, Katherine had replied with, 'He's a good match for you, Linota. He's handsome, he's rich and has a prominent place in the King's court. He is well placed to bring our family back into eminence. With your beauty you will be able to entice him into offering marriage. You need only give him some encouragement.'

It hadn't mattered how many times Linota had told Katherine she was beautiful and could probably attract a good suitor, perhaps even the Earl, for herself, Katherine just hadn't believed it. Katherine thought she looked like a boy and no amount of flattery could change her mind.

Since the journey had begun, Katherine hadn't pressured her to entice Borwyn any more, which had the strange effect of increasing Linota's guilt over it. Linota knew how much Katherine wanted her to make a good match and so she had tried a few times to start a conversation with Borwyn.

The problem was...well, the problem was Borwyn was so serious. Whenever she tried to engage him in light-hearted conversation he answered her politely, but his eyes never twinkled in amusement whenever he looked at her; neither did he make her laugh in return.

Resolve filled her belly; she would do better when they stopped at the next tavern for a rest. She would smile and laugh and be as charming as she possibly could and she had to hope that was enough to engage the man. Maybe when she had broken through his reserve, she would find someone whose company she enjoyed or, if that was too much to hope for, at least able to share the same space peacefully enough. At least then Katherine couldn't say Linota hadn't tried when Borwyn didn't offer the marriage proposal Katherine was sure was coming.

She tilted her face up to the sky. For now she would enjoy the winter sun against her skin.

'You are looking very pleased with yourself,' said a deep voice to her left.

Her heart skipped a beat and her lips involuntarily curved upwards. She didn't need to turn to know who had ridden up beside her. Borwyn might never smile at her, but Erik's blue-eyed gaze was never without an amused twinkle. Every afternoon he would ride next to her and keep her company. She loved how he always made her laugh and, she admitted to herself, these interludes were the favourite parts of the day.

'That's because I am very pleased with myself,' she replied lightly. 'Only five days ago I didn't know how to ride a horse.'

'And here I was thinking you'd obviously had a full knight's training you ride so well.'

Laughter gurgled out of her. This was what all of their exchanges were like; he teased her and she played along. Even though everything between them was light and relaxed, her heart still raced whenever they spoke. If only Borwyn was like his steward, she would marry him in a heartbeat.

'I expect Borwyn will want to recruit me to his

guards,' she replied, trying and failing to keep the laughter out of her voice.

'He was only saying the same himself yesterday evening.' Erik grinned, his eyes sparkling with humour.

'Excellent. I suppose I shall drop my sister off at Castle Swein and join the rest of you for your return trip to Borwyn's fortress where I shall take up my new position.'

Her heart thumped as she thought how much she would like that to happen. Not to travel to the fortress as Borwyn's wife, but as Erik's friend. A friend whose company she could enjoy without censure or reproach.

She glanced around at the men who travelled with them. She knew her own riding technique did not really rival theirs. She could not match their straight-backed dominance, but it didn't diminish her achievement in her eyes, although she knew that, even if she was better than all of them, it wouldn't matter. She would still be a woman who had no control over her own life and who could never join in as an equal.

Erik rode next to her in silence for a while. It was a relaxed stillness, not taut like her exchanges with Borwyn, which had her searching her mind for boring platitudes just to fill the silence.

After a while she glanced across at Erik. He was deep in thought, his gaze fixed unseeingly at a point in the distance. Dark stubble covered his jaw and the sun highlighted faint creases around his eyes. Although he'd been smiling at her mere moments ago she couldn't shake off the feeling that there was something beneath the surface upsetting him, which was odd, because she didn't know him well enough to make assumptions about what was going on in his mind.

Their conversations were light and friendly and fun, which was exactly what she needed as she started this new and exciting time in her life.

Late at night, while Katherine slept soundly beside her, she admitted to herself that she wanted to get to know him more. She wanted to know exactly how silky his hair was to the touch and whether the stubble across his jaw was soft or bristly. In the cold morning air she would remember that all this wasn't possible. There was nothing stopping her being his friend, though, and friends helped one another, didn't they?

Linota wrapped her fingers around her reins and then let the straps out again, watching as they slowly unfurled. Other than her sister, she had no friends. She didn't know whether it was right or wrong to ask Erik about his burdens. Would she be overstepping some invisible boundary she knew nothing about?

She reached up and tugged at her braid. She had finally broached the subject of wearing it looser with Katherine. Katherine had agreed to try and she was definitely getting better at tying Linota's hair up so it wasn't tight against her scalp, but it was still a relief to undo it at the end of every day and she itched with the urge to untie it now. How lovely it would be to let it flow along behind her as she rode instead of leaving it constrained like this.

'Are you comfortable, my lady?' asked Erik.

She glanced across at him. He didn't appear to have taken his eyes from the horizon and yet he was aware of her discomfort. Perhaps he also felt this strange connection between them.

She tugged at her braid again. 'I cannot abide having my hair tied up so tightly. I would much rather wear it loose.'

She waited, expecting a funny retort in response, but only silence greeted her statement.

He ran his hand over his face and stroked his long fingers along his jaw. It was hard to guess at what he was thinking, but he looked annoyed. She couldn't fathom why, when there had been nothing in her comment to irritate him.

'Imagine it was loose,' he said when she'd given up waiting for a response. 'It would be everywhere, flying into your face, probably even into mine. Poor Alban, riding behind you, would become entangled in it and be flung from his horse.'

Linota turned in her saddle and saw Alban, a young page, riding close in her wake. He caught her gaze and a deep flush crossed his ruddy skin.

'I think you've made a conquest there.' His words were light, but there was something about his tone that was off.

She waited a few heartbeats and then said, 'Are you quite well, Master Ward?'

He turned to her suddenly, his bright blue eyes meeting hers. Her breath caught in her throat. Gone was the usual sparkle of laughter and instead something else lurked there, intent and watchful. Her heart quickened. She couldn't have turned away from him for all the wealth in England.

He blinked and the spell was broken. She turned away, raising her fingers to her lips.

'Everything is fine, Mistress Leofric. Why do you ask?'

'You look…' She wanted to say sad, but she didn't think he would like it. She settled on, 'Preoccupied.'

She held her breath as she waited for his reply. She wondered if he would confide in her, whether they could make this friendship deeper.

'I'm merely hungry and thinking how long it will be until our evening meal. I've stopped at the tavern we're aiming to reach this evening. I know you enjoy a good cut of meat and their roasted pheasant is particularly rich and succulent. I think you will enjoy our evening repast.'

Her heart sank and she had to grip hold of the pommel to steady herself. She'd hoped for a moment that he would be serious with her and tell her what was troubling him, but she had been mistaken. It shouldn't matter that he hadn't. There was no reason to expect more than a polite response. She'd hoped he would be different from everyone else though, that he would treat her like an adult rather than the naive girl everyone else saw when they looked at her. While she was hoping to make a friend, he was merely keeping her company on the long journey.

'Did you know that we are currently on Borwyn's land?' asked Erik pleasantly.

'Having no memory of life outside Ogmore's fortress, no, I didn't,' she said sharply.

Erik didn't pick up on her changed mood, which only had her tightening her fists as he continued with his commentary about the scenery. This was the fifth time he had done this in as many days.

Every time they rode together he would tease her gently for a while, causing her heart to do the strange flutter it only did when talking to him. Then he would turn to the topic of the Earl of Borwyn and his greatness, whether it was to do with the Earl's land or his wealth and influence.

These interludes were strange. Erik's voice would change, becoming less chatty and more like a priest reciting evening prayers.

It was almost as if Erik was trying to *sell* Borwyn to her. But that couldn't be true. She was the penniless daughter of a treasonous father and an insane mother. Although Katherine wanted a match between Linota and Borwyn, Linota couldn't see what the Earl, who had only given her polite interest so far, would gain from the match.

There was no way Erik could be pointing out the Earl's assets to make *him* more *appealing* to *her*.

Maybe this was Erik's way of passing the time, but it sounded a little to her like the merchants she'd heard from her chamber window, hawking their goods to uninterested passers-by and she couldn't, for the life of her, understand why.

Chapter Three

Linota peered into the fast-moving stream. It rushed past her boot-clad feet, speeding towards an unknown destination. The riding party had stopped to rest near the water for the horses to take a well-earned drink. She dropped a twig into the swirling current and watched how it spun quickly before disappearing out of sight.

She rocked back on to her heels and glanced around at the men milling about nearby. Some had their arms crossed over their chests; others were staring at the surrounding countryside. The deep rumble of masculine laughter she'd become used to over the days of travelling with them was missing.

Today was different, although nobody would tell her why, no matter how many times she asked. When she'd awoken this morning she'd been alone in her bed, which was very unusual. She'd pulled her clothes on quickly and headed down to the taproom of the inn they'd been staying in. No sooner had her feet hit the wooden floor of the room than Katherine had bustled over to her and informed her that there had been a change of plan.

Instead of heading to their brother's home in Castle Swein, they were changing destination and were now travelling towards Borwyn's fortress.

Until now, the journey had taken place at a sedate pace with frequent stops. Today, they had raced along; only stopping when it was clear Katherine could not handle the speed.

The new destination didn't bother Linota. It gave her a chance to see so much more of the kingdom than she'd ever dreamed possible. But it was clear she was the only one being kept in the dark as to why the change in direction was happening and that really irritated her.

Even Katherine knew. Her slim shoulders were tight with tension and her eyebrows had settled into a permanent frown. But when Linota had approached her, Katherine had only said not to worry and that had Linota curling her fists in frustration.

Once again, Linota was the cosseted little sister who had to be protected from unpalatable truths. She knew she shouldn't be upset, Katherine had treated her this way for as long as she could remember, but there was no getting around the unsettled feeling in her stomach. She hated being kept in the dark. It hurt that Katherine still saw Linota as someone to be sheltered from unpleasantness.

Her sister shielding her wasn't unusual. Katherine had practically raised her and had seen it as her duty to protect Linota from hurtful gossip and their increasingly violent mother. Linota was grateful, from the bottom of her heart, for the stability Katherine had created, but they were out of their mother's reach now. They were free and Linota didn't need that looking after any more. She needed to be her sister's equal.

She squinted into the horizon where the sun hung low in the sky. She caught sight of Erik and her heart skipped a beat. Even as she chided her body for such a reaction she still couldn't tear her eyes from him. He'd not spoken to her today and she'd missed the way he made her laugh over the simplest thing. She realised that she'd been craving his company and the thought scared her. He should be no different to her than any of the other men travelling with them, but she already knew that he meant more to her than anyone else outside her small family.

Erik began talking intently to Borwyn, both of them frowning, their bodies half turned away from one another. She didn't need to hear the conversation to know that whatever was going on was causing discord between the two men.

She turned away from them. They wouldn't tell her what was going on either: she was alone.

She wandered further downstream. The water was pooling here, swirling in a circle before tumbling down over rocks and rushing off into the distance. She nudged a stone with the edge of her boot. It plopped into the water and plummeted to the bottom. She fought the sudden urge to kick all the rocks around her into the murky depths while screaming at the top of her voice— anything to gain someone's attention. She clenched her fists. She was being silly and acting like the child everyone obviously thought she was. Instead of staring moodily at the water she should walk up to her sister and demand answers. She was no longer a vulnerable child, but a fully grown adult, who could and should share the burdens of those around her.

She spun on her heel and stopped abruptly.

Men on horseback were emerging from the surrounding woodland. Men she had never seen before and who weren't stopping to engage in conversation, but who were thundering through the rough gathering, trampling over discarded travel bags and narrowly avoiding stampeding over Borwyn's men.

Linota inhaled sharply as one of them sped past Katherine, brushing so close to her that she was pushed into the stream, her mouth wide with shock.

Linota started forward to get to her sister.

As she moved a man, a thick, black beard obscuring his face, caught sight of her from atop his horse. In that split second he seemed to reach a decision.

He turned his horse in her direction. His black gaze locked with hers and there could be no mistaking his intent.

Far away from her, Katherine began to scream.

Linota twisted and began to run, but her dress caught around her ankles and she tripped, hitting the ground with a hard thud.

She scrambled to her knees, but the mud was slippery and she couldn't seem to get purchase.

The horse rider was getting closer, the ground shaking from the pounding of the horse's hoofbeats.

In the distance she heard Erik yell, 'Get up, Linota. Run to me.'

She looked towards his voice. He was running towards her, his arms pumping wildly as he sprinted. He cleared a fallen log. He was so close, she stretched out an arm.

'Get up,' he yelled again.

This time she managed to scramble to her feet, only for a large hand to grab the back of her cloak.

She screamed Erik's name, the sound tearing out of her as her whole world shifted.

She was lifted bodily and thrown across the front of a horse. Her head smacked against the horse's neck and her legs flailed wildly over the other side. And then she was moving, Katherine's screams following her as the ground sped beneath her eyes.

Bile rose in her stomach as the strong stench of an unwashed body hit her.

The horse veered sharply to the left. The world spun and black spots appeared before her eyes. Her heart raced painfully fast as if it would burst from her ribs.

They entered woodland, but the rider didn't slow, even as twisted roots lined their path. Behind them she could hear the thundering hooves of other riders following closely.

She started to slip and she hoped she would fall. A broken neck would be better than whatever these men had planned.

A rough hand gathered up the fabric of her cloak and pulled her back into position.

She was both desperate to stop moving and willing the ride to never end. She didn't know what fate awaited her when the riders reached their destination, but nausea was building up inside her. She needed to rest her head to stop the world from spinning violently.

* * *

After what felt like a lifetime of racing through the densely packed trees, the riders eventually began to slow before finally grinding to a halt.

Linota was hauled down from the horse's side and dumped on to her feet. She staggered and fell to her knees, retching, her stomach spasming violently.

'I told you not to injure her,' said an irritated male voice.

'She's not hurt,' said another voice nearby. A hard hand gripped the back of her dress and hauled her to her feet.

The world spun and she staggered again, but the iron grip on her clothes forced her to remain upright. From the stench, she guessed she was being supported by the same man who had slung her across his horse with ease. Nausea caused bile to rise once more. She bent over at the waist and braced her hands on her knees.

Slowly the world came back into focus.

'She is hardly in the best of health,' said the original voice. He sounded cross and Linota held on to that. At least one person here wanted her to remain well.

'You didn't say nothin' about her being in good shape. She's in one piece, ain't she? I think me and me men did well, considerin' we snatched the girl in front of the Earl and all his sword-carryin' cronies.'

Around her, men jeered in agreement.

Linota's stomach settled and she forced herself to stand up straight. She would meet her foes face on. If this was where her life was to end, then she would face it with dignity. Not one of them would know how violently her knees were trembling.

She took a slow look at her surroundings. Four men were seated atop their horses. A tall, thickset man was next to her, gripping her cloak tightly. She recognised him as the man who had been riding towards her as she had tried to get to Erik. It was evidently his horse she'd been unceremoniously dumped across.

She took a small step away from him, but he roughly pulled her back until her body was flush with his. The pungent stench of his sweat mixed with the sourness of his breath overwhelmed her. She turned her face away. Her whole body convulsed as she retched again.

Somebody nearby laughed. She closed her eyes tightly, willing her body under control.

She slowly opened her eyes and looked towards the man who appeared unhappy about her condition. He didn't look much of a threat, short and rotund with a straggly beard—a strong shove would probably knock him over. Despite his appearance, he seemed to be the leader of this ragtag band of men.

He caught her gaze and sketched a short bow. 'Mistress Leofric, I apologise for your rough treatment. Please believe me when I say that I mean you no harm.'

She licked her lips. They were so dry. She longed for a drink, but she would be damned before she asked these men for anything.

'Who are you?' she croaked.

'I am Simon de Bevoir, my lady.' The portly man bowed again and a bubble of laughter rose up her throat. He looked ridiculous. She'd been abducted, thrown unceremoniously over a horse and hadn't been able to stop gagging since they'd stopped moving, but the man responsible was acting as if they had met at a grand feast.

De Bevoir paused and she wondered what he was waiting for her to say. Perhaps he thought she would say that she was pleased to meet him, but she was most assuredly not going to do that.

De Bevoir ran his hand down his straggly beard. 'You will be staying with us for a while, I'm afraid. But you don't need to be frightened. Neither I nor my...' de Bevoir waved his hand at the men as he searched for a word to describe them. 'None of us will hurt you. I swear it on my honour.'

Her knees trembled, but she forced herself to stand firm. 'If I'm not to be hurt, why am I here?'

De Bevoir sucked on his teeth. 'That I will not tell you. You're a small part of a much wider plan. You may as well make yourself comfortable. We won't be moving from this place until tomorrow. Gamel—' he addressed the man who held her in place '—see to Mistress Leofric's comfort.'

Gamel gripped Linota's arm painfully hard and pulled her in the direction of a fallen log.

'Sit there and stay out of our way,' he grunted.

Linota stumbled as he shoved her away from him. She managed to right herself before she fell. By the time she was stable Gamel had moved away from her and was fiddling with the bindings on his saddlebag.

Now she wasn't moving the cold of the day began to creep through her clothes. She shivered and pulled her arms tightly around her. None of the men turned in her direction. Would they notice if she ran away?

She took a small step away from the log and froze before she could take another one. Riding slumped over the horse had robbed her of all sense of direction.

She would surely starve or freeze to death if left to her own devices. De Bevoir had promised her no harm would come to her. Was she the naive little girl everyone thought she was to believe him?

Her limbs were locked, seized with indecision. Although she made no movement it sounded to her as if her heart was beating so loudly everyone in the clearing must be able to hear it.

'Please sit, Mistress Leofric,' said de Bevoir, appearing at her elbow. 'It's going to be a long couple of days. It would be best to conserve your energy.'

The decision made for her, Linota sank, almost gratefully, on to the moss-covered log.

De Bevoir nodded and walked away from her, but now she knew that she wasn't as unobserved as she'd first thought.

Once the horses had been seen to, the men relaxed slightly, slumping down on the ground or leaning against some of the trees at the edge of the clearing. After a while she stopped listening to their talk—there was nothing to be gleaned from their conversation, which seemed to focus on women and horses. No reason was given as to why she had been taken.

Her teeth started to chatter in earnest as the men passed around a flagon of ale. She was seemingly forgotten. As the evening wore on the men slouched as the alcohol took effect. Even de Bevoir, who had initially held himself aloof from the others, began to join in.

Linota swayed as exhaustion rushed over her. Her eyes stung with the effort of keeping them open. She wanted to give in to her body's demand to sleep, but the fear of what might happen to her if she lost consciousness forced her to keep her eyes open even as they burned.

'She's a comely little thing,' said Gamel, his voice nearer to her than she'd realised.

She jerked upright and blinked. She had been dozing. In that time, de Bevoir and several others had succumbed to sleep.

In the darkness of the evening she could make out Gamel looming over her, his eyes two dark pools above his bushy beard.

'De Bevoir said we ain't to touch her,' said another man.

'De Bevoir's not just asleep, Fletcher, he's passed out. The weasel ain't got no stomach for ale. I don't think he'd wake up if we 'ave a little play with our new friend.'

Fletcher grunted. 'It has been a long while since I had a woman.'

'I bet you ain't never had one as sweet as that,' said Gamel, nodding in her direction, his gaze locked with hers.

Linota was desperate to run, but her legs weren't responding to her thoughts. It was as if she was watching the events from someone else's eyes.

Gamel staggered towards her. Behind him, Fletcher laughed. 'You ain't gonna be able to perform, old man.'

'I will and I'm gonna go first,' growled Gamel.

The fear that had kept Linota frozen to her seat suddenly pumped through her. It rushed through her veins, waking her from her trance. She sprang from her woodland seat and ran into the surrounding forest.

Away from the clearing the darkness of the forest blinded her. She didn't care. Her only thought was to get away.

Behind her she heard muffled cursing and many heavy footsteps following after her. Her breath came quickly in shallow gasps as she tripped and tumbled over gnarled roots.

She fell and cried out when she banged her knee. She pushed herself up again. She had to get away, the alternative was unthinkable.

Her face was wet and she wiped her tears away with the back of her hand. She couldn't afford to be upset now; the tears would only blind her further. The darkness hindered her, but it was also her friend. If she couldn't see, then neither could her pursuers. She only needed to keep moving.

The footsteps seemed to be closing in, but she didn't turn to look as she ran on. Something grabbed at the back of her cloak and she screamed.

She pulled away, darting to the left. Her lungs hurt now. Every breath was laboured. She couldn't keep going for much longer and yet she couldn't stop.

A fist closed around her braid, yanking her neck backwards. Pain burst across her skull. She reached behind her and pulled, trying to release her hair, kicking out with her legs as she did so.

A rough hand slapped her face, sending her spinning. She reached out a hand to stop herself from falling, but she was too late. The ground rushed up to meet her. Her head hit the ground and the world went black.

She was airborne, her head resting against a solid chest, strong arms holding her tightly. A scent vaguely familiar and comforting filled the air around her.

Everything was fuzzy. Her legs and arms burned

and her head throbbed, but the arms holding her were warm and secure.

Something terrible had happened, but she couldn't remember what it was. She only knew she had been running. She couldn't think what from, only that her life depended on getting away.

Her cloak slipped and cold air rushed over her ankles, pulling her from her dreamlike state. She gasped as memories tumbled over her. She'd been escaping from those men who wanted to do unspeakable things to her. And now she was caught.

She *had* to get away.

She struggled, but the arms only tightened around her, her captor increasing his speed. A moan escaped her lips. She might be weak, but she wouldn't let those men do what they had been planning. She pushed harder.

'Are you awake?' a voice asked softly.

The voice was familiar, but it didn't belong to either Gamel or de Bevoir. She stopped struggling for a moment and squinted into the darkness. It was impossible to make out any features of the man who carried her. The darkness in the forest was absolute.

Perhaps sensing her confusion, the stranger spoke.

'It's all right, Linota. It's me, Erik. I've got you. You're safe now.'

'Erik,' she breathed. 'How...?'

She reached up and encountered his jawline. His stubble was softer under her fingertips than she'd imagined during the long hours of riding next to him. She traced the edge of his face until she found his chin. She heard his soft inhale as her fingers touched his lips.

The soft kiss against her hand was so gentle she would have missed it if all her concentration hadn't been on the spot where their bare skin connected.

He moved his head slightly and she dropped her hand, not sure what she'd been thinking when she'd touched him so intimately.

'I can walk,' she said.

He stopped. 'Are you sure? You weren't conscious when I found you.'

'I'm sure,' she said, although she didn't really want him to put her down. She was cocooned in his arms, safe from the horrors of the evening, but now that she was regaining consciousness it didn't seem fair to make him carry her. They would travel faster if she was also on foot.

He slowed to a stop. 'We'll need to hurry.' He lowered her gently to the ground.

Her legs nearly went from under her. His arms came around her waist and she leaned into his strength, resting her head once more on his chest.

'I can carry you,' he murmured into her hair.

'No, give me a moment.'

She stood in his embrace, her legs trembling whether from fear or some other emotion she wasn't sure. Gradually her strength returned, but even then she was reluctant to pull away from him.

'Linota, we need to keep moving,' he said eventually.

Heat rushed over her face. Here she was clinging to him when they were running for her life. He must think she was pathetic.

'Sorry,' she muttered. 'I'm fine now.'

She pulled away from him and she heard his arms drop to his sides.

'Where are we going?' she asked as he began to walk, her falling in behind him.

'For now I'm trying to put some distance between us and those men. When I'm sure they are no longer following us I will try to get us back to my horse, Cai. From there, I should be able to find the path and hopefully re-join the others.'

Over the snapping of twigs and the occasional hoot of an owl his words sunk in. They were lost in the woods, in the dark during one of the coldest seasons she could remember.

'How did you find me?' she asked when the silence crowded in on her, threatening to swamp her completely.

'I started chasing after you as soon as you were taken. I followed you into the woods, but as darkness fell I lost the trail. I kept going. I couldn't bear the thought…' He muttered something under his breath. 'I didn't want you to be alone with those men any longer than possible. But Cai threw a shoe, he was limping and so I had to stop. I tied him up and was about to press on with my search when I heard you scream.' They walked in silence for a moment. 'It wasn't difficult to find you after that. The sounds of the men chasing you could be heard throughout the woods. I heard you fall and I was able to make out one of the men scooping you up. I wanted to run him through for daring to lay his hands on you, but I've left my sword with Cai.'

Linota heard Erik kick something and mutter under his breath. It sounded like a curse over his carelessness, but she couldn't be sure.

'I followed you back to their camp. The men seemed concerned that you weren't waking up. In the end they laid you on the ground and continued with their drinking. It was easy enough to creep in and pick you up while their attention was diverted.'

'What diverted their attention?' she asked, sure from Erik's voice that he must be responsible.

'I was careless about my sword, but I'm not completely useless. I started a fire on the other side of the clearing, close enough to their horses to spook them, but not enough to cause the animals any pain. While they were dealing with it I picked you up and walked away. It may be a while before your absence is noticed. I hope that they think you escaped by yourself, that way they will search the surrounding area first.'

Something soft and feathery brushed her cheek. She leapt forward and collided with Erik's back.

He turned quickly and pulled her into his arms, his body rigid next to hers. 'Did you hear something?' he whispered above her head.

'No, something…something touched me on my face.' She shuddered.

Katherine's tales of ghosts roaming the earth filled her mind. She pressed herself into Erik's lean body, no longer caring what he thought of her.

'Touched you?' His voice was soft in the cold winter air.

'Yes.'

'It was probably a bat.'

She let out a shaky laugh. 'Of course it was. I'm sorry. I don't know what's the matter with me. I'm shaking all over and jumping at shadows. I don't know how to make it stop.' She stepped closer, hoping he would take this as a sign she needed to be comforted and not that she craved his touch.

Erik's hand came up and he began to draw long, comforting circles on her back. She wanted to stay there, nestled against him for ever, breathing in his comforting scent.

'No, it's me who should be sorry for dragging you through the night when you've had such a terrifying ordeal. I will find somewhere for us to shelter and then we will rest.'

He stepped back and his hands skimmed over the length of her arms, tracing over the skin of her hands and coming to rest with his fingers entangled with hers. Her heart slowed at the contact, skin on skin. His hands—rough, calloused—dwarfed hers.

'Come,' he said quietly.

He kept one of her hands in his as they moved slowly through the woodland. She stayed close to his side, partly because of the warmth, but also because she wanted to.

A few times her eyes drifted closed. Erik slipped an arm around her waist, supporting her. Every bone in her body ached, but she forced herself to keep going. If she stopped, Erik would have to carry her and she couldn't bear the thought of being a burden to him when he had already done so much for her.

When taking another step finally seemed impossible to Linota, Erik came to a stop.

'Here,' he said.

She blinked a few times, but she couldn't make out what had caught his attention.

'What is it?'

'There's an overhang. It should provide us with enough shelter for the night and hide us if those men attempt to come after us.'

He tugged her gently and she followed gratefully.

Erik crouched and patted the ground. She sank down next to him. She no longer cared if a whole army of bats wanted to touch her all over. All she wanted to do was sleep.

'You lie down first,' said Erik, gently guiding her into position. She was grateful for his support. She didn't think she could move now if her life depended on it.

Erik's large body lay down next to her. She could only make out the shape of him as he tucked an arm behind his head, his face turned towards the sky. She wanted to reach out and trace the lines of his face again, to feel that soft stubble beneath her fingertips. She wondered whether he would welcome her touch. Perhaps he would begin to see her like a woman... Or would he be shocked by her desire to touch him, to feel his lips against her again, but this time with a different intention?

She kept her hand to herself. She didn't need to add the embarrassment of his rejection to everything else that had happened to her that day.

'Are you warm enough?' asked Erik.

'I'm a little cold.'

She jumped as an arm came around her waist. It disappeared as quickly as it had arrived.

'I'm sorry, I did not mean to alarm you,' said Erik. 'I'm not going to hurt you. I only wanted to warm you up.'

Her heart pounded in her throat, but it wasn't from fright. She had never felt less frightened in her whole life. That brief touch had awakened something inside her, something she had not experienced before. Her whole body yearned for him to touch her again.

'I… I'm not alarmed by your arm,' she stuttered. 'I jumped because… I thought it might be another bat.'

His body shook in silent laughter and she closed her eyes tightly. Why had she said bat? She should have chosen something believable.

She wanted that arm back around her and not just for warmth. How naive and young she must sound. Back at Ogmore's fortress she'd often spied him from her chamber window. Catching a glimpse of him had been one of her favourite pastimes. She'd observed the way women were always fluttering around him. There was one woman who never missed an opportunity to drape herself around him in some way, whether it was curling herself around his arms or touching his chest, laughing up at him invitingly. That woman would know exactly what to say now to get Erik's arm to come around her once more. Linota's mind, however, was completely blank. She curled her knees up to her chest and sighed.

She was no longer tired, only cold and lonely.

'Mistress Leofric, I am neither a bat nor a hedgehog,' said Erik, laughter lacing his words. 'May I put my arm around you to keep you warm?'

Heat spread across her face and she was glad for the dark so that he couldn't see her delight at his words.

'Yes, please,' she said quietly. 'And I think you should call me Linota. Mistress Leofric sounds too formal now that we are lying in the mud together.'

Once again she felt laughter rumble through him and she felt ridiculously pleased. She'd never seen the clinging woman make him laugh in return for her efforts.

His strong arm slipped around her waist once more and she felt him tucking his cloak around her body.

'Are you sure you're warm enough?' she asked.

'Aye,' he said gruffly. 'You don't need to be afraid of me, though. If you'd like to get closer, I promise I will not take advantage of you.'

She slid nearer as her heart thudded in disappointment. Here she was, hyper-aware of his body, and he had no designs on her at all.

Her forehead brushed the solid wall of his chest and she settled. She might not ever cause his heart to flutter when he saw her, but maybe this experience would result in a friendship. She would have to be content with that.

Chapter Four

Something hovered on the edge of Linota's consciousness. She tried to prise her eyes open, but they were weighed down with sleep. In this half-dreamlike state she was aware of a coldness seeping into every part of her body, freezing her toes and settling deep in her lungs. She stirred, trying to fold in on herself, to curl deeper into her covers and to warm even just a little part of her.

'Linota,' said a deep voice next to her ear.

Her eyes snapped open immediately.

Erik was so close, his face almost touching hers. This near she could see flecks of ginger running through his brown stubble and thin lines at the corner of his eyes.

'Erik,' she said on a breath.

His gaze snagged on hers and the lines around his eyes deepened for a moment, then he frowned.

'We need to be quiet,' he whispered. 'I think somebody is out there.'

Her whole body stilled. Instinctively, she shifted closer to him.

He brushed a strand of hair away from her cheek, his fingertips lightly touching her skin, causing a delightful tingle to race down her spine. She frowned. How could her body be feeling such things when their lives were in danger?

He glanced at her face and snatched his hand away.

'Sorry,' he muttered and then added. 'Please don't worry. I won't let any harm come to you.'

She nodded, her mind still on his gentle touch and the way he had taken his hand away so quickly. What had she done to cause him to act like that? She wanted to get his touch back, but she didn't know how. Perhaps her enjoyment had been written all over her face and that had horrified him. Where he'd only intended comfort she had taken it for something else. She edged slightly away from him. She needed distance to think.

The small space didn't allow her to back away far and the tiny sliver of a gap she managed to create did not help clear her mind.

Erik's broad shoulders filled the tiny crevice in which they had wedged themselves. A creeping vine of ivy hung just above his head. She fixed her gaze on that and tried to rid her mind of all thoughts and feelings, forcing her body to calm and her pulse to return to normal.

They waited in silence. The only sound was Erik's calm breathing. She concentrated on the steady in and out, willing her body to be as still as his.

She had almost succeeded when the sound of horses slowing to a stop could be heard close to where they were lying. She cringed into the back of the crevice.

The hiding place didn't seem big enough to cover them completely from whoever was out there.

'I paid you quite handsomely, Gamel.'

Linota flinched as de Bevoir's nasally voice filled the morning air. Erik's hand came to rest on her hip. She risked a glance at his face. Sweat beaded across the skin of his forehead, his jaw pulled tight as he stared at the roof of their hiding place. A thrill of fear raced down her spine. Even though Erik was a hardened warrior, he obviously thought that de Bevoir and Gamel posed a real threat. Last night she had been in even greater danger than she'd thought.

'You had one simple job,' de Bevoir continued. 'Get the girl and keep the girl. It wasn't difficult and yet you've failed.'

'She must 'ave 'ad help, de Bevoir. That fire ain't starting by itself. They can't 'ave gone far.'

'You said that last night and yet we still haven't found her and this so-called accomplice.'

'A slip of a girl like that ain't finding her way out of a sack.'

If de Bevoir replied it wasn't loud enough for Linota to hear.

Last night Linota had found the rotund de Bevoir slightly ridiculous, with his polite manners and straggly beard. That had been a mistake. The cold calculation now in his voice sent chills racing up her spine and she shivered.

When there was no further conversation Linota tapped Erik on the shoulder. She was surprised to see anger burning brightly in his eyes.

'Can we move now?' she mouthed.

He shook his head and mouthed a reply.

She frowned to show she hadn't understood his meaning. He leaned over, his stubble brushing her cheek, his breath whispering across her skin. She managed to hold herself still as her body longed to arch into the sensation.

His whisper was as soft as a summer's breeze. 'I haven't heard their horses moving. I think they are still in the area.'

Linota's fear disappeared as Erik's nearness swamped her senses. She could feel the length of his hard body down the fullness of hers. His hand still rested gently on her hip, steadying her.

He moved away from her and she followed instinctively. She heard his sharp inhale as her body aligned with his. He looked down at her, the anger in his gaze replaced by something else. An emotion she didn't recognise but which had her body tightening in response. His eyes flicked to her mouth and back up again. Her heart beat as if it wanted to take flight. Her fingers trembled and she reached up to place her hand on his arm.

He flinched and dropped his hands from her body, increasing the space between them. Her stomach swooped with disappointment and she turned her head away so that he wouldn't read it in her expression.

She'd been so sure, when his gaze had dropped to her lips, that he was experiencing the same intense feelings as she was: an overwhelming desire to run her fingers over his whole body, to experience what it would be like to become one with him.

But of course he wasn't. He was a man used to

women throwing themselves at him. Perhaps their enforced proximity had flared a momentary attraction for him until her touch on his arm had reminded him who she was.

It was probably for the best. If he had kissed her like she'd desperately wanted him to, it might have caused her to fall deeper for him and that would only end in heartbreak—her heartbreak, not his.

She rolled on to as much of her back as possible and stared up at the overhang above her. A spider scuttled across the craggy roof and she shuddered.

She needed to get out of this tiny space and away from Erik whose presence crowded her senses.

As the long moments passed her desperation increased until it felt as if she were trying to crawl out of her own skin.

After what felt like a hundred lifetimes they eventually heard the sound of horses moving away from them.

She raised herself on to one elbow until a hand on her shoulder stayed her movements.

'We need to give them enough time to move far away from here,' said Erik quietly.

She sagged back down and waited, her eyes fixed on the spider, which was now spinning an intricate web above her head.

She didn't turn to look at Eric once.

Finally, he appeared to be satisfied with the amount of time that had passed since they last heard de Bevoir and Gamel.

'Let's go,' he said.

He rolled away from her quickly and out into the

open. Although she'd been desperate to get away from
him, she immediately missed his warmth and the security his large body had given her. She crawled after
him, her body stiff after a night in the cramped space.

'It's so cold,' she murmured, her breath turning to
white puffs in front of her.

'We'll warm up once we start moving.' Erik strode
off in a seemingly random direction, not waiting to see
if she was following.

She scrambled to her feet and scurried to catch up.
'Where are we going?'

'I'm hoping to find Cai. I left everything with him.
I've got a handful of coins, but we'll need more if it
takes us a while to meet up with the others. We'll have
to eat.'

At the mention of food her stomach roared to life,
sending her a sharp reminder that she hadn't eaten in
over a day, apart from a dried oatcake she'd forced down
during her ride. She'd been so cross with Katherine for
not telling her what was going on that she hadn't had
much of an appetite. How petty that anger seemed now.

She rubbed her growling stomach. One of her mother's favourite punishments for Linota and her sister had
been to withhold food, so Linota knew what it was like
to feel hungry. At least she'd thought she'd known. This
hollow feeling was something entirely different. The
stabbing pains shot through her and there was nothing
she could do to ease them as she followed Erik further
into the woodland.

Erik didn't appear to notice her discomfort. He strode
on ahead of her as if the intimacy of the night hadn't
happened.

She trailed after him, trying to ignore the way her gaze kept catching on the breadth of his shoulders or the strength in his arms. She would do well to remember that, although she found him endlessly fascinating, she was just a young woman for him to protect. She would never be like those sophisticated women she'd spied hanging around him and with whom he'd seemed to find enjoyment if the smiles he'd thrown in their direction were anything to go by.

When the silence between them began to grate against her skin she moved quicker so that she was walking alongside him. 'How do you know where to look for Cai?'

'The sun was setting in that direction when I left him,' said Erik, pointing into an endless wall of tress. 'So it makes sense to me to head this way.' He nodded in the direction they were walking. 'If we are lucky, we haven't strayed too far away from where I tied him up.'

'And if we're unlucky?'

Erik's jaw tightened. 'Then we will find our way out of this woodland and make our way to the nearest town. The settlements around here are all within Borwyn's land. I've visited most of them on behalf of the Earl many a time. I will be able to find someone who will help us, I'm—'

Erik grabbed her arm and pulled her behind a tree.

'Wha—?' she began.

She stopped as Erik placed a hand over her mouth. 'Someone's coming,' he whispered into her ear.

Linota was acutely aware of his hard body pressing into hers, but he seemed completely oblivious to the way they were moulded together. His gaze squinted off into the distance, focused on something she couldn't see.

Linota sighed internally. All Katherine's protests that Linota was one of the most beautiful women at Ogmore's fortress must have been sisterly bias. She'd always thought so, but Erik's obvious indifference proved it. He wasn't aware of her as a woman at all.

No matter how much she strained her hearing, all Linota could make out was the sound of a small animal rustling through the leaves near her feet.

She waited for Erik to admit that he was wrong, but the hard lines of his body stayed taut. This close to him she could see the tendons in his neck straining as he continued to peer into the distance. She closed her eyes so that she was no longer studying him. This intimate knowledge of his body wasn't doing her any good.

'There,' he said eventually.

She tilted her head, but she still couldn't hear anything out of the usual.

'Damn,' he muttered. 'They have Cai.'

'Who?' she whispered against his hand.

'I'm not sure.'

Whoever it was, they were moving very quietly through the forest. Only now could she make out the faint snapping of twigs as they moved closer. As the sounds grew nearer she could hear a low conversation between two deep voices.

'De Bevoir ain't gonna be happy to find out we were followed after we took the girl,' said one voice.

'The horse don't prove we were.'

'And what, the owner just vanished in a puff of smoke? You're a damned idiot. Of course we were followed. Look at this beast. This ain't some common nag. It's a warrior's horse. De Bevoir will blame us for the mistake, even though we followed his exact instructions. If he thinks we failed, we ain't getting paid.'

'So we let the horse go and pretend we never saw it.'

There was a silence.

As Erik concentrated on the strangers' conversation his hand loosened against her mouth. His fingers trailed down the length of her neck until they rested at the base of her throat. A wave of pleasure spread through her body at the gentle touch of skin on skin. The rough bark against her back, the birds in the overhead trees, it all fell away as her whole body stretched towards his absentminded caress.

One of the strangers spoke again and she jumped, earning a quizzical look from Erik. Heat rushed over her skin and she forced herself to retain eye contact.

'The horse is probably worth more than de Bevoir was ever going to give us. Let's leave the others to chase for the girl and her protector and make away with this prize.'

There was another silence, much shorter this time.

'Aye, all right then. But you ain't be double-crossing me. We're in this together.'

'Of course.'

Linota rolled her eyes.

She wouldn't trust either man. They were both only interested in what they could get rather than the lives that were at stake. Erik grinned at her and the air whooshed out of her lungs. The full force of his smile turned her knees to liquid.

'This makes things easier,' said Erik quietly, as the pair moved away.

Linota frowned, trying to concentrate on her surroundings and not the new sensations running through her body. 'How is this better for us? Surely those men taking Cai makes it harder?'

'Now we know all the men aren't chasing us. We follow these two until I can set up a decent ambush. Then I take back Cai and we ride on.'

'How are you going to manage that? They have your sword and their own.'

Erik still hadn't moved away from her. His body still pressed her gently into the tree. He looked down at her and raised an eyebrow, his eyes filled with amusement. 'You really think it would be difficult to defeat those two?'

Linota smiled at his confidence. 'If you're that sure, why not get Cai back now?'

The amusement in his eyes faded. 'We're too close to the others. If I don't manage to silence them, those two could bring the rest of the gang running and we'd be back to the beginning. Or worse, in my case, because it sounds as if they want to keep you alive, which means they'll probably want me dead. That way I can't save you again or reveal your location to Borwyn and his men.'

Erik said the words lightly, but dread curled in Linota's stomach. She couldn't be responsible for Erik's death, not when he had gone to such lengths to protect her.

He finally stepped away from her. Cold air rushed

over her and she shivered. She pulled her cloak tightly around her.

As she followed Erik through the forest she made sure to concentrate on where she placed her feet and how she moved through the undergrowth. The two men didn't know they were being followed and she didn't want to be the one to draw attention to the two of them following close behind. Erik might be confident he could fight them without his sword, but she didn't want to be the reason he found out if that were true or not.

The men ground to a halt and seemed to be arguing about which direction to take. One seemed keen to take the horse to the nearest settlement and get a quick sale, the other wanted to walk a little longer and get a better price.

'What would you prefer them to do?' whispered Linota as they watched the altercation.

'I'd prefer them to head to the nearest hamlet. I want this over with. Heading further away means we're out in the open for longer.'

Linota shivered. She did not want to encounter Gamel again.

'Are you cold?' asked Erik, his blue eyes turning to look at her.

She was about to shake her head. She was cold, but not desperately so. It was the thought of Gamel's lecherous gaze that had goose pimples running down her legs. But before she could think of what she was doing, she nodded instead. She wanted him to curl his arms around her and pull her to him, warming her with his body as he had done in the night.

For a long moment he looked at her, his gaze skimming her face as if he were trying to read her thoughts. She held her breath. His hands twitched against his thighs and her heart skipped a beat as she waited for him to move towards her.

In front of them the two men started walking again. Erik's gaze flicked away from her as he watched their progress.

'It looks like they've made a decision.' Without sparing her a second glance, he began to follow them once more.

Linota fell in behind him, her steps heavy with disappointment. She'd wanted him to hold her and, although she knew it was ridiculous, she felt cheated.

If they were able to recover Cai at the next settlement, then it would be no time at all until they reunited with the rest of their party. She knew that should make her glad. Her time with her abductors had been terrifying and being surrounded by Borwyn's ferocious guards would make her safe once more but…it would also mean her life returning to normal. And in that life Katherine was relying on her to make a good marriage to a wealthy nobleman, hopefully Borwyn himself. She wouldn't be able to sleep in the arms of the man that she chose, especially a steward who was rumoured to be an unclaimed bastard.

Linota knew she was being selfish. Katherine was probably out of her mind with worry. They'd never been apart before. Linota had heard the screams her sister had made as she'd been dragged away. Katherine would not want to let her out of her sight once they were reunited.

Deep down, Linota knew it was a gift to be loved so much, but sometimes that love could be constricting. It was as if she'd spent her whole childhood tightly wrapped in ribbons and now she was beginning to experience what is was like to have them loosened. She wasn't sure she could go back to being the biddable sister.

Not for the first time Linota wondered how different her life would have been if her father hadn't been executed for treason. Braedan and Katherine would have been first to make fine marriages. Perhaps that would have left her, as the youngest child, free to marry for love.

'I hate traitors,' she said, her thoughts bursting forth.

Erik glanced across at her. If he was puzzled about her outburst, he didn't say.

'Is that because of your father?' he asked.

'My father wasn't a traitor,' she said quickly.

Erik didn't respond.

Her fists curled involuntarily. Since her father's death she'd known that she was the only person who believed in his innocence. She'd hoped, rather than expected, that Erik would have regarded her father as innocent without her having to explain, purely because he'd come to know her.

She wanted Erik to know what her father was really like, not the man he was portrayed to be by all the malicious gossipers whose whispers followed her and Katherine on the rare occasions they walked around the fortress.

'Do you believe he was guilty just because the King said so?' She knew it was unfair to ask this of him. Lord Leofric had been found guilty of treason and to say otherwise was a crime against the Crown.

Erik rubbed his jaw. 'I think…that a man can be put into an impossible situation. One where he has to make a decision that, no matter the outcome, will hurt someone. He may have to make choices that some would see as traitorous, but others would see as honourable. Sometimes it is not black and white, only grey.'

Linota stepped over a gnarled root. The trees were thinning out now, so they must be nearing the edge of the wood. Her time alone with Erik might nearly be over. For some reason it was important to her that Erik understood her point of view right now. She wanted him to know the truth about her family.

'I don't agree. I think there is only a right decision and a wrong one. I *know* that my father was not guilty of treason. He was the loyalest, kindest man who ever lived. He was betrayed by his so-called allies who spread lies about him. The King believed them rather than my father and he was murdered.'

Linota had never spoken about her father before, not even to Katherine. But now the words were spilling out of her, ideas and thoughts she'd kept from everyone, feelings she'd kept buried for years.

Although no one spoke of Lord Leofric any more, she remembered the man who told her stories while she sat on his knee. She remembered how he had protected her from her mother, who was already showing signs of insanity long before his execution.

'My father was a great man. He was not a traitor. It was the men who betrayed him who were guilty of treason, not him.'

Erik held a bramble aside so she could step through.

'How can you be so sure?' he asked. 'You must have been a very young child when he died?'

'He was hanged, Erik, before my eyes. I was not so young that I cannot remember every horrific detail of it. I can still hear the sound he made when the trap door fell away. I was ten years old, not a baby like everyone seems to assume.'

Erik stopped for a moment and leaned against a tree, a frown creasing his forehead. 'I'm sorry, Linota. No child should have to witness such a thing.'

'No, they shouldn't,' she said, sweeping past him, stopping a few steps away from the tree and gazing back at him. 'My happiest memories come from when he was home and he would take me about on his horse. We would ride across the countryside, him holding me tightly in his arms. He would tell me the most fabulous stories. I can still remember them all and no one listening would doubt that he knew right from wrong. When I have children I am going to tell them every single one of his tales so that they know they must always make the right decision.'

Erik pushed himself away from the tree and continued walking. 'Instead of dwelling on your father's death, perhaps you should give thanks for your fortune at being loved by him. Some of us are not so lucky.'

It was Linota's turn to stop abruptly. 'You know who your father is?'

Heat washed over her as she realised what she had said. She had acknowledged that he was an unclaimed bastard. Although she didn't have friends she knew this was not the kindest thing to say. Katherine would be disappointed in her if she knew.

Erik turned to her and his lips twitched without humour.

'Aye, I know who he was. He's dead now. Come on, I believe we're nearly there.'

'Who was he?' Linota asked, curiosity getting the better of her manners.

Erik's shoulders shook. 'I'm not discussing that with you. Suffice to say he was not a good man.'

'Why won't you tell me? If he's dead, it can't do any harm.'

'Can't it?'

'I wouldn't tell anyone. I can keep a secret.'

'How many secrets have you had to keep up until now?' asked Erik, amusement dancing in his eyes.

Linota paused, her foot suspended in front of her. That was a good question. Other than her belief that her father was innocent of the crimes of which he'd been accused, she didn't really have any secrets to keep. After her father's fall from grace and the removal of the land and wealth from their family, Linota's brother had gone to the Earl of Ogmore, with whom he had served as a page, and begged him to take in his sisters and mother. Ogmore had agreed in return for Braedan's unswerving loyalty.

Linota was grateful to have had a home, something she had often repeated to herself over the years when the bleakness of her restrained circumstances threatened to swamp her.

Unable or unwilling to face people after their family's fall from grace, their mother had kept the two sisters largely confined to their rooms for eight long years. Linota supposed that if she had any friends she would

keep from them the truth that her mother was bordering
on insane. It would reflect badly on her and Katherine
and would likely hinder their chances of good marriages, something Katherine was particularly fervent
about. She wouldn't tell anyone of the beatings Katherine had endured or the near starvation the sisters had
been through, but it was a moot point. She didn't have
friends or confidants other than Katherine who knew
all anyway.

'Fine,' she said. 'I haven't had to keep secrets up until
now, but I know that I can and I would keep yours.'

Erik grinned and Linota's heart felt lighter.

'I trust you, Linota, but it is a long story and not
one I like to dwell on. And certainly not one I want to
think about just before I mount an attack on those two
buffoons.'

'Are we about to start?' she asked eagerly. They had
been walking for so long she had almost forgotten what
lay at the end.

'*We* aren't going to start anything. *I* am going to find
a comfortable tavern for you to wait in and then *I* am
going to get my horse back.'

'But—'

'No. I'm not going to put you at risk and there is no
argument.'

'Do you know where we are?' she asked as a small
settlement came into view, the men having disappeared
among the buildings.

'It's Afon, which, unfortunately, is not somewhere
I've had much reason to stop in before. I know there
is an inn, but not where it is. It can't be hard to find,
though, there are only a handful of buildings here.'

Two boys stopped playing with a dog to stare at them as they approached.

'Where's the tavern?' asked Erik.

The taller of the two boys, his cheek streaked with mud, pointed to the left.

'Thanks, lad,' said Erik, flicking him a small coin from a pouch on his belt. 'For another one can you tell me where I can buy a horse?'

'Tha's funny,' lisped the boy, his two front teeth missing. 'Two men jus' asked 'bout horses. I told 'em go to Murry's stables, he always wants to buy or sell summat.'

'Where will I find Murry?'

'Near the tavern. He owns both.'

'Thanks, lad.'

Erik threw him a slightly bigger coin and the boy fell on it. Likely he'd never had so much money in his short life.

Linota hadn't either.

'Do I really have to stay in the tavern?' she asked as they made their way down a narrow street. 'The men won't be expecting you and so it will be easy to get your horse back.'

'I'm glad you have such faith in me,' said Erik drily. 'But, yes, you do have to stay in the tavern. It is best that they don't see us together. I don't want them going back to this de Bevoir character and telling him they've seen you alive and well in Afon.'

'Oh, I…' She trailed off.

'Oh, what?' he said, coming to a stop.

'I imagined you were going to kill them.'

Erik raised an eyebrow. 'In the middle of the settlement? I don't think that would be wise. I don't want to hang after all. I'm sure I'll think of something less violent, but it would make me happier if I knew you were safe.'

He folded his arms in front of him; the set of his jaw showed her that he wasn't going to back down from this. Fine, she would agree this once but only because she was so hungry and she would finally be able to get a meal in the tavern.

'All right, I'll stay hidden this time,' she said.

His shoulders relaxed and he nodded briefly.

Linota followed him as he began striding in the direction of the tavern once more. She knew it was reasonable for her to wait inside. It was for her safety, but she had the unsettling sensation that there was something more, something she was missing.

As the tavern came into sight she was unable to shake the feeling she had just made a huge mistake.

Erik leaned his back against the tavern wall and let out a long steady breath. He couldn't fall apart now, not when he'd achieved so much.

Linota was safe. He needed to focus on that. But for as long as he lived he would not forget the sound of her screaming his name as she was carried off. The sound had pierced his soul, almost cleaving him in two.

If he hadn't been so distracted yesterday morning those paltry men wouldn't have got away with something so brazen. But he'd been thinking only of what Jarin's change in direction would mean to him and trying to think of anything to stop the Earl returning to his own fortress.

De Bevoir had given Erik a small task in return for his niece—keep Jarin away from his fortress for a week—but somehow, and Erik had absolutely no idea how, Jarin had found out there was some sort of plot against him. Erik had tried all the arguments he could think of to keep Jarin from returning home, but all of his reasoning had failed. Jarin was heading towards whatever de Bevoir was planning and there didn't seem to be anything Erik could do to stop him.

The chances of Erik ever seeing his niece were rapidly diminishing.

He'd been frantically trying to come up with a new plan when Linota had been taken and then Erik no longer cared what Jarin was up to. De Bevoir could do what he wanted. The only thing of importance was getting Linota before those men could cause her harm in any way.

Jarin had yelled some instructions to him as Erik had thundered past on Cai, but for the first time in his life he hadn't stopped to listen to what his liege had to say. His only thought was to get to Linota; nobody as beautiful and as pure as her should spend even a second with those vile individuals.

He'd lost track of them after the men had taken her into the woods and he was nearly crawling out of his skin with despair when Cai had thrown a shoe.

When Linota's scream had sounded in the night air it had shot right through him, piercing him like an arrow to the heart. The sound would haunt his nightmares, but at least it had brought him to her side.

Everything inside him had stilled when he'd seen her lying lifeless on the ground, the ragtag band of men standing around her. He'd almost charged into the clearing and killed the bastards with his bare hands.

He'd managed to stop himself when he realised that Linota wasn't dead. He'd still wanted to tear them all limb from limb, but he'd held himself in check, waiting for an opportunity to get her back that didn't involve mass destruction. Then the group of men had parted, apparently relaxing after they realised Linota was only unconscious. As they'd done so, Erik had caught sight of Simon de Bevoir and his mind had buzzed with questions. Why had de Bevoir taken Linota? What was he hoping to achieve? Did he know how much Erik lusted over her? Was it another way to blackmail him into submission?

Erik hoped the reason had nothing to do with him because otherwise his feelings for Linota were far more obvious to those around him than he'd realised.

He rubbed his forehead. He needed to clear his mind and think, but there wasn't much time. His first priority had to be getting Linota to safety. De Bevoir must have a plan involving her and Erik would be damned if the man got his vile hands on her again.

And he had to keep de Bevoir away from Borwyn. If Jarin found out that Erik was in league with his enemy's right-hand man, then his friend would, quite rightly, never forgive him.

As for Linota, he'd heard what she'd had to say about traitors. She abhorred them. She had made it abundantly clear that there was never any justification for betraying your friends. There was no turning away from the fact that he had done just that to Borwyn, no matter how honourable his intentions. He was going to the devil far quicker than he'd imagined.

He inhaled deeply and tried to get his thoughts into some semblance of order. He pushed himself away from the tavern wall. He needed to get Cai back without alerting those men as to who he was. He hoped, rather than believed, that no bloodshed would be necessary.

He took a last look at the tavern, grateful that Linota had agreed to stay. He'd thought she would argue, but he'd managed to make sure she was installed in a private room which she'd locked from the inside. She was safe and she had food. He didn't need to worry about her for now.

He followed the line of the building and found the boy's information was correct. The stables were next to the tavern. The smell of unclean stalls was almost overpowering as he took a step towards them.

Some of the tension he was holding in his shoulders fled when he rounded the corner and saw Cai swishing his long, dark tail, seemingly unharmed.

Erik squared his shoulders. It was time to put on the persona he'd used around everyone since becoming a man. Pretending to be more confident than he felt usually produced the result he desired. If that didn't work this time, then he would use his fists. Three against one was reasonable odds for him.

'My good men,' said Erik, striding into the stables. 'There seems to be some misunderstanding. This horse is mine.'

Cai whinnied in welcome and stretched towards Erik as if to confirm his statement. Without giving the two men time to argue, Erik seized the reins and rubbed Cai's nose.

'Hang on, we found...' began one of the men.

'Him in the woods, I know,' said Erik serenely, as if he didn't have a care in the world. 'Cai threw a shoe last night. I tied him up in order to come into town for assistance, but I got lost and spent a very uncomfortable night out in the cold. Thank you for bringing him into town for me. Here, for your troubles.'

Erik flicked a coin to each of the men. It was nothing to what they would have received if they'd managed to sell Cai, but as he wasn't insisting the two men be punished for stealing his horse he hoped they would go quietly.

'Sir,' he said, addressing Murry as if the two men had agreed and were already going about their day, 'I trust you will be able to provide a shoe for Cai. I have urgent business in... Middlesex and I need to be on my way as soon as possible.'

Murry made noises about being able to do just that, seemingly accepting that Cai was Erik's horse. Although Erik's clothes weren't the finest silk, they were still a better quality than de Bevoir's men and Cai was obviously a wealthy man's stead. Murry probably recognised that he would get more from Erik than the two dirty men who had come trying to sell him a horse of dubious origin.

The two men shuffled around in the background for a few moments, but when it became obvious that neither Erik nor Murry were going to give them any more attention they sidled out into the mid-morning bustle of the main street.

Murry muttered something about bad blood, but Erik didn't comment. He was just glad the whole thing had been resolved without a fight.

Now he needed time and space to think about what to do next and he knew exactly where he was going to go to get that.

Chapter Five

'Are you comfortable?' Erik murmured into her hair.

'Mmm…' Linota shifted slightly in the saddle. 'I'm fine.'

Fine didn't quite cover how she felt. She *was* comfortable. In fact, she was *too* comfortable. Erik's strong arms were wrapped around her and she was snuggled against his chest, his cloak encasing both of them. She'd be content to stay like this for ever, with the warmth of his body seeping into hers.

'You got Cai back quickly,' she said, trying to distract herself from her inappropriate thoughts.

A laugh rumbled through his body, the movement causing pleasant tingles to ripple through her. 'It wasn't difficult. They weren't the cleverest men I've ever met.'

He lapsed into silence.

He was different this afternoon. Much quieter. Which was fine, he obviously had a lot to think about, but the lack of conversation allowed her imagination to run wild. As they'd left the small settlement together she'd wondered whether they looked like a married couple, riding towards their home, and the idea had sent a thrill running through her.

Her head kept reminding her that she mustn't have these thoughts and feelings about Erik. There would never be a future for them in which resting in his arms would be as normal as breathing. But her body wasn't listening. Her fingers itched with the urge to trace the length of his arms, to feel the muscles that held her tightly.

He rode briskly, not stopping for a break and only speaking once to ask if she was warm enough. To distract herself from Erik, Linota tried to concentrate on the passing scenery. There was only so much attention she could give to endless trees and after a while she gave up trying. She'd have to spend the rest of her life without Erik, why not enjoy the sensation of his arms around her right now? She allowed her back muscles to relax and sink into him. She held her breath, waiting for him to pull away, but he didn't and after that she thought of nothing but him.

The sun was starting to set when he finally pulled off the rough path they were following.

'We'll be able to stop soon,' he said.

'Where are we going?' She'd assumed they were heading for Borwyn's fortress and was unnerved by how thrilled she was that they weren't. Whatever happened later, tonight she was going to spend more time alone with Erik.

'I…' He cleared his throat. 'I have a place. It's small. I…the thing… I… Nobody knows about it.'

She twisted in the saddle and looked up at him. A

faint blush had spread across his cheekbones and her heart squeezed at the sight.

'What I'm saying is it's not luxurious,' he said, not looking down at her. 'I bought it for... I bought it as a place to stay whenever life at the fortress gets...overwhelming.'

Linota turned away from him. His confession had embarrassed him and she didn't want to make him feel foolish by staring. She'd never thought of him as the type of person to need a sanctuary. He always seemed relaxed in his surroundings, whether riding through the forest or training with the men at Ogmore's fortress. She knew him as a casual, carefree man, someone whose eyes twinkled as he spoke. His reputation as Borwyn's right-hand man suggested he was fearless, a formidable man not to be provoked. A bolthole seemed incongruous with the man she'd come to know.

She wanted to ask him more, but his obvious discomfort held her tongue. The time for questioning would come.

It wasn't long before a peasant's cottage came into view. They slowed and came to a stop in front of it. Linota did her best to keep her expression straight. This simple dwelling was another surprise. Even knowing he had a refuge she still hadn't expected this rustic dwelling for the hardened warrior.

'I'll stable Cai if you would like to let yourself in.' Erik jumped down and helped Linota off the horse.

Once her feet were settled on the muddy ground he strode off, tugging Cai after him, not glancing back to see what she was doing. He let himself into one end of the dwelling and disappeared from sight.

She looked around her, trying to get a sense of what this building was used for. The air was still with no sign of any animals around, no sense of anyone else around, for that matter. Whatever Erik used the place for it wasn't for keeping livestock or a hidden army.

She made her way over to a wooden door at the opposite end of the dwelling to where Erik had recently disappeared and shoved it open.

A little light, left over from the evening, spilled in through the opening. She wasn't sure exactly what she'd been expecting—something thick with dust, perhaps, or maybe the sour scent of damp—but the inside was very neat and clean with only the faint whiff of old wood smoke. An unlit fireplace was brushed out with no signs that it had been used recently. A long, wooden table took up one side of the room. She made her way over to it and ran her hand over the smooth wooden top. It was a beautifully made piece with a long bench of equally good-quality workmanship tucked underneath.

Linota stilled as she looked them over, her heart beating painfully in her chest as a horrible thought occurred to her. Could Erik possibly be married or betrothed? Was this home set up for the woman he loved? She'd never thought to ask him if he had a wife and no one had mentioned it either way. She'd seen him flirting with women but, of course, that meant nothing. Plenty of men were unfaithful. The giddy feelings she'd been experiencing whenever she was around him suddenly seemed ridiculously naive.

The more she looked around the more convinced she

became. This was not some place Erik had acquired on a whim. There were little details throughout the cottage that spoke of love and care and a fine attention to detail.

How foolish she was to have felt comfortable in his arms. This confirmed that all the gentle flirting had been nothing but a kindness on his part. She was so inexperienced in the world that she'd taken that care and made it into something else in her head. And, even though she'd always known they couldn't be together, she'd still tucked away every little compliment he'd given her. She'd been so foolish.

She twisted her fingers into her skirts. She didn't want him to come in and find her dithering and slightly heartbroken over her discoveries. She needed to be active, to show that she didn't care that he had a woman in his life who wasn't her.

A small stack of wood was piled next to the fire. She made her way over to it and started to pile the sticks in the way she'd seen her sister do. It couldn't be that hard to light a fire and it would give her something to concentrate on other than her heart constricting in pain.

'You are being silly,' she muttered to herself as she selected some of the smaller logs. 'Even if he did adore you, you couldn't marry him anyway. So stop this nonsense and get on with things.'

'Did you say something?' said Erik.

'Ah!' she yelped, dropping the logs she'd carefully collected.

'Sorry.' He moved towards her. 'I didn't mean to startle you. Here, let me help.'

Linota stood back as Erik arranged the logs and then placed tinder around the base.

'Please pass me the strike-a-light.' He held up his hand. 'I keep it just above you.'

She reached up to the shelf above her. There was only one object to hand, which was lucky because she didn't want to show her ignorance at not knowing what he was talking about. Lighting fires had never been something she'd done and now she was regretting letting Katherine take charge of everything. If only she'd learned some basic skills, perhaps she wouldn't have been so much at the mercy of those men and now she wouldn't feel so crushingly naive and young. Erik's woman probably knew exactly how to light a fire and defend herself against marauding men.

Erik's fingers brushed her skin as he took the strike-a-light from her, sending a delicate tingle across her skin. She snatched her hand away. Up until now she had enjoyed his light touches, even though they had been innocent, but if he had someone special in his life...

She missed what he did to start the fire, but soon the kindling had caught and yellow flames were licking the logs. The first wave of heat reached her. She sighed and held out her hands to the blaze even though it was still too small to really make a difference to her temperature.

Erik lit a couple of candles and placed them on the long table.

'I don't have much in the way of food here, but I can probably rustle up a couple of oatcakes from Cai's saddlebags if you're still hungry.'

'I ate enough at the tavern, thank you.' Linota didn't think she could eat anything right now. Her stomach was still in knots over her recent deductions.

'Ah, right. Shall we warm ourselves by the fire then?'

Erik pulled two chairs up to the hearth. He disappeared into a far corner and returned with a rug. He settled it over one of the chairs. 'Sit on this and I'll wrap it around you.'

Linota's heart stuttered over his gentle care. *He's either married or betrothed,* she reminded herself. *Don't take this gesture as any more than solicitude over a guest.*

She rearranged the rug around herself and stared into the flames, absentmindedly running her fingers over the arm of the chair. The wood was as smooth as silk under her touch.

Next to her Erik shifted in his seat. 'Are you comfortable?'

'Oh, yes, this is an incredibly comfortable chair. Your wife has excellent taste.'

Her heart skipped a beat. She hadn't meant to be so blatant, but the words had flown out of her without her permission.

Erik laughed softly. 'I don't have a wife.'

'Oh, your betrothed then?' She glanced across at him quickly. He was watching the flames with a small smile playing over his lips.

'I am not betrothed to anyone. As for the chairs, I made them myself.'

'Really?' she said, sitting upright and running her fingers over the smooth wood once more. 'But they are beautiful.'

'I am not just Borwyn's mindless thug.' Erik smiled at her, but she had the impression he was only pretending to laugh at himself.

'I never thought you were. I only imagined that your

work for Borwyn would keep you almost constantly busy. I can't see when you'd have the time to make such exquisite pieces.'

Linota didn't say, but she'd pictured him spending his free time fighting or spying for Borwyn. Any time he had left after that was for seducing willing widows, like the one who had hung on his arm at Ogmore's fortress and whose adoring eyes Linota had thought about scratching out more times than she would care to admit to herself.

'I find working with wood, carving something out of nothing, calms me.'

Linota continued to run her hands over the arms of the chair, imagining the effort it would take to make something so perfect. She tried to dismiss the image of him working over the wood, the strong muscles of his forearms flexing as he moved. Even though she knew he didn't have a wife, such thoughts were inappropriate.

'Did you make that little horse carving? The one I saw on my brother's wedding day?' she asked eventually. She didn't remember exactly what the little animal had looked like, only that it was made with the same dedicated care.

There was a long pause. She remembered how strangely he had reacted after the horse had fallen from his belt. She frowned at the fire. It was such an innocuous item and yet it seemed to hold mysterious claim over him.

'Yes,' he confirmed after such a long pause she'd thought he wouldn't respond. He didn't elaborate further. Her mind buzzed with questions, but she kept her mouth shut.

Erik threw another log on to the fire, the bright sparks lighting up the side of his face. Linota wished she could reach across and touch him. She wanted to know what was going on in his mind. There were so many different sides to him. He was Borwyn's enforcer and right-hand man, the one who was willing to get his hands dirty while Borwyn stayed out of such affairs. He was the man whose laughing eyes took nothing too seriously and who had kept her entertained during the long afternoons of riding. But he was also the man with such an incredible artistry, a side to him he clearly kept hidden from everyone else.

Linota looked around the space. Most of the room was thrown into darkness, but the light from the fire and the flickering candles showed a space that had been well maintained and obviously cared for.

'Why do you have such a place if not for a wife?' she asked when she could stand the silence no longer.

Erik laughed bitterly. 'If I had a wife, do you think she would want to live here when she could live in luxury at Borwyn's fortress? Besides, who would have a bastard like me? I only survive on the good graces of my…of Borwyn. If we were to fall out, I would have nothing.'

Linota wanted to argue that she would have him. That she would be honoured to have such a man as her husband, but she knew that Katherine and Braedan would feel the same way as Erik. He wasn't good enough, in their eyes, to marry her, despite the fact that, until very recently, their family circumstances had been just as bad. Now that they were on the rise her siblings

would only want her to marry someone from the no-
blest families, not an unclaimed bastard.

Her throat ached with the unsaid words, the silence
stretching painfully between them.

Erik's shoulders dropped and she wondered if he had
been waiting for her to give voice to the thoughts which
were stuck inside her.

'It's getting late,' he said quietly. 'Let me show you
where you can sleep.'

Linota's heart began to race.

Last night they had slept next to one another. Would
they do so again this evening?

Erik led her to the back of the room and she followed
slowly. Her pulse pounded violently in her throat. A
dark staircase took them to a narrow loft. A narrow bed
was pressed up against the far wall. It was too small for
the two of them to fit on it together and her fluttering
heart took a deep dive.

Erik rooted around in a trunk at the bottom of the
bed. 'Here are some blankets.' He held them out to her.

She took them from him, folding the soft fabric over
her arm.

'I'll bid you goodnight, then.' Erik moved over towards the top of the stairs, taking the light with him
and the breath caught in her lungs. This was a horror
she hadn't prepared for.

'I can't.'

He paused. 'I'm sorry?'

'I can't be on my own in the dark. I've never been
left alone. I mean, Katherine has always been with me.
I can't… The nightmares… They're so bad.'

She didn't want to describe to him what horrors she

faced when she closed her eyes. Night after night her father would hang before her very eyes. The dreams didn't come so violently if Katherine told her a story before they both fell asleep, but if she ever woke up to find Katherine not beside her in the bed then panic would set in. Her whole body would tremble, her lungs would close and she would gasp for breath. It had happened so often that she knew she wasn't going to die from the slow suffocation, but whenever it occurred it truly felt as if she would this time.

Erik stepped back into the loft and set the candle on the trunk. He folded his arms and stared down at the floor. 'I'll stay with you until you fall asleep.'

It wasn't ideal, but she could hardly ask for more without sounding as if she were offering him something, something that, however much she desired him, she wasn't ready to give.

'Thank you,' she said quietly.

Erik lowered himself on to the floor, leaning his back against the chest as she arranged the blankets on the bed. She climbed into them without taking her clothes off and turned on her side, curling up into a ball.

The night was still, the only sound in the small room Erik's steady breathing and the faint crackle and spit of the fire below.

'Talk to me,' she said quietly.

His boots scraped across the floor as he shifted. 'What about?'

'Tell me about this place.'

There was a long silence. She was getting used to this reaction from him. For all of his jokes and smiles, he always thought about what he was going to say when the topic was serious. She lay there patiently, waiting for him to be ready to talk.

He cleared his throat. 'I'll tell you about it if you promise me that you won't repeat what I say tonight to anyone else.'

Linota tucked her hands between the folds of her skirt, trying to get them warm. When she'd asked her question she hadn't meant for him to reveal secrets. She was hoping to find out how he'd come to buy it, but now that the opportunity presented itself to learn more about him she couldn't resist.

'I swear on my honour that I will not tell a single soul what you tell me this evening.'

His boots scraped again as he moved once more. When he spoke it sounded as if he had turned to face her, but she could not make his features out in the darkness.

'I bought this cottage for my sister, Mary.'

Whatever she had been expecting it wasn't that. A story about smuggling, perhaps, or something vaguely unlawful, perhaps like this was where he brought enemies of Borwyn to torture them or married women he wanted to seduce. A sister was so mundane she was almost lost for words.

'I see,' she said eventually. 'Does she not like the idea of living here?'

Perhaps his sister valued the rich living in Borwyn's castle or maybe she was exiled in some terrible disgrace, not allowed to come back into Borwyn's lands until she had undertaken some sort of penance. Linota's mind whirled with questions. She chewed her lips, forcing herself not to bombard him.

'She doesn't know about it,' said Erik quietly.

Linota tucked one arm beneath her head. She was warming up now under the swaddle of blankets.

'Why doesn't she know?'

Erik cleared his throat twice, a sign Linota was beginning to recognise as one he made when he didn't really want to talk. She was really getting to know him now and the more she knew the more she realised how hard it would be to be parted from him.

'She doesn't know because…well, partly because she is dead, but she didn't know of its existence before that either.'

Linota said nothing. His words were so stark. He'd spoken without emotion, but this cottage, with all its fine attention to detail, showed just how deeply he did care. The beautiful furniture and the comfortable bed spoke of a man who had done everything he could to provide his sister with her own private, comfortable space. She longed to slip from the bed and wrap her arms about his body. He might be a warrior, but he could still hurt.

She couldn't imagine the pain of losing a sibling. According to Katherine, their mother had birthed more children than the three who had survived into adulthood. They had all died before Linota was born and, as she was their last child, she didn't miss these babies who had gone long before her. Katherine often said she believed it was these deaths which had gradually changed their mother into the way she was, a cruel and vindictive woman who appeared to enjoy making Katherine and Linota's life a living hell.

'I am sorry for your loss. I've only known Braedan and Katherine as my siblings. I don't know Braedan well. He's fourteen years older than me and had left our father's home long before I was old enough to know him. But Katherine… If something happened to Katherine it would devastate me.' She took a steadying breath. 'Did your sister die recently?'

Erik heaved out a rough sigh, which told Linota all she needed to know. He did feel the pain of her death no matter how hard he might try to hide the fact.

'The truth is, I don't know when she died. I only found out about it recently. My sister and I were both unwanted bastards in a fortress that didn't take kindly to burdens. I tried to protect her as best I could, but I wasn't very big or strong as a child and I couldn't be with her all the time. I had to work so that we could eat. I took all the jobs I could find. My mother wouldn't allow us to stay near her and so we slept and ate wherever we could. We were always on the move, trying to find somewhere safe to stay.'

Linota had never thought about Erik's early childhood. He'd appeared at Ogmore's fortress as a fighter, a warrior with whom no one would argue. His broad shoulders and muscled body showed a man to be feared and respected. She couldn't imagine him as a little boy scrabbling around trying to find food for himself and his sister.

'What happened?'

'I don't know if we had the same father.' He huffed out a bitter laugh. 'The man who sired me wouldn't claim me as his own, despite the fact that I look very much like him and his legitimate children, but that didn't stop him…well, let's just say he wanted me disciplined as if I were his son. He was a cruel man who delighted in the misery of others. He didn't take any notice of Mary at all, for which I was grateful. I can't imagine what he would have done to a daughter... She looked nothing like him and my mother was rumoured to have had several lovers. My mother always claimed she was his, but she wasn't truthful so...'

There was so much pain in Erik's voice that tears pricked Linota's eyes. How could anyone treat two children so badly? If she was ever blessed with any she would make sure they knew how much they were loved, every single day.

'What was Mary like?'

'She was gentle and kind.' Erik's voice was softer now and full of love. 'She adored animals, especially horses. I carved the horse you saw for her and made it into a necklace. She never took it off.'

Linota could hear the pride in Erik's voice and her heart bled for him.

'Unfortunately for Mary, she took after my mother in looks. I may not have liked my mother, but even I could tell she was extraordinarily beautiful. Men would flock to her like bees to flowers. If she changed the colour of her clothing, that colour would become instantly popular with the women of the fortress. As soon as Mary began to develop womanly features the male attention on her was intense and continuous. Men assumed she would be like my mother and offer her favours to the highest bidder. She was barely out of childhood and was terrified by the attention. Keeping men away from her was how I learned to fight.'

The urge to climb out of bed was even stronger now.

The pain was so evident in his voice. She forced herself to stay where she was, though. She wasn't sure the hardened warrior would want sympathy and in the darkness she didn't trust herself not to try to kiss away the pain.

'When my mother realised her daughter was getting more attention than her, she went to my father and asked him to arrange a marriage for Mary. I'm not sure my father would have raised himself to be bothered, but I was brought before him because I'd been caught brawling over her. Either he wanted to please my mother or he wanted to cause me pain because a marriage was arranged for her quite quickly after that. Mary begged me to save her. I promised that I would, but I failed.'

'No, that is not true. You didn't fail anyone. You can't have been much more than a boy yourself. How were you to go up against your father?'

'I could have taken her away from the fortress to somewhere safe, away from my father and poisonous mother.'

'Where would you have gone? Two young children alone in the world would not have lasted long. You would have been killed and Mary would have ended up in a far worse situation than an arranged marriage.'

Erik laughed although the sound did not sound joyful. 'You are kinder to me than I deserve. Maybe it's true that I couldn't have saved her when we were children, but I should have found her long ago and brought her here where she would have been safe.'

'Do you know anything about the man she married?' asked Linota.

'I don't know anything about what happened to her

from the moment I last saw her. As I told you, I failed Mary.'

'You didn't fail. You were only a boy. For all you know her marriage was happy.'

She was determined to show him that he wasn't to blame. His hateful parents were the ones who should carry the shame of letting down both of their children.

Erik grunted. 'My father would not have wanted Mary to be happy in her marriage. He was not that type of man.'

'He sounds like an awful person. I am sure that he is in eternal hell now for all his sins. Who would want his children to be so miserable? More to the point, who would have that level of control to arrange such a thing?'

Erik didn't answer. Silence stretched between them.

Linota gasped. Suddenly it was obvious who his father was. It only astonished her that it had taken so long for her to realise.

'Does he know?' she whispered into the darkness.

'Does who know what?' said Erik, a layer of caution lacing his words.

'The current Earl of Borwyn. Does he know who your father was? Does he know that you are half-brothers?'

Erik inhaled sharply as the truth thudded between them. 'It didn't take you long to work that out. Did you already know?'

'Of course not! As I've said before, I've hardly left my chambers for the last eight years. Whenever I do, gossip follows me round, but that's about me and my father, not about yours. How on earth would I have known? Does everyone?'

Erik tapped his heel against the floor. 'I don't think Jarin knows I'm his half-brother. He's never mentioned it. I've wanted to ask him, but I can never find the words. Jarin is a good man, kind and thoughtful, but he has his own problems and is focused on himself and solving those. I don't think it would occur to him that I am his half-brother. I've overheard snide comments about myself—as I said, I look very like the late Earl— but nothing is said directly to my face and certainly not when Borwyn is around. He's a powerful man now.'

'How are you and the Earl friends, then?' Linota was about as far away from sleep as it was possible to be. Now that Erik had trusted her with his secret she wanted to know everything. 'You seem very close.'

'After Mary left I found I wanted to know my other siblings. My two older legitimate brothers, who have since died, were as bad as our shared father, cruel and self-centred. Jarin was, and is, different. He is rational and kind. The other two liked to use their fists to solve problems. They thought nothing of taking a woman whether she wanted their attentions or not. I came across Jarin when he was hiding from our father. He had just borne the brunt of our father's rage and was covered in bruises from the beating he'd received. I helped him find a place to hide and recover. Over time we became close friends.' The chest creaked as Erik shifted his position. 'I should have discussed my parentage in the beginning, but now that time has passed it feels…uncomfortable. It makes no difference. I am loyal to him and would consider him a brother with or without our shared father.'

'But if you were an acknowledged Borwyn, you could have your own land. You wouldn't need—'

'How can I be acknowledged now that our father has died?' said Erik, his voice raised to almost a shout.

Linota froze. She was being too intrusive. Erik had trusted her with so much. She mustn't push him on something so sensitive. She waited in silence for him to calm down.

Eventually he spoke again, quieter this time. 'I would be lying if I said I don't sometimes look at what Jarin has and wish I had some of it but… Jarin has more responsibilities than you and I can imagine. I wouldn't want to take his place for all the money in the kingdom. Now, we've discussed enough of my past. I think it would be best if we tried to get some sleep.'

She heard a creak as Erik settled back against the chest, his boots scraping across the floor as he straightened out his legs. There were so many questions she wanted to ask, but she recognised that the time for confidences was over. He had come to the end of his story and she needed to be grateful that he'd given her so much already.

Her mind was so full of swirling thoughts that she didn't think she would ever drop off to sleep, but she was warm and safe and before long heaviness tugged her under.

Chapter Six

Linota's breathing finally settled into the heavy rhythm of deep sleep. Erik stood slowly, careful not to make any noise. He really did not want to wake her. As much as he enjoyed talking to her, her questions this evening were so probing. A few more and he would spill everything, even the secrets he had buried so deep inside him they hadn't seen the light of day in years.

Before he could make it to the stairs, he stopped. Despite his best intentions, his gaze was drawn to her sleeping form. Her body was curled so tightly she resembled a hibernating dormouse. He smiled. He wished he could watch her sleep, not just from this position but next to her. He longed to see her hair fanned out across the bed, her fingers curled in relaxation, but he didn't deserve such a simple pleasure.

He crept over the edge of the loft, careful to avoid creaking floorboards, and ghosted down the stairs.

He hadn't meant to tell her so much, to open his soul to her but he'd wanted someone to know him. Hell, he wasn't being honest and he might as well be with himself if he wasn't going to be with everyone else—he'd wanted *her* to know him.

He'd wanted her to see his childhood, all the deprivation and the struggle, so that she would understand him, so that she would know why he was going to such lengths to get his niece to safety. He closed his eyes tightly. He could never tell her about Isabel. To do so would reveal him to be a traitor to his half-brother and closest friend and she would never forgive that. She had made it very clear that there was only right or wrong in her eyes and even he knew that, despite his good intentions behind his actions, what he had done to Borwyn was definitely wrong.

Downstairs the fire had burned down to embers. He threw on a few logs, prodding the flames until they roared again. He sat down on Linota's chair, pulling her blanket around him. He fancied he could still smell her on the cloth. He leaned back against the chair and closed his eyes. Tomorrow would be a long day and he should rest. His muscles pressed into the hard confines of the chair. Whenever he had trouble sleeping he would picture carving a hunk of wood into something pure. Tonight his mind wouldn't focus on it. All he could think of was Linota sleeping upstairs in his bed, her body soft and warm.

He opened his eyes and stared blankly at the dark ceiling. He was falling for Linota. Hell, he'd already fallen. She'd had his heart from the moment he'd first seen her and there was nothing he could do about it. To see her married to Borwyn would kill him, but he owed it to his brother to promote the match. Even without her sizeable dowry she would be a perfect wife for him, beautiful, intelligent and kind. She would be a wise countess, someone who would be an asset to Borwyn whether dealing with the townsfolk or travelling to court.

Even before she'd been abducted by de Bevoir he'd had to keep reminding himself of this fact. Every time he spoke to her, he got carried away, unable to stop himself flirting with her, desperate to make her laugh. But he'd known he'd been wrong to do so. If he was betraying Jarin, then the least he could do was make sure Linota was amenable to becoming Jarin's wife. The dowry and alliance were vitally important to Jarin's future as Earl. Erik's flirtation with Linota was a double betrayal.

And Erik would have to get used to the idea of Borwyn sharing Linota's bed.

A weight pressed down on his chest. He couldn't breathe. He strode over to the door, wrenching it open and stepping outside. The cool air rushed over him, biting against his skin. He inhaled deeply, relishing the cool air burning his lungs.

A twig snapped.

And then another.

Erik pulled his dagger from its sheath and held it out in front of him; peering into the darkness.

'I take it you have the girl.'

Erik's grasp tightened on his dagger as de Bevoir's nasally voice seeped into the night air. How did de Bevoir know where to find him? Had they been followed the whole time?

'Where are your men?' he growled.

If they were anywhere vaguely near here, he was

going to gut them where they stood for daring to touch Linota.

There was a snort of disgust to his right. 'I got rid of those imbeciles as soon as I realised you had taken the Leofric girl. I know you think nobody knows about this place of yours, but it is my business to know things. I cut those men loose. It is simpler this way.'

'What do you mean, *simpler*? This is already out of control. You never said anything about involving an innocent woman in this insane plot of yours.'

Erik heard de Bevoir move until suddenly he was standing in front of him. Erik could just make out the shape of his body in the darkness.

'Our agreement was that you would keep Borwyn from returning to his fortress for a week.' De Bevoir paused. '*You* failed to do that. Borwyn will reach the fortress within a matter of days, which does not suit me *at all*. I have had to take preventative action. Linota Leofric is part of that plan.'

Erik's hand shook as his grip on his dagger tightened.

'Linota Leofric has nothing to do with Borwyn,' he growled. 'She is a complete innocent.'

There was a pause. 'That's not quite true, is it?'

Erik clenched his jaw, but said nothing.

'Oh, I know the girl is an innocent,' de Bevoir continued. 'I'm sure we can both agree on the purity of her body and the beauty of her features. She's almost a paragon of virtue. But it is not true that she is *nothing* to Borwyn, is it?'

Erik froze. Surely de Bevoir couldn't *know* about Linota's dowry.

It had only been Jarin and Erik in the room when

Ogmore had made his substantial and surprising offer. Neither of them had told a soul. Jarin didn't want anyone to know about his straitened circumstances. Only Erik knew some of the details and even he didn't know everything. It was the direness of the situation that made Ogmore's offer so appealing to Jarin and he wouldn't want that common knowledge. Erik was loyal to Jarin and wouldn't tell a soul.

So surely de Bevoir couldn't know that Borwyn was considering marrying Linota Leofric for that very reason.

In the darkness Erik heard de Bevoir laugh softly. It was a sound completely devoid of humour. 'It will save us both time, Erik, if you know that I, like you, have spies everywhere. Although I would wager mine are better informed than yours. You lack certain… experience. Suffice to say, I know about Ogmore's offer of a substantial dowry on both Leofric sisters and I know that Borwyn needs the money and the support. My liege and others on Borwyn's many borders have been mounting a steady stream of small skirmishes.' Erik's chest tightened. This was a living nightmare. De Bevoir knew everything. 'Borwyn's had to overstretch himself all over his land. He must be close to breaking point by now.'

De Bevoir laughed and this time he did sound amused. 'The young Earl is nothing like his father. He is not ruthless enough to survive as the lord and master of such a large swathe of land. It won't be long before all those who had land taken off them by the late Earl begin to take advantage of his son's weaknesses.

Lord Garbodo wants to get his land back before fighting really sets in.'

Erik fought to keep his stance firm even as the overwhelming urge to lie down swept over him. He and Jarin had been fighting and plotting for months to try to get the borders into a semblance of order. Approaching Ogmore for support had been their last resort. Without Ogmore's aid de Bevoir was right. Jarin was not going to make it. He would lose everything he had been striving to hold together.

Jarin had not been prepared to inherit the estate; that should have been the responsibility of his older brother. In his own twisted way the Earl had cared about *that* son. At least to the extent that he had shared his vast knowledge of how the estate worked. The two of them had shared a passion for hunting and wenches, too. They were the exact opposite of Jarin, who was thoughtful and compassionate.

When his older son and the next one in line had died the Earl had been left with a son he despised and Erik, whom he hated even more. Jarin had tried to be the man his father wanted, but by then it was too late. The animosity between the two of them had been great and unfixable. The old Earl had wasted his remaining years tying Jarin in knots, gaining great amusement from sending Jarin on pointless errands. He'd ignored Erik completely.

Jarin should have appointed an experienced steward when he'd inherited everything. Someone who would have seen Lord Garbodo's plot coming months ago and could have advised him on a sound strategy to save the Borwyn estate. But he hadn't. He'd named his closest friend as his right-hand man and Erik had let his brother down in every way.

He rubbed a hand over his chest, but it did nothing to relieve the tightness building there, threatening to choke him.

'Why not take both girls?' asked Erik. He needed to keep de Bevoir talking. Given enough time he might be able to come up with a plan to sort this problem once and for all.

'Come now, Erik, we both know that Borwyn is not going to choose the older sister. She looks like a boy. He's not going to be able to stomach bedding that.' De Bevoir paused as Erik's heart sank. De Bevoir had confirmed what he already suspected. Nobody would want to marry Katherine Leofric when Linota was also on offer. He glanced up and realised de Bevoir was watching him intently. His hope that his emotions had not played across his face were dashed when de Bevoir added slyly, 'I know you prefer the younger sister, too.'

'I don't…' Erik paused; denying his attraction to Linota wouldn't help.

De Bevoir obviously had spies everywhere and Erik had perhaps not been as discreet in his admiration as he'd believed. Or perhaps de Bevoir was fishing for information. Whatever de Bevoir was playing at, it was best to keep his feelings hidden. No one could know how much he was falling for Linota, not de Bevoir, not Jarin and especially not Linota herself. He'd seen the desire shining from her face. He could kiss her and she would respond, but then he would be betraying Jarin further still.

Besides, if he kissed her, he would only fall for her

even harder. It would be even more difficult to give her up when she married Borwyn.

'I promise not to hurt the girl, Erik,' said de Bevoir, his manner changing briskly. 'I will only ransom her for the money I was going to take from Borwyn's coffers. Either way will bring Borwyn to financial ruin. When my liege takes back the land which belongs to him, Borwyn won't be able to raise an army to reclaim it. No lives will be lost fighting over a stretch of land that is historically Garbodo's anyway. You will almost be doing Borwyn a favour.'

De Bevoir made everything sound so reasonable apart from one point from which Erik would not be moved. 'I will not hand Linota over to you.'

'You may not like me, Erik, but I am a man of my word. No harm will come to Mistress Leofric.'

'No.'

'Then you can say goodbye to ever meeting your niece.'

'You don't want Isabel.'

'I don't, but it is in my power to make sure she has a happy future or...perhaps one that is less than desirable. I'm a reasonable man, but I don't like to be crossed. If you make this difficult for me, then I will make it hard for you. Deep down you and I are the same. You know what you have to do to survive, as do I. At the moment, your niece is the best negotiating tool I have and I will keep it that way until this is over.'

Erik tucked his dagger back into his belt. Much as he wanted to he wasn't going to hurt de Bevoir, at least not until he had Isabel. Then de Bevoir had better run and hide because nothing would stop Erik from hunting him down. He rubbed his jaw where his stubble was quickly becoming a beard. He needed time to think, but time was one of the many things he didn't have. 'I will hide Linota from Borwyn.'

'I don't see how that will work.'

Erik closed his eyes tightly. He was about to make his deal with the devil even deeper, but this way he could keep two people safe. He'd worry about his own soul later.

'I have somewhere she can go. I can hide her from Borwyn. I will not inform him that I have rescued her and I will be your go-between.'

'You will give him the ransom message and ensure he hands over the amount I request?' asked de Bevoir dubiously.

Erik inhaled deeply. 'I will. I swear it on my sister's eternal soul.'

Even in the darkness Erik could feel the weight of de Bevoir's stare. 'Don't let me down, Erik. The life of your young niece depends upon it.'

Erik nodded. 'I won't.'

De Bevoir regarded him for a long moment and then nodded. 'Very well. Meet me at the old tannery when you arrive at Borwyn. We will discuss our next move then.'

De Bevoir turned and disappeared back into the darkness. Shortly afterwards, Erik heard the sound of hoofbeats moving away from the cottage.

Hi kicked the wall. He'd had the chance to end de Bevoir, to run him through with his dagger. He could easily have hidden the body in the undergrowth surrounding his cottage. No one would ever have found out what he'd done. But then he would never find his niece and there was nothing he wouldn't do for his sister's child.

If he found she didn't exist, he would rip de Bevoir apart with his own hands.

He paced away from the cottage and dropped to his haunches. The silence of the night closed in around him, the darkness pressing down from all sides. He was getting deeper into this situation and he wasn't sure how he was going to come out of it with his honour intact.

He stood, rubbing his chest again. The truth was, he wasn't.

There was virtually no way his betrayal would remain uncovered. He would probably lose his privileged position and the respect of his only friend. But that wasn't the worst of it. Linota with her pure heart would be devastated by his treachery. He inhaled deeply. If it meant that she still lived once all this was over, even if she despised him as a liar and traitor, it would be worth it. The world would be a dark place indeed without her in it.

He stepped back into the cottage and grunted as something solid barrelled into him.

'Linota?'

Slender arms slid around his waist and clung on tight. Despite his good intentions, his arms wrapped around her shoulders, pulling her close towards him.

'I awoke and you were gone. It was so dark.' Her whole body shuddered against his. 'I came downstairs and you weren't here either.'

Her small curves fitted perfectly against his body, just as he'd imagined so many times. She was so beautiful, so innocent. He didn't deserve her trust, but he would do everything to keep her safe. De Bevoir would never be allowed to touch her again. He didn't trust the man not to try to take her again.

'It's all right. I'm here now.' He bent his head and rested his cheek against her soft hair.

He meant the gesture to be comforting but he soon realised his mistake. Desire he'd been fighting for so long rushed through him, hot and intense. His body tightened and his fingers shook as he fought with the urge to bury them deeply in her hair.

'I'm sorry you were scared,' he said, battling to keep his lust under control. His voice sounded rough even to his own ears.

He needed to step away from her before he did something foolish. He slowly released her, trailing his hands gently down her arms. Her fingers, small and shapely, caught his. Despite his good intentions he linked his hands with hers. Her skin was so soft against his. He traced a small circle on the back of her hand with his thumb. He felt, rather than heard, her soft gasp.

He'd had women before, although not as many as had offered themselves to him. He was choosy about who shared his bed. He knew some women found his roughness attractive. None of those women had ever made his heart pound like this from such a simple touch. She was an innocent. She would have no idea what she was doing to him. How the very sight of her nearly sent him to his knees with longing, how he loathed his half-brother, at this moment, for being able to marry her if he wanted to.

'Erik,' she whispered.

His name on her lips was his undoing.

'Linota,' he groaned, pulling her back towards him.

His lips passed over her forehead and down the soft curve of her cheeks. Half expecting her to step away, he moved slowly. Gently, so as not to scare her, he placed the softest of kisses against her mouth.

She didn't pull away or scream in horror.

He kissed her again, longer this time, but just as softly. Beneath him her mouth moved in response.

He pulled away, but she followed him, pressing a kiss of her own. He could taste her inexperience in the tremble of her lips. He knew he was even worse than a traitor, he was the worst of men, for not pulling away, but he couldn't. Her sweetness called to him, pulling at his soul and demanding he take more.

He reached up, drawing over the line of her jaw with his fingertips. He could feel her pulse beating wildly in her neck. He slanted his mouth over hers. She moaned as he traced the seam of her lips with the tip of his tongue. Her mouth parted and he swept in, groaning in pleasure as she welcomed him.

He cupped her head, her silken hair falling over his fingers.

'Linota,' he groaned again, her name almost a plea.

He moved his lips from her mouth, along her jaw, her breath coming in quick, breathy gasps as he dipped to the length of her neck.

She wanted him as much as he did her. That thought was nearly his undoing. His body screamed to take her while his mind roared a reminder of her innocence.

Her fingers fluttered at the nape of his neck, the touch so soft and gentle. So innocent.

His mouth reclaimed hers.

This kiss was nothing like he had ever experienced before. He'd thought he knew all about pleasure, but he'd been wrong. Kissing Linota was otherworldly. He could drown in her body and die happily listening to her soft moans of delight.

There was a reason he shouldn't be doing this. It tugged on the edge of his consciousness, taunting him in this perfect moment. He pulled her tighter against him, pressing their bodies together. The voice screamed louder in his head, reminding him of his loyalties, reminding him that he was a better man than this.

He lifted his mouth and rested his head against Linota's forehead. Their loud breathing filled the room. He should step away. He would step away, in a moment, when he was stronger.

'I'm sorry. I shouldn't have...' He tailed off. He didn't want to apologise for what had happened between them. It was the purest thing he'd ever experienced and, although it was wrong of him to take advantage of her, he couldn't bring himself to regret it.

What he wanted to apologise for was the fact that he was lying to her, that he was also taking advantage of her innocence.

He couldn't tell her about his deal with de Bevoir. Linota had made it very clear that she thought betrayal was the worst crime imaginable. She had said that there could be no excuse for betraying someone. If she found out the truth of what he'd agreed to, she would hate him. And he wouldn't blame her.

He was a bastard in every sense.

He dropped his arms and stepped away from her.

'Erik?'

He hated the vulnerability in her voice. He'd put that uncertainty there by his actions. He only had to hope he hadn't completely destroyed the easy camaraderie they shared. He loved the way her eyes lit up every time he made her laugh and he didn't want to lose that.

'I'm sorry... I... I'm sorry I left you alone.' He pushed his hands through his hair, dismayed to find that they were still unsteady. 'I'll come up and wait for you to settle again.'

He heard her hesitation and held himself rigid. He wouldn't be able to stop himself if she closed the gap between them and brought her mouth back to his. He had to hope that her inexperience with men would save them both from what could only end in disaster.

'Come,' he said sharply.

He strode across the tiled floor and quickly climbed the stairs to the loft.

He pretended to rummage around in the chest at the foot of the bed while she slowly climbed back under the covers. When he was sure she was lying down he closed the lid with a snap.

'You need to rest now,' he said. 'Tomorrow is a long day.'

'What about you?' she asked softly.

'Once you're asleep I will head downstairs and rest as well.' He had to get away from her before the temptation became too great.

'Please don't go,' she whispered.

He really should head back downstairs. He could imagine Linota's slender figure, lying there, cocooned among the covers and her cloak, and remember how it fitted so neatly against his. Knowing what her lips felt like under his made the situation even worse. But he could tell by the strain in her voice that she really was afraid of being left alone in the dark and he would be the worst kind of bastard if he left her to face her fear alone.

'I won't be far away,' he said gently, in a last desperate attempt to put some distance between them.

'I have nightmares. Bad ones. My father…he's—it's—' she stuttered. 'My mind replays the moment of his death, if…if I'm lucky. If I'm not, it's him and Katherine with the noose around their necks. I won't… Just please don't leave me.'

Erik closed his eyes. He'd never sleep so close to her but unable to join her in the bed. The night would be one, long torture. But he owed her this comfort. It was his fault she was here and that she'd suffered an ordeal at the hands of those men. Besides, he'd survived sleeping next to her last night. He could do it again.

'Very well, I will stay.'

'Thank you,' she whispered.

He pulled a blanket out of the chest and spread it across the narrow strip of floor available to him.

'Goodnight, Linota,' he said firmly. He did not want to talk to her any more. The more they conversed the more he liked her and he was already in danger from liking her too much for his own sanity.

'Goodnight,' she said quietly.

He closed his eyes tightly. *Let this all be over soon so that my life can go back to normal.*

But even as he prayed he couldn't ignore the heavy

weight settling in his stomach as he imagined a time when it wouldn't be just him and Linota, alone together without anyone to come between them.

Chapter Seven

Linota woke slowly. The edges of a dream tried to tug her back under with its promise of soft lips and strong arms. She snuggled deep into the soft blankets, her eyes scrunched tightly, but persistent birdsong stole into her mind and kept her hovering on the brink of wakefulness.

She was comfortable and warm, warmer than she'd been in a long time. She didn't want to wake and face the day. She shifted, the movement bringing her closer to full awareness.

Nearby, the unmistakable sound of a deep, masculine sigh filled the air. She blinked awake and listened intently. Now that she was properly awake she could make out Erik's steady breathing. He must have stayed with her all night; the thought warmed her heart even as she warned herself against reading too much into it. He'd said he would keep her company, but she'd imagined he would leave again when she was asleep.

She rolled on to her side. Dawn must be breaking, but it was still hard to see much in the darkness of the cottage. Below her, on the floor, Erik was still asleep, his arm flung high above his head. She wished for a little more light so she could see his face. She'd like to know what he looked like when he was soft and unguarded with sleep.

She raised her fingers to her lips. She could still feel the imprint of his mouth against hers and the way his soft stubble had grazed the sensitive skin of her neck as he'd kissed the length of her jaw. It had been beautiful and not nearly enough.

She'd seen men and women together, sometimes kissing, sometimes more.

Linota and Katherine's chamber window at Ogmore's fortress had overlooked a large section of the castle grounds. With nothing much to do each day they would gaze out of it, watching people come and go, interacting with one another, not realising they were being observed from up high. The two of them had seen a lot of life in that small section of the world.

They'd been able to see couples who'd thought they were being discreet by hiding in alcoves, their bodies pressed tightly together. The act had both intrigued and repulsed them. It looked so messy and ungainly, almost as if the couples wanted to eat each other. More often than not the scenes had reduced Katherine and her to helpless giggles. They'd not been able to understand why anyone would want to engage in such a pastime.

It had been different altogether to experience it for herself.

His lips had been firm and dry. They'd drifted over her mouth with the gentlest of touches. It hadn't been enough. Her whole body had screamed out for more, even though she didn't know exactly what it wanted.

He'd kissed her again, more firmly this time, but it didn't repel her the way she'd thought it might. Instead it was as if her whole body had wakened. As if it was purely made for kissing Erik Ward in the confines of his cottage.

She rolled on to her back and stared at the dark ceiling.

Last night had changed her world and not just because of the kiss. Erik had trusted her with a secret so big that she didn't know how she would keep it inside, yet she knew that she must. Betraying his confidence would make her the type of person she despised.

In her very limited dealings with the people of Ogmore's fortress she had never heard the rumour that Erik and Borwyn were related. It didn't mean that nobody knew, only that the rumours weren't rife.

Now that she knew it was so obvious. The two men were so alike, both tall and broad-shouldered with dark blond hair and striking blue eyes. But to her mind Erik was the more attractive of the two. It was in the sparkle of his eyes as they danced with humour and the quirk of his lips whenever she said something that amused him. It was also in the way he moved, as if every step was thought through. He prowled like a cat stalking its prey and when there was a threat he moved with a deadly speed and precision.

Her heart squeezed at the thought of his sister. He'd bought this place for her, not only to be safe, but also to get her away from life at Borwyn's fortress. Much as Linota admired her own brother, he had never done something so generous for her and Katherine.

There were so many different layers to Erik Ward. She wanted to spend time getting to know each one, to really understand the man whom most people saw only as Borwyn's right-hand man and sometimes attack dog.

She turned back to look at him. He hadn't moved. She wanted to crawl out of bed and join him on the floor. Yes, to kiss him again, but also to put her head against his solid chest, to hear his heartbeat and to feel his arms around her once more.

He came awake with a grunt and a deep inhale. He rubbed a hand over his face and then turned to face her.

For a long moment he said nothing, only looking across at her in the semi-darkness of the room.

'Good morning,' he said eventually, his voice husky with sleep.

'Hello.' Heat rushed over her. She wondered how his lovers greeted him in the morning. Was there something she should say that didn't make her seem gauche and naive?

The uncertainty paralysed her bones, leaving her unable to say anything further.

They'd kissed last night and shared secrets, but in the dim light of the early morning that seemed as unreal as an insubstantial dream.

Erik threw off his blanket and pulled himself into a sitting position.

'I'm getting old,' he said, rubbing his lower back. 'I ache all over.'

Linota laughed at his disgruntled expression. 'I think that has more to do with sleeping on the floor than your age.' She tilted her head, looking at the strong lines of his body. 'How old are you?'

He ran a hand through his rumpled hair. 'I think I lived for twenty-nine summers, but it is not as if my mother kept records. I could be slightly older or younger than that.'

Linota's stomach twisted. She hadn't meant to bring up bad memories for him by asking his age.

'Ah, look at your face,' said Erik, his lips curving into a smile. 'I'm not upset so you needn't look so pained. It doesn't really matter not knowing how old I am. It's not something that bothers me.'

Linota didn't answer. For all her mother's awfulness, the woman had never denied Katherine or Linota their birthright. She had never felt that her mother didn't *want* her. That she didn't like Linota was pretty evident, but her mother was proud of the Leofric heritage despite what had happened.

'Please, Linota. There is no need to look so sad. I am content with my lot.'

Linota nodded and smiled, pretending that she was fine, but how could she be when she could imagine how much he was hurting? How could he be content when the sister he had obviously cared deeply about was dead?

Erik pushed back his blanket and stood, folding the cover neatly and returning it to the chest.

'I'll see if I can rummage us up some food and then we had best get going. I hope that we will reach Borwyn today.'

Linota climbed out of the bed and started folding

her own blankets. 'Do you think the others will already be there?'

Erik stilled on the stairs. She glanced over at him. He appeared to be gazing intently at a spot on a wooden beam that ran along the low roof. 'I hope so,' he muttered eventually.

Linota frowned as she put the blankets back in the chest. His reaction had been a bit…off. Almost as if he didn't want the others to have arrived at Borwyn.

She shrugged. She must be imagining things. There was no reason for him not to want to be reunited with everyone else.

She ran her fingers over her braid and wished she had a mirror. She no doubt looked a mess. For a moment or two she fretted over it, heat stealing over her cheeks when she realised she wanted to look pretty for Erik.

She was being ridiculous. In her tatty dress, which was years old and patched up in several places, she wouldn't be able to hold a candle to the women who fawned over Erik. There was no need to give her hair even the slightest of considerations. She made her way downstairs, trying to smooth the tendrils that had escaped the braid, all the while telling herself not to be so foolish.

'Did you find anything to eat?' she asked as she stepped into the main living area. The fire was going once more and she edged closer to it.

'A couple of apples.' He held them up for her to see. 'They are past their best, I'm afraid. I only picked them before Jarin and I left for Ogmore, but I still haven't worked out the best method for storing them so they don't rot quickly.'

He handed one over; its skin was wrinkly under her fingertips. She bit into it. The fruit was soft, but still tasty. The way her stomach was rumbling she would have eaten it if it was rotten.

'Are there apple trees around here, then?' she asked, wiping juice from her chin.

'Yes, a couple outside. I'm thinking of planting more, but…' He shrugged.

They chewed in silence while she mulled over what he'd said and what he hadn't.

'Do you visit here often?' The house was too clean not to be visited regularly, but if he hadn't found his sister why did he bother?

'When my other duties allow it.'

'Do you bring women here?'

He spluttered on a mouthful of apple. 'What?'

Something strange and unpleasant clawed at her heart. Now that she'd thought about it, she couldn't get the image of Erik sitting around his exquisitely made table, talking and laughing with some nameless woman. She hated the way the idea made her stomach burn. What was happening to her? Why did she care so much?

'Do you have a comb?' she asked sharply.

A comb would suggest a woman's presence.

'I'm afraid I don't. And…' He pushed a hand through his hair. 'I haven't brought anyone else here other than you.'

He looked up at her. Their gazes caught and held. Her heart began to beat painfully in her chest. What was happening here? It couldn't be good, whatever it was.

He blinked and she managed to tear her gaze away from him.

She moved over to the fire, pretending to warm her fingers while she finished her apple.

Erik disappeared upstairs and she didn't turn to watch him leave the room. She finished her apple and licked her fingers free of juice.

She heard the heavy clomp of his boots returning downstairs and sucked in a breath. She would not let him know how much his presence affected her.

'Are you ready to go?' he asked, smothering the fire until it was out.

'Of course.' She smoothed her skirts unnecessarily and took one last look around the room. She wanted to remember every detail so she could picture him here once they had parted for the last time.

Outside the air was crisp with cold. She pulled her cloak tighter, but it did nothing to stop the cruel wind cutting through her clothes and chilling her skin. She shuddered and immediately wished that she was back in the cottage, curled up by the comforting fire.

Erik had been heading over to the barn where he'd stabled Cai, but he stopped when she didn't immediately follow him.

He retraced his steps and stood in front of her. His gaze swept over her body. Her body tightened under his penetrating gaze. Her heart began to race. Her fingers itched with the urge to reach up and touch the soft curls of his hair.

She waited. He leaned forward and took the edge of her cloak between his thumb and forefinger. She held her breath, waiting for his hand to slip beneath the fabric and pull her to him.

'I hadn't realised this was so thin,' he said, rubbing the fabric lightly. 'Let me see if I have something warmer for you to wear.'

He disappeared back into the cottage and she let out a long breath.

Once again she'd proved to herself just how foolish she was. While she was thinking of nothing other than kissing and being held, he was thinking about practical matters. She needed to concentrate and stop fantasising about things that would never happen.

Reappearing, he handed her another cloak without comment. She shrugged into it while he led Cai out into the open. The horse snorted and shook his head, seemingly as displeased to be outside in the cold as Linota. She pulled the new cloak tightly around her; it was thicker and warmer and smelled faintly of Erik. She wanted to bury her nose into the fabric and inhale deeply, but she forced herself not to. She didn't want Erik to witness her pathetic behaviour.

Erik vaulted on to Cai's saddle and then leaned down to pull her up behind him. 'If it's easier, you can hold on to me as we ride. It will be more comfortable for Cai if you move with me.'

Cai broke into a gentle trot and Linota slipped her arms around Erik's waist. She could have held on to the saddle to gain purchase, but the chance to hold him innocently was too good an opportunity to pass up.

Even through the layers of clothing she could feel the firm muscles of his stomach and a strange yearning opened up inside her. She wanted to run her fingers over the bare skin of his chest, to feel those muscles against her skin. She closed her eyes as the intense longing washed over her.

Seemingly oblivious to the exquisite torture she was going through, Erik tried to engage her in conversation.

'You're very quiet this morning, Mistress Leofric. You're normally much chattier than this. Is everything all right?'

'Everything's fine and I thought we agreed that Mistress Leofric was too formal for our situation. I fully intend to keep calling you Erik, Erik.'

She felt his quiet laughter rumble through him. 'All right then, Linota it is. Do you ever shorten it to Lin?'

No one ever had, but she liked the idea of him having a private name for her.

'You could call me Lin,' she mumbled into his back. She straightened. 'How about you? Does anyone ever shorten your name?'

'Erik doesn't really lend itself to being shortened.'

'What about Rik or Rikky?'

'Absolutely not! Anyway, Rikky is longer than Erik so that defeats the purpose.'

She passed the rest of the early morning by coming up with increasingly ridiculous nicknames for Erik, pleased every time she got a chuckle out of him. She delighted in making him laugh and knew it was something she would never get tired of doing.

She only stopped when he threatened to call her Ot from now on.

The laughter between them slowly ebbed away and was replaced with a deep contentment. Being with Erik was easy. There was no tension, no worry that she might say the wrong thing and upset him. She sensed that he would not whisper behind her back or listen to nasty rumours about her family.

'Did you know,' asked Erik, when they had been riding for some time, 'that Borwyn is one of the largest landowners in the country? Only the King has more and only the Earl of Ogmore has similar reach and influence.'

'I did know because you have already told me.' She waited a moment and then added, 'Why do you do that?'

'Do what?' said Erik. 'Talk to you about things? I thought you might be interested.'

His words were light and dismissive. It was only because she had her arms around his waist that she knew his body had tensed. There *was* more to this than idle chatter.

'No, you didn't. There is something else going on here and I want to know what it is.'

Erik laughed, but the sound was nothing like his real one—the one she was coming to love. 'There is nothing going on, Lin.'

'Do you promise me?'

There was a long silence and her heart thudded painfully.

'I...'

'Erik, please... If there is something going on I need to know about it. I'm not a child.'

'Damn it, Linota. I know you are not a child. Every moment of every day I am aware of the fact that you are a woman. This has nothing to do with your age.'

Her heart fluttered at his words even as her brain reminded her to keep pressing for answers. Something was off and she needed to know what it was.

'Then what is it? Why does it sometimes seem to me as if you are trying to sell me Borwyn and his land?'

Erik huffed out a long breath. 'I'm sorry. I don't mean it to come across that way, although I suppose I am doing that, in a way.'

Her breath caught in her throat. 'Why?'

Erik groaned. Linota almost felt bad for pressuring him, *almost*.

'Why?' she said again, firmer this time, her arms tightening around his stomach.

'It's because...' He shifted in the saddle. A pool of dread settled in her stomach. 'Do you know about the dowry?'

'Dowry? What dowry?' She pulled away from him slightly. 'Do you mean mine? Because I can assure you I don't have one. Everything was taken from my family when my father was executed for treason. And I mean everything. We were left with the clothes we were wearing and nothing more. I have nothing. I suppose my brother might be able to provide something now he has married, but it won't be big.'

Erik cleared his throat.

Linota dropped her arms. She found she didn't want to be holding him when he was so obviously hiding something big from her.

'Erik, tell me. Or I will...'

'You will what, exactly? Run off into the woods because that went well for you last time? I should also warn you that I can outrun you quite easily with or without Cai.'

'I shan't trust you any more,' she said quietly.

He was silent for a moment. 'You don't fight fairly, Linota Leofric. How can I deny you now?'

Although she no longer held him their bodies rubbed together as Cai moved through the woodland. She wanted to rest her head against the middle of his solid back. She was sure she didn't want to hear what he was about to say and her head throbbed with a sudden exhaustion.

'Ogmore has settled dowries on you and your sister. They are quite substantial.'

Her heart pounded. 'How substantial?'

The sum he mentioned was so vast she had to ask him to repeat himself.

'Why?' The amount made no sense to her. Ogmore had shown no interest in Katherine or her in the eight years they'd been sequestered in his fortress, never intervening to put a stop to the semi-incarceration. The sum he was suggesting was akin to a dowry he would provide a daughter.

Erik cleared his throat. 'Now that your brother has married his only daughter I understand that Ogmore views you and Katherine as family.'

The world appeared to spin as Linota absorbed this. Katherine and she had been alone for so long and now it appeared they had a wealthy protector. For the life of her she couldn't decide if this was a good or a bad thing.

'Is there anything else?' she asked, pleased at how calm she sounded despite the roiling inside her stomach.

'Ogmore has promised Borwyn a strong alliance as part of the union.'

Linota inhaled sharply. 'So it's not my imagination. You are trying to sell Borwyn to me.'

She pressed her hand to her chest. Her heart was still beating even though it felt to her as if it had cracked in two. She was as naive and as foolish as she had originally thought. While she'd imagined Erik and she had been developing a bond, he had been trying to sweet-talk her into marrying his half-brother. Of all the ridiculous things!

While she'd been slowly falling for him, he had been plotting for her to become his sister-in-law. She was so...hurt, angry and... She couldn't even frame the emotions churning around her at the moment. She needed to get away from Erik. Preferably far away.

'Is there anything else?' she asked.

Erik flinched. 'No,' he said flatly. 'That's it.'

Tears pricked her eyes as she realised she didn't believe him. There was something else he was keeping from her, she was sure of it. A tear fell down her cheek and she wiped it away with the back of her hand.

'Please may we stop for a moment?' she asked politely.

'We really need to keep going. I want—'

'Erik, I have to stop,' she snapped. 'I cannot keep going with this new information swirling around my head. Let me down, please.'

'Lin... Linota, I—'

'No, you don't get to talk to me at the moment. Anything you have to say, absolutely anything, will only make me feel worse. Stop Cai so that I can get off, please, or else I will jump down and you will have to explain my broken neck to my sister. Believe me, there is nothing as frightening as my sister in a protective rage—not even a fully trained knight would go against her.'

'All right,' said Erik, slowing Cai down with a gentle tug on the reins. 'You can get down, but only for a short while. We need to reach Borwyn by nightfall.'

Linota nodded against Erik's back. He must have felt her movement or else he believed her threat to jump down because he brought Cai to a stop. She leapt down before he had a chance to help her. Her knees jarred as she landed on the ground, but she barely noticed the pain.

She stalked away from Cai.

'Stay where I can see you,' called Erik.

She ignored him, striding through the trees with large, angry steps.

How dare he! He'd laughed with her, made her feel special. He'd even kissed her, knowing all the while that she was Borwyn's potential bride.

Did Katherine know? Linota doubted it. Katherine would have been thrilled by the knowledge. With a dowry that size behind them they could both make fantastic marriages, which was what Katherine had always wanted. Any nobleman in the country would want that connection with the Earl of Ogmore, never mind the wealth the man would gain through the dowry. It wouldn't matter what she wanted. Her hopes and dreams would be completely smothered in the grab for that much wealth and power.

And it wasn't even as if her dreams were huge. She didn't care for the trappings that came with being a great nobleman's wife. She'd never wanted to help run a fortress or even a smaller castle. All she'd ever wanted was to be loved—to have someone to hold her when she was scared and to laugh with when she was happy.

She stumbled over a log and realised she was crying. She wiped away the tears. It was no good being this upset. It didn't change anything. She took a deep, shuddering breath. Erik wasn't to know that she was falling for him. He hadn't asked her to and, aside from the kiss, he had never given her any reason to hope that his feelings were any deeper than momentary desire.

She'd known all along that even if he had they could never be together. Braedan would not countenance such a match. They were trying to raise the Leofric name, not bring it down. An unclaimed bastard would not do as a husband for her, even without the dowry.

She came across a narrow stream, the edges of which were lined with ice. Sitting down on the frozen ground, she watched the water flow beneath her. It was strangely calming to think this stream would carry on its path no matter what went on in the world around it.

A snapping of a twig behind her had her sighing in resignation. Erik had found her. The time for her sulk was over. She needed to carry on as if nothing had ever happened between them. As if she hadn't been falling for the man, hadn't been willing to risk the wrath of her sister and brother just to be with him.

She stood slowly and turned.

She opened her mouth to apologise for her outburst and then froze.

It wasn't Erik who had followed her.

It was Gamel.

Chapter Eight

Gamel moved quickly, pressing a hand over her mouth before she could scream for help.

'Don't even think about it,' he growled in her ear. 'You've caused me no end of trouble, you little whore. De Bevoir ain't gonna pay me after your disappearin' act so now I'm gonna get me a new deal.'

He pushed her hard against a tree. The rough bark bit into her back and she whimpered in pain.

'I'm gonna take what's my due and then I'm gonna sell you to a whorehouse, which is exactly where you belong.'

She squirmed against him, desperate to be free.

He laughed at her attempts. 'You're gonna give me what I want and don't think lover boy is gonna come to your rescue. He's busy moonin' after you. Givin' you some time to think. We'll be on our way before he knows you're missin'.'

Gamel unclasped her cloak and it dropped to the ground. The world swam as Linota tried to get breath into her lungs. It was so hard. Gamel's hand still covered her mouth and her nose didn't seem to be able to take a deep enough breath. She was going to die without ever seeing Erik or Katherine again.

Gamel reached down to gather up her skirt and she kicked out, her booted foot connecting with his shin.

'You bitch,' he hissed, raising his hand to smack her.

She screamed Erik's name, before the rough hand of his fist came down on her cheek.

'Please,' she muttered, shoving against Gamel and managing to break free of his grasp. 'Please.'

She shifted back towards the stream, Gamel following her closely. Surely Erik would have heard her scream. He couldn't be too far away. She only had to survive until he found them.

Gamel lunged for her. She dodged and pushed him at the same time. He lost his footing on the ice and went crashing to the ground.

He didn't get up.

Linota's breathing was coming quick and fast. She leapt over Gamel just as Erik came bursting through the trees.

'Linota,' he cried.

She flung herself into his arms and began to sob as his arms came around her and held her tightly.

'I think I've killed him,' she said against his chest.

'Good,' Erik growled. 'The bastard deserves to die.'

'I don't want to be a killer,' she sobbed.

Erik stroked her back. 'It's all right, my love. It's all right.'

Behind them, Gamel groaned.

'You've not killed him. He's moving.' Erik made to

step towards Gamel, the steel in his voice leaving her in no doubt of his intentions.

'No!' Linota grabbed his sleeve. 'Please. I don't want you to kill him on my behalf. I want us to go.'

Erik growled, his arm rigid beneath her fingers.

'Please, Erik.'

He glanced down at her. His eyes were swirling with rage. She licked her lips as her body tightened: laughing he was beautiful, furious he was devastating.

'Please,' she whispered.

'Very well. I won't kill him, but...' He stepped past her and kicked the prostate man, who slumped back to the ground. 'If he comes after us again, he will die.'

Linota nodded.

'Come on. Let's get you back on Cai.'

Erik bent down and picked up her cloak. He slipped it over her shoulders and did up the clip for her. She was grateful for the action because she didn't think her own fingers would manage it. Even knowing she wasn't a killer didn't stop them from trembling violently.

Erik put his arm around her and she leaned into his firm body. He pressed her to him as they made their way to Cai.

He helped her up on to the horse, but this time he vaulted himself up behind her. He snuggled her close to his chest and kicked Cai into motion.

Linota only realised she was crying again when Erik murmured against her hair.

'Please stop, my love. You are killing me.'

'I need to wash him off me,' she said. 'I feel as if he is still crawling all over me.'

'We'll be in Borwyn's township before the day is

over. I will arrange for a large bath to be brought to you straight away.'

She squirmed. 'I can't wait that long. I need to get him off me now.'

'My love, he's lying in a stream. He's not on you any more. I know it feels—'

'No, I don't think you do know how it feels. His touch has made me unclean. I do not need the water to be warm, only for it to wash him away.'

He nodded against her head. 'All right.'

He turned Cai towards the left. 'There's a lake, but, Linota…'

'Yes?'

'I cannot give you any privacy. I must stay with you. I know it isn't ideal, but…'

'It's fine, Erik. I trust you.'

He muttered something under his breath, his words rumbling through her even though she didn't catch his meaning. She wasn't worried. If he was preparing her to marry his brother, then he would hardly take advantage of her now.

A small lake came into view and she leaned into him gratefully.

'Thank you, Erik.'

'I think I'm going to live to regret this,' he said as he swung his leg over the horse and dropped to the ground.

He lifted up his hands to her and she slipped down from Cai. She expected him to let go of her as soon as her feet hit the ground, but he held on, gazing down at her. Words seemed to hover on his lips and she waited expectantly. He swallowed and let her go, stepping away from her. She dipped her head, hiding the disappointment she was sure was shining in her eyes.

'I'll wait here,' he said, nodding to Cai's saddle and turning to face it.

She stared at him for a long moment, but he only gazed intently at the saddle as if it contained some important mystery he needed to solve.

Her hands moved to the clasp of her cloak and she unclipped it, her fingers still unsteady. She flung the cloak over Cai's neck, not wanting it to get wet from the icy ground.

Her fingers went to the ties of her tunic.

Next to her Erik cleared his throat. 'Please could you get undressed away from Cai,' he said, his gaze still not moving from the saddle.

Her heart fluttered as the skin of his cheeks turned a dark red. The experienced warrior was blushing.

Perhaps he wasn't immune to her after all. It might only be desire, not love, but desire was better than nothing.

'I don't want my clothes to get wet,' she said. A wave of heat swept over her cheeks and she realised she was blushing as well. She wished she'd thought of something more seductive to say, but then…maybe something simple would work.

'Perhaps you could help me with my ties,' she said, turning and lifting her hair out of the way.

'Linota,' growled Erik.

Despite herself she smiled. That was not the tone of a man who was completely unmoved by the situation. It sounded as if he was very much on edge.

Good. It should not just be she who had to suffer the torment of wanting something she could not have.

'Please, Erik. My fingers are still trembling.'

He was muttering darkly again. She couldn't make out the words, but the tone sent a thrill to her stomach. This was dangerous territory. She could end up hurt beyond measure, but if a lifetime of duty was in front of her, then didn't she deserve, if only for an afternoon, a bit of pleasure for herself?

Firm fingers began to tug at the tunic's bindings. Her nipples puckered as the tunic fell free from her body. Erik flung it over her cloak.

She could hardly ask him for help with her dress. It was loose fitting and easy to remove. She quickly pulled it over her head. She nearly lost her nerve then. The thin fabric of her linen undergarments was no match for the cold air which rushed over her.

Before she could concede defeat and pull her dress back on, she stripped off her remaining clothes and boots.

Behind her she heard a sharp gasp and triumph soared in her belly.

He was not immune to her!

Keeping her eyes firmly on the body of water, she made her way over to it. The icy ground was sharp against the soles of her feet, but she welcomed it. Her whole body was alive with this moment.

Her toes touched the icy water and she gasped at the shock of the first contact. The cold was exactly what she wanted. She knelt by the lake's edge and began splashing cold water over the skin of her arms and stomach. The icy droplets stung, but the sensation was glorious.

This was no longer just about washing away her encounter with Gamel. With each splash she was washing away years of confinement, of worry about what was going to happen to her as the years passed with no hope of ever escaping her chambers. It was washing away her duty and the need for her always to be the good girl, the daughter and sister who always did as she was told.

'Linota, that's enough.'

She glanced up from her position by the water. Erik was holding open her cloak.

'You're turning blue,' he said, a small frown between his eyes.

'It feels great, Erik. You should try it.'

'Come on, Lin.'

He leaned down and draped the cloak around her shoulders and pulled her into a standing position.

'Your whole body is shaking.' He wrapped his arms around her tightly and tugged her back towards Cai.

'I feel as if everything is washed away, Erik. All those years of worry. I'm like new.'

'You sound as if you've had too much ale,' he said, tucking her up close to Cai and rubbing her arms briskly.

'I feel as if I have.' She smiled. She was weightless; the ties that normally held her together were gone. She was giddy and floating all at once. It was glorious.

'You're starting to scare me, Lin.' He reached up and touched his hand to her forehead. His fingertips were so warm it felt as if she had been branded.

'You're so warm,' she murmured.

Without thinking she leaned her whole body into him. The hard leather of his tunic bit into her nakedness.

He groaned into her hair as she rested her head against his chest. Beneath his clothes she could hear his heart racing.

Later she would have to be good. She would have to take the generous dowry Ogmore had gifted her and her sister and marry a wealthy nobleman, but why couldn't she have this moment for herself? She knew Erik had lovers, why couldn't she be one of them?

She reached up on tiptoes and brushed her lips against his. It was a gentle, innocent touch, but it made her heart race.

'Lin, please. Stop,' he whispered against her mouth.

Despite his protest he didn't move away. Only a wisp of air separated their lips. She brushed against his mouth again and then once more. Slowly, almost imperceptibly, his lips moved in response.

Tentatively, she reached up and traced the length of his jaw with her fingertips, slipping her hand into the hair gathering at the nape of his neck. She ran her fingers through its soft length. His eyes closed, his lips slightly parted.

She lightly skimmed the back of his neck with her fingernails.

He inhaled sharply against her mouth.

She smiled and felt his answering one against her lips. 'What are you doing to me, Linota?'

'I want to know what it is like to feel passion,' she whispered against the skin of his neck. And love. She wanted to feel loved, but she would not say that to him. Not ask him for something he couldn't give her.

She trailed her lips along at the base of his throat and he groaned.

'Linota, I...' His mouth settled over hers and he kissed her gently.

And she knew she was winning.

Thrilling tingles raced up her spine as his tongue lightly swept along her lips. She knew what to do now. How to make them both feel good. She opened her mouth and he grunted, his kiss turning demanding. Every moment something inside her tightened and she became lost in a world of lips, tongues and teeth.

She was no longer in control of her body. Her hands were everywhere, running through his hair, over the width of his shoulders and grasping at his muscled arms. She came to the bindings of his tunic and her hands played with the ties. She wanted to pull back the layers of his clothing; she longed to be skin to skin. To feel whether he was burning up, just like she was.

As if he could read her mind his hands slipped beneath her cloak, so warm against skin she hadn't realised was cold. He skimmed over her hips and lightly traced the length of her back. She arched into him; he groaned. The sound almost as if he were experiencing pain.

One of his hands lightly skimmed the curve of her buttocks and she moaned into his mouth, surprising herself with the decadent sound. Her breasts felt heavy and she longed to feel the touch of his fingers there. She would beg if she had to.

His thumb brushed the underside of her breast and she gasped as pleasure surged through her.

Abruptly he pulled his hands from her body and stepped away from her.

Cold air rushed over her body and she inhaled sharply.

Erik leaned over and pulled her cloak tight over her body.

'You should get dressed,' he said briskly. There was no sign in the tone of his voice that the last few moments had happened at all.

'Erik—'

'No, Linota,' he shouted, pushing a hand roughly through his hair.

His gaze met hers. Fury burned in their depths. She stepped back against Cai, her heart pounding wildly.

'Sorry.' He reached a hand up to her cheek, but stopped just before he made contact. 'I didn't mean to scare you. I only want you to stop. This is hard enough as it is without you...' He gestured to her body, which was naked beneath her cloak.

'But, Erik, I—'

He held up a hand to stop her. 'Linota, you will have to use your future husband to find passion. It cannot and will not be me.'

'By husband do you mean the Earl of Borwyn?'

Erik rubbed a hand down his face and closed his eyes. 'Yes, I mean Borwyn. He would be a good match for you.'

An icy hand clutched her heart. 'Do you want me to marry your brother?'

Erik's gaze met hers and she flinched at the anger she saw burning there. 'He is not my brother, is he? He is my half-brother and therein lies the problem. An unclaimed bastard cannot have what he wants. Do I want you to lie with another man? No, the very thought makes me want to tear the world apart. Do I want you to be happy? Yes, and if that happiness depends on a good marriage to a decent man then I will make that happen even if it is the last thing that I want.'

She looked at him and for the first time she believed she was seeing the real man behind the tough, cynically amused façade. He might be a warrior, but he was as hurt by his parents' actions as she was by hers.

She met his gaze. All the hurt coursing through her was reflected in his eyes. He was right—just because they desired one another didn't mean that they should act on it.

This was an infatuation. She had to hope it would pass.

'I'm sorry,' she murmured.

He nodded brusquely and moved away from her.

She climbed back into her clothes. The high she had experience from washing herself in the icy water slowly ebbed away, leaving her empty and flat. Her clothes chafed on her newly sensitive skin.

She straightened after pulling on her boots. 'I'm ready,' she called.

'Great. We should be able to get to Borwyn town before nightfall.' His tone was light, but his eyes were bleak.

She wanted to reach out to him, but he had made his feelings clear. He thought the best thing for her was marriage to his brother. Katherine also believed this to be true. Linota wondered what Borwyn thought about it. Perhaps he, too, agreed on their mutual fate. From her brief interactions with the man he had come across as practical. The dowry would help him and the alliance with the influential Earl of Ogmore was something to be prized. He'd want the match for that alone.

Borwyn came across as an honourable man. She supposed she could be happy with him. There would be no passion in the marriage; there was no spark between them. He didn't make her stomach churn with excitement whenever he came near; he didn't make her laugh so much her sides hurt. But she knew he would treat her kindly and there would be no violence from him.

As Erik helped her back up on to Cai she told herself she was lucky. Marriage to such a man was a good thing; she'd heard of unions that were a living nightmare. Her new sister-in-law had been married to a man who had been staggeringly unkind to his young bride. His only saving grace was that he had died, leaving Ellena free to marry again. Borwyn would not be like Ellena's first husband. He would treat her with respect because that's how he was towards everyone. Linota should be glad.

Her heart didn't appear to be listening to her head, though. A hard lump settled around it, hurting with every beat.

Chapter Nine

The journey to Borwyn's township was exquisite torture. Erik's body roared at him to finish what it had started with Linota while his mind urged him to climb down from Cai. He knew it made sense to walk alongside the horse rather than subject himself to more contact with her beautiful body, but he couldn't quite force himself to do it. If their time together was going to be limited he would rather spend it torturing himself than miserably alone.

Every time Cai jolted, Erik's body rubbed up against her. He had to tighten his jaw to stop himself from groaning out loud. He should have made her ride behind him, then he wouldn't be subjected to her tantalising scent or have her silken hair brush his chin.

He wanted to run his lips down the length of her long neck and to trace the fine bones of her ribs. He was desperate to finish the exploration he'd begun, to have allowed more than his thumb to brush the underneath of her breast. It would have been the work of a moment to follow her curves with his fingertips, to brush over her exquisite nipples, to hear her moan as he did so.

She would have let him.

She would have allowed him to pull the cloak from her body and to explore all her soft skin with his lips and tongue. And… That thought did nothing to ease his torture.

When he'd caught a first glimpse of her at Ogmore's castle he'd been transfixed by her ethereal beauty. She'd stopped in her tracks to stare at the bright, winter's morning sky and he'd almost started to move towards her until he'd stopped. Such a delicate creature would not want some untamed warrior leering over her.

But that hadn't stopped him staring at her until she'd disappeared from sight, his blood pounding in his ears. He'd never seen a woman whom he'd wanted with such visceral need before.

Someone had yelled his name; it was his turn in the training yard. It was the first time in years that he'd lost a practice sword fight. The men he'd been sparring with had been remorseless in their taunts, but he hadn't cared. All he could think about was her.

He'd known such a beautiful woman could not have remained unwed, but he'd hoped, prayed even, that she would be a widow. He'd known then that if that had been the case he would stop at nothing to be her next husband.

When he'd found out that she was Linota Leofric, youngest unwed sister of the man named The Beast because of his fighting prowess, he'd still held out hope. Sir Braedan was a hardened warrior, but Erik knew he was probably his equal on the battlefront and that the knight would respect Erik on that front.

He'd desperately searched the castle, trying to catch sight of her again, but for weeks she'd remained hidden from him. He'd known all about their family's history, but he didn't care. If anything, it made it better for him if she was disgraced. Sir Braedan might even have welcomed an offer to take one of his unwed sisters off his hands. Erik wasn't a wealthy man, but his connection to Borwyn made him an influential one.

He'd begun to make plans. Small ones. He would talk to her, show her he wasn't the hard man he was made out to be or the womaniser some thought him. He imagined there would be no greater achievement than making her laugh. He tried not to think of a future in which he could gaze at her night and day. Having hopes and dreams had not worked out well for him in the past.

One day he'd thought he'd caught sight of her golden hair fluttering from a window, high above the castle grounds in the heart of the keep. Someone had confirmed that the Leofric sisters were mostly confined to their chamber, only allowed out occasionally. After that he'd imagined her up there, watching him. He'd tried harder and won more games than any of the knights who also competed in the training yard. No one mocked him for losing concentration again.

He'd gained the attention of many a woman, but not the one he had wanted.

He was still holding out hope when everything changed.

Whenever he thought about being called into Ogmore's private room to discuss negotiations a wide pit opened in his stomach.

He'd walked in with his half-brother. Jarin's natural optimism had been subdued and Erik had been trying to rally him. Ogmore had called *them* for negotiations after all. There must still have been something the wily old Earl was going to offer Jarin.

But Borwyn had been sunk in gloom. He'd come to Ogmore's fortress thinking that he was going to be offered Ogmore's daughter's hand in marriage. *That* union would have been perfect, the two great houses uniting and forming a formidable alliance across large swathes of land. But Ogmore had allowed his daughter to wed in a love match to a man much lower in status than Borwyn. To a man who wasn't even noble. Sir Braedan was only a knight but, and this turned out to be crucial, he was also Katherine and Linota's older brother. It was this kinship that had ruined Erik's tentative hopes for his own future because a relative of Ogmore did not marry an unclaimed bastard.

Erik hadn't known all this as he and Jarin had strode towards Ogmore's rooms. He remembered slapping Jarin on the back and saying, 'It will be all right. You will see. Ogmore won't want to lose an alliance with you. As far as he and the rest of the kingdom know, your power and reach matches his.'

'He won't want it if he ever realises what a precarious position I am in.'

'What you're facing now is a momentary problem, it will pass. You're being tested by our rivals. It's natural when an heir takes over. They want to get the measure of your strength. We'll find a solution. We always do.'

Jarin had smiled, but the gesture hadn't reached his eyes. 'I should never have inherited. We both know I'm not cut out for this. I want to help people, not rule them. My father knew it. It's one of the many reasons why he hated me.'

Erik's heart had constricted. It was not like Jarin to sound so defeated. Erik had vowed to himself that he would do whatever he could to help his brother. It would be a punch in the face to their shared father if Jarin succeeded in making the Earldom even more successful than it had been during the late Earl's lifetime.

Erik hadn't realised that making that oath would cause him so much pain.

Ogmore hadn't wasted any time.

'I'm sure you want to know what I can offer you, Borwyn,' he'd said, sitting on a huge, gilded chair while Jarin and Erik were forced to perch in front of him on a narrow bench.

Erik had hated Ogmore at that moment. Jarin was Ogmore's equal and here he was being treated like a child.

'I would still like to form an alliance with you,' Ogmore had continued.

Erik had fought to keep the snarl from his face. Ogmore had no more daughters for Jarin to marry, unless he had some of his own bastards hidden from life in the castle and that wouldn't do for the Earl of Borwyn.

'My new son-in-law has two sisters, the Mistresses Leofric.'

Erik's heart had stilled, his mind roaring an emphatic *no*.

Ogmore had carried on, oblivious to the turmoil he

had caused. 'They are of marriageable age. I'm suggesting your betrothal to one of them under the same terms as if you were marrying my daughter.'

Erik's heart had started to pound violently then. He clutched the bench tightly, his knuckles turning white. He'd wanted to roar, to stand up and tear every hanging from the room, but he'd stayed silent.

Jarin was like a statue next to him. If Erik hadn't known him well, he wouldn't have realised just how tense his brother was. For the first time, in a long time, he didn't care. There had to be another way to make an alliance with Ogmore, there had to be!

'I am not aware of the girls,' Jarin had said nonchalantly, as if they were discussing the weather. Erik had glanced at Jarin then and realised his friend was telling the truth. He did not know who the Leofric sisters were. The beauty of Linota had not burned itself into his soul.

Ogmore had tapped the arm of his chair with one long finger. 'They are younger than my daughter and have been kept closeted for some time. As you are no doubt aware, their father was executed for treason. Their mother is…unwell, shall we say. It has made their prospects bleak, but now that their brother has become part of my family I have decided to take an interest in them.'

'I see.' Nothing in Jarin's voice suggested how he was feeling.

'Sir Braedan and my daughter have offered for the girls to go and live with them at Castle Swein. I have arranged it so that you can escort them. It will give you a week to get to know them. At the end of the week you may either offer for one of them or walk away.'

Jarin had only nodded.

'If you walk away, I will still let it be known that I stand beside you as an ally, but you won't receive any backing from me in terms of wealth.'

'I see,' said Jarin.

'I will, after a week has passed, let it be known that the girls have dowries attached to their names. I am sure that they will, therefore, have many offers of marriage after that.'

Erik forced himself to remain seated even as Ogmore's words hit him harder than a sword to the stomach.

The dowry put Linota out of Erik's reach. There was no way he could ask for her hand in marriage now. It didn't matter if Jarin decided against wedding her because some other lucky nobleman, who would be very keen to strike up an alliance with Ogmore, would and there was nothing Erik could do about it.

The pain hadn't ended there.

Jarin had thanked Ogmore for his offer and then swept from the room. Erik strode after him, despite feeling as if he was bleeding from several open wounds.

They'd stopped in the first unoccupied room. Jarin's rage was so potent Erik was sure the room would burst into flames.

'It's an insult,' Jarin had hissed. 'To suggest that the Earl of Borwyn marry into such a ruined family.'

For the first time Erik had wanted to ram his fist into his friend's face until he bled. How dare he call marriage to Linota an insult!

Jarin should be getting down on his knees and thanking God that he was being handed one of the most beautiful women in the kingdom, along with more wealth than most men could even comprehend. At that moment he had hated his half-brother. The reaction had shocked him because Jarin had been the one constant in his life. The first person to treat him with respect, the one who had raised him from lowly kitchen hand to steward of Jarin's vast estate. He owed everything to Jarin and his generosity.

He'd tried to tamp down on his own feelings as Jarin had railed against his future. Erik knew he must support Jarin with every fibre of his being. Without this match, Jarin's future as the Earl of Borwyn was in serious peril. The money in his coffers was almost gone and without it Jarin couldn't raise an army to protect his borders. It wasn't just Jarin's life on the line, but many of the innocent villagers who made their homes on the edges of Jarin's land.

It would be hell to watch Linota marry Borwyn. And Borwyn would choose Linota. The older sister didn't hold a candle to Linota's beauty. It would rip his soul to pieces and destroy what little contentment he had built up in this world. To see her produce the next heir to the Earldom would cut him deeper than any sword.

He'd known all this and had made peace with it. At least he'd thought he had.

As their journey across the country had progressed he'd allowed himself to spend time with Linota, to get to know her and to make her laugh. He couldn't marry her, but he could be her friend and that would have been enough.

But now... Now he knew what it was like to kiss her, to hold her in his arms and touch her delicate skin. He knew how her eyes would crinkle at one of his jokes and how she would look at him as if she could see straight through his bravado to the man who lurked behind it. The person he allowed no one else to see but her.

It would be agony to see her married to Jarin, an unending hell he could never escape.

But he'd already betrayed his brother once. It didn't matter that his very soul rebelled against the idea of betraying his closest friend. If Isabel was anyone other than his sister's daughter he wouldn't even consider deceiving Jarin, but he could not let Mary down again.

He couldn't compound matters by stealing Linota from Jarin as well. If they wed, Linota would still be untouched. He could give his brother that.

The winter sun started to set. Cai moved steadily beneath them, taking them to the only place Erik had ever called home. 'We're not far from Borwyn now.'

'I'm looking forward to a proper wash,' Linota said brightly, although he was sure he could hear the strain in her voice. Strain he'd helped put there by his actions.

He closed his eyes tightly, glad she was facing away from him and couldn't see his face. Up until this point he hadn't lied to her, not really. He'd only omitted the fact that he knew about de Bevoir and what he was up to. This was the point where he was going to betray her trust in him. Even though he knew they would never be together it still hurt to deceive her.

'I've been thinking,' he said slowly, weighing his words carefully. He didn't want to scare her, but he did want her to doubt her safety. 'We don't know why you were snatched by Gamel and his men. If it has anything to do with your new dowry, then I think it is best you are kept hidden for now.'

She said nothing in response.

His stomach squirmed at her silence. He was the worst kind of monster, frightening her in order to keep his bargain with de Bevoir. When this was all over de Bevoir was going to pay the price for having caused so much pain and anguish.

Erik could risk it and tell Linota the truth, but, knowing how she felt about betrayal, he doubted she would be amenable to his plan. And he could not jeopardise Isabel's safety.

He had to keep reminding himself of that. Even if she found out and hated him for his actions, it would not make a difference to their future.

'What do you have planned?' she asked eventually and his heart crushed at the trust in her voice.

'I have a friend, Emma. She will take you in and keep you safe.'

Her whole body stilled. 'Emma?'

He cleared his throat, heat rushing over his face. He had made it sound as if he was on intimate terms with Emma, which was crude considering he had been stroking Linota's bare skin not long ago. It was true that Emma was an ex-lover but that had been years ago. They had been friends for a lot longer.

'Emma and her husband, Clayborne Payne, own a bakery in Borwyn town,' he clarified. 'They make the most delicious bread you have ever tasted. You won't go hungry during your stay.'

Linota's shoulders stayed rigid and he hated himself just a little bit more.

'Won't it be safer for me to stay with you at the fortress?'

Erik closed his eyes, glad once again that she couldn't see his face. The desire to stay with her and never leave rushed through him. But for his plan to work she needed to be kept away from the fortress. Nobody could know that Linota was safe and well even though he would do everything in his power to make sure she did, indeed, remain that way.

'Until whoever is behind your abduction is caught, it is not safe for you to be out in the open.'

At least that much was true.

'Will you stay with me in the bakery instead?'

'I cannot. They would not have room for me. Besides, I think it is best I return to the fortress. Something dangerous is afoot and I need to get to the bottom of it before anyone else gets hurt.'

'Oh. I don't really want to be apart from you.'

Her slender hand reached out and encircled his arm. He could only just feel the pressure of her touch through the thick fabric of his clothes, but it didn't stop goose pimples rushing over his skin.

'I understand,' he said thickly. 'I know this ordeal has been frightening for you, but I will keep returning to let you know what's happening. I shan't leave you completely alone.'

Her little sigh of disappointment hurt him more than any physical wound he'd ever received.

He knew she didn't feel the same way about him as he did about her. He'd had enough women. There were those that wanted to use him to slake their lust and those that thought they were in love with him. A woman who asked for passion was not one who wanted a husband.

She wouldn't even want to be his friend when she knew everything.

Their parting would be a wrench for him, but she would be reunited with her sister and would soon forget about the man who had kept her safe for a couple of days. Their kisses would be a tale she would tell herself when her husband bored her. A sweet reminder of a brief adventure she'd had when she was young.

'Please promise me you won't leave me for long.'

'I won't.'

Linota didn't press him and he was glad. He wasn't sure if he was promising to come to her or refusing to promise that he would. It was something on which he did not want to dwell.

Borwyn's walled town came into sight as a vibrant sunset finally faded into softer pinks.

'I didn't realise Borwyn's settlement was on the sea,' she said as they rode along the path, Cai's hooves kicking up puffs of sand.

'Borwyn's assets rely heavily on being an important trade route,' he told her.

'Hmm,' she murmured, staring out towards the now darkening water.

He smiled against her hair; he guessed trade routes weren't exactly the most scintillating topic of conversation. This was part of the adventure she wouldn't be telling her grandchildren about.

'I've never seen the sea before,' she mused.

'What do you think of it?'

She was silent for a moment. 'I'm not sure I like it.'

'Really?' asked Erik, surprised but pleased the conversation had taken a different turn. He couldn't imagine having a strong opinion about the sea. It had always just been there. 'Why's that?'

'It's like a dark, black pit, yawning into the distance, waiting to ensnare unworldly travellers.'

Erik's arm tightened around her. 'That's a very dark opinion. I suppose it has been known to take a life or two, but it also keeps the town in a steady supply of fish, meaning there is still food even in the worst of harvests.'

She wriggled in the saddle. 'When you put it that way…no, I still don't like it.'

Erik brought Cai to a slow walk and then stopped him altogether.

'I think we should walk the rest of the way. Cai is very recognisable and I'd be known as soon as I stepped into the town. Without him we can sneak through and should be able to get to the bakery without anyone spotting us.'

Guilt pierced his heart as Linota slid down from Cai's back, her unquestioning trust making his betrayal even worse.

He ran his fingers over Mary's carving, which he wore close to his heart. He needed to remember exactly why he was doing this, why he was using the woman he had fallen so deeply for. Mary's daughter was an innocent child, relying on him to rescue her from de Bevoir and his liege, Garbodo. He could not let her down even if it meant lying to Linota.

He quickly tied Cai up, whispering words of comfort into his horse's mane even though Cai seemed completely at ease at being left alone again.

He tucked Linota under his arm, loving how she

perfectly fitted against him even as the thought tortured him.

'The southern gate should be open at this time,' he said.

'Will there be a guard?'

'There should be, but I suspect he will be in the tavern.'

'Ogmore would never allow such a dereliction of duty,' said Linota, sounding scandalised.

His muscles tightened. 'Borwyn and I don't either. Since Borwyn inherited his father's lands there has been trouble on some of his more distant borders and all the best soldiers have been sent to reinforce Borwyn's position. Unfortunately, that has left us with the weak or lazy soldiers at home. It's… We're working on it. It is not an ideal situation, but it will work in our favour this evening.'

'I'm sorry. I did not mean to criticise.'

He found her fingers and pressed them lightly, letting go before he could hold on to them for too long. 'I know. I'm sorry if I sounded harsh. It is a problem Borwyn and I have been battling for a while now. An alliance with Ogmore would certainly help strengthen our position.'

'Oh,' said Linota quietly.

Erik wanted to kick himself. He'd made Linota think about a match between her and Borwyn and that had been the furthest thing from his mind. But perhaps it shouldn't have been. He should really use this moment to remind her of all the things she would gain as Borwyn's wife. With Linota tucked securely under his arm he couldn't bring himself to do it.

* * *

Emma and Clayborne's dwelling above their bakery was small but cosy. Erik had no qualms about leaving Linota there; Emma would mother her and make sure she ate well. He'd had to let Emma in on some of the details, but not all. It would be better for her if Emma didn't know everything. She could be trusted and that was why he was content to leave Linota in her custody.

As he'd been leaving, Linota had turned her big blue eyes towards him. The expression in her eyes had almost sent him to his knees to beg for her forgiveness for getting her involved in this. He'd wanted to stay, to pull her into his arms and to press his mouth to hers once more, but he knew he wasn't worthy of this or even her respect.

Instead, he had bid her a cheerful goodnight and let himself back out into the cold night air.

The streets of Borwyn's town were quiet. Given the cold weather and the time of year it wasn't surprising, but it was still eerie. He was used to the streets bustling with people as traders called out their wares and shoppers tried to find the best deal.

De Bevoir had said he would be waiting for him at the disused tannery. It irked Erik to know that de Bevoir had seen enough of the town to be aware that the tannery had been out of use for a little while. What use was there in having informants in the town if they didn't tell him about Garbodo's right-hand man being around? If Borwyn and he had known about de Bevoir's visit earlier, they might have been able to put a stop to the plot before ending up in this situation.

He ran lightly through the streets, welcoming the

stretch of his muscles after so long in the saddle, only slowing as the tannery came into sight.

The building looked deserted from the outside. The wooden door was hanging off its hinges and no lights flickered from within.

If de Bevoir had crossed him in this, Erik was going to hunt him down and make him wish the two of them had never met.

He ducked through the narrow entrance and stood just inside the doorway as his eyes adjusted to the darkness.

'You've taken your time,' said de Bevoir, stepping out of the shadows.

Erik crossed the room before he could think. Pinning de Bevoir up against the wall, he held his dagger to the man's throat. 'We had a run in with one of your men. Gamel decided he wanted Linota for himself. Did you send him?'

De Bevoir swore under his breath. 'That lump's an idiot. Of course I didn't send him.' Erik relaxed his grip slightly, but still held the knife up. 'Linota is worth far more to me as a virgin than as despoiled goods,' de Bevoir said.

Erik clenched his fists, fighting with himself not to punch de Bevoir or to gut him. How dare he talk about Linota as if she were something you could buy at market!

'She is still a virgin, isn't she?' queried de Bevoir.

Erik punched de Bevoir in the stomach, his mind black with rage.

De Bevoir doubled over and gasped for breath. Erik stepped back, sheathing his dagger. He wanted to grind the man into pulp for his insinuations, but he had questions. Questions that needed answering tonight. He wasn't going to get those answers if de Bevoir was unconscious or dead.

'That was uncalled for,' said de Bevoir when he was finally able to catch his breath.

'Don't ever speak of Linota like that again.'

'It was a valid question. No, don't hit me again. Try to act like a reasoned man rather than a beast without a brain! No wonder Borwyn is in such a mess with a knave like you advising him.'

Erik's fist was curled so tightly it hurt. He took a step away from de Bevoir so he wasn't tempted to plunge that fist into the man's stomach once more.

'I've seen the way you look at her,' de Bevoir continued. 'It's as if you want to consume her. And, despite your pitiful heritage, she looks at you as if you were actually someone and not the pathetic bastard you are. Oh, stop growling like that. It makes you appear even more ignorant than you are.'

Erik ran his hand over his face. He knew he was as pitiful as de Bevoir suggested when, despite his overwhelming rage towards de Bevoir, he was enraptured by the idea that Linota looked at him as if he were somehow worthy of her.

He shook his head. It would not do to think of her or allow himself a tiny glimmer of hope. There could be no happy ending. Even if it was true he would certainly destroy that when she discovered that he had been lying to her.

'So is she still a virgin then?' de Bevoir asked Erik again. 'After all, you've spent two nights in her company. I hear that ladies swarm over you, probably hoping to enjoy a bit of rough once they're bored of their noble husbands.'

Rage had blood pounding in Erik's throat. 'Don't speak of Linota like that!' De Bevoir could throw all the insults he wanted at Erik—Erik was used to it—but de Bevoir wasn't fit to lick Linota's boots.

De Bevoir laughed, ignoring Erik's anger. 'This has all been very interesting. I hadn't realised you'd fallen for the girl.'

Erik growled, furious at himself for revealing his feelings in front of de Bevoir. If anything he had just put Linota in even more danger.

'I want to see Isabel,' he said, changing the subject abruptly.

'That's not possible,' said de Bevoir, all trace of amusement gone from his voice.

'Because she doesn't exist?'

'Of course she does.'

'Then prove it. The necklace you gave me means nothing. You could have taken that from Mary easily enough, alive or dead. She was hardly a ferocious fighter. I'm working for you, betraying my liege and lying to an innocent woman all for the promise of a girl I've no evidence has ever existed. If you don't show her to me, then our deal is off.'

There was a long silence. Erik leaned his shoulder against the stone wall and waited. He was not going to back down from this request.

'Very well,' said de Bevoir eventually. 'I will fetch the girl and bring her here for you to see. You will wait here. If, at any point, I hear you following me, then you will not see Linota again. It doesn't matter how many bakeries you hide her in.'

Erik said nothing as he listened to de Bevoir leaving the building. He'd been so sure that no one had seen him coming into the town. It was unnerving to realise that someone had been spying on his movements. There must be many more Garbodo informants than he or Borwyn had realised. When this was all over security was the first thing that needed to be improved. Jarin and he could not be taken unawares again.

He moved over to the doorway and listened. De Bevoir's footsteps headed in the direction of the sea. He tapped the wooden door with his fingertips and began to count. He'd reached one thousand twice over when he heard returning footsteps.

He moved away from the door.

Two men he didn't recognise stepped into the room. He pulled his dagger out once more and held it tightly.

'De Bevoir says you're to come with us.'

Erik nodded; he'd expected something like this. He moved towards them.

'You're to wear this.'

One of the men held up a sack. Erik froze.

'You don't wear it, we don't take you.'

Erik released a long breath and sheathed his dagger. He reached out and took the sack, its coarse material rubbing against his fingers.

He fitted it over his head, wondering whether he was making the worst mistake of his miserable life. Half expecting a sword to run him through, he jumped when a meaty hand grabbed his upper arm. He scowled into the darkness as he was led out of the tannery. He was pathetic. The sooner he got a grip on this situation the sooner it would be over.

The two men said nothing as they led him through the streets. He'd begun counting again as they'd left the tannery. He was now far over a thousand and reckoned they must be leading him a merry dance as they traipsed the streets of Borwyn. They were no doubt trying to disorientate him. It would have worked better for them if he didn't know the streets of Borwyn more than he knew himself. He'd run wild here as a child and pounded them as he got older, looking for a little light relief from the trials of the fortress.

The smells and the dips in the streets were as familiar to him as the inside of the fortress. They had passed Emma's bakery only moments ago and now they were turning into a side alley.

He was roughly pulled through a narrow doorway, his shoulder jarring against the frame. Inside, his boots scuffed on a wooden floor. There was no warmth; no fire had been lit to keep the winter's night at bay.

His niece had better not be staying in these conditions or there would be hell to pay.

'De Bevoir is waiting for you upstairs.'

He was spun in one direction and the rough sack was pulled from his head. He blinked, but no light shone in the room, making it impossible to see his surroundings.

He took two steps and found the edge of a staircase; the steps creaked heavily as he made his way to the top. The two men followed closely behind, saying nothing.

By the time he reached the loft his eyes had adjusted a little, enough to make out de Bevoir waiting for him in the darkness.

'This is all very excessive,' said Erik as he came to a halt.

'I've seen you fight. I know what we are up against and I know you wouldn't hesitate to turn on me if you thought you could get your niece back without betraying Borwyn. I am not stupid.'

Erik nodded. It was good to know de Bevoir wasn't underestimating him. The knowledge would help him when he plotted his revenge.

'Isabel is in the room behind me. Wait... You can't go barging in there. At the moment she is unharmed, but if you make any moves to take her then that will change. The men inside the room, and those behind you, are loyal to me. They are not as useless as Gamel and his men and have orders to kill the child if you make any sudden movements.'

De Bevoir stepped in front of him and slowly opened the door.

Weak candlelight spilled out on to the floor in front of him. Erik took a brief moment to look around. The dilapidated state of his surroundings told him that this dwelling was probably abandoned, narrowing down the possibilities of where they were even more.

He slowly stepped into the room, careful not to appear aggressive, no doubt in his mind that de Bevoir would follow through on his threat to hurt Isabel.

Two men lurked in the shadows, but Erik didn't pay them any attention.

A woman sat on the dirty floor, a candle to her left. In her arms lay a sleeping child, her dark, curly hair falling in waves about her face. He took a cautious step towards them, his foot causing a floorboard to creak loudly. The little girl's eyes fluttered open and his heart constricted.

Time fell away and he was a small boy again, looking into his sister's innocent face.

There was no doubt in his mind that the girl was Mary's child. The likeness was unmistakable, the big, brown eyes as beautiful as his sister's.

He reached out a hand and the child cowered into the woman's lap.

'That's enough,' said de Bevoir.

'But—'

Erik wanted to talk to Isabel, to find out if she was being treated well and if there was anything she needed.

The men in the shadows stirred and Erik dropped his arm.

'You wanted to see her and now you have. We have a deal. Stick to it.'

Erik hesitated.

'Don't,' warned de Bevoir. 'We're leaving.'

De Bevoir's hand brushed his sleeve, but Erik shrugged him off. He turned abruptly and strode down the rickety staircase. De Bevoir followed, close on his heels.

'I want this resolved quickly,' said Erik when they were back downstairs.

'That suits both of us. Tomorrow we will give Borwyn the ransom message for Linota. You will make sure Borwyn gives me what I want and I will give you Isabel. Everyone is happy.'

Pain thudded around in Erik's chest. 'Except Borwyn.'

'Garbodo isn't greedy. He is only after the land that should belong to him anyway.'

Erik snorted in disbelief. De Bevoir ignored him.

'Besides,' de Bevoir continued, 'Borwyn will get the lovely Linota as his virgin bride. I'm sure that will more than make up for the brief inconvenience of losing insignificant land in the north.'

Erik curled his fists, his muscles straining with controlled violence.

'Put this back on,' said de Bevoir, holding out the sack.

'There's no need. I know where we are,' said Erik and he strode for the door without looking back.

De Bevoir didn't stop him.

It was a small victory, but not a significant one.

De Bevoir still had the upper hand and Erik could do nothing about it.

Chapter Ten

Linota edged nearer to the hearth, tugging her blanket even tighter around her.

The smell coming from the downstairs bakery had caused her stomach to rumble all day. A round loaf was in front of her now, but despite her hunger she'd been unable to force more than a few mouthfuls down.

The day had passed with an agonising slowness; the low hum of customers coming and going from the bakery was the only indication that time was passing at all. She'd woken this morning curled in a nest of blankets, imagining that Erik would come to her with news just as soon as the sun had fully risen.

But he'd yet to arrive and the shop below was closed for the day.

She'd been naive to agree to stay in the bakery. She should have insisted she return to the fortress with Erik. But, and she felt foolish for admitting this even to herself, she'd imagined staying in the bakery would give her more time to spend with Erik. She'd been wrong and she was bitterly regretting her acquiescence.

She heard the creak of the stairs and rushed to the top to see who was coming. The air rushed out of her lungs at the sight of Emma carrying a trencher laden with a hearty-looking stew and thick-cut hunks of bread.

'Hello, pet,' Emma said when she caught sight of Linota peering down at her. 'I thought you might be hungry so I've brought you up a little something.'

'Thank you,' said Linota, taking the trencher and setting it on the floor near the fire next to her uneaten loaf. 'Is there any word from…?'

She looked up at Emma and heat rushed over her skin at the pity she saw on Emma's face.

'No, pet, there's no word from Erik yet, but he did say he might be a while. I wouldn't worry.'

Linota twisted her fingers together. 'I think I should go and—'

'No,' said Emma forcibly.

Linota frowned. 'No?'

'You can't be wandering round the town. It's not safe and you've no idea where you're going.'

Linota laughed. 'I can hardly miss the fortress.'

Even in the darkness last night it was hard to miss the giant edifice looming over the walled town that stood in its shadow.

Emma bustled over to the fire and prodded it violently. Sparks flew into the air and a few flakes of ash settled on Linota's sleeve. Emma leaned over and brushed them off. 'I don't want you running into those men again. Gamel might get lucky next time you encounter him. Now you must try to eat something. You're practically skin and bones.'

Despite Emma's words of warning Linota wanted to

rush out of the room and out on to the street below. Only the good manners Katherine had drummed into her all of her life kept her in the room with her host. Emma settled down in front of the fire, rubbing her chapped hands together. Linota sank down next to her and tried to force down some of the mutton stew.

'Tell me more about your brother,' said Emma, resting her elbows on her knees. Emma seemed fascinated by Linota being related to such a fearsome and renowned warrior when, in Emma's words, Linota was such a tiny little thing.

Linota bit back a sigh. She didn't really know Braedan that well and had already told Emma all that she knew about Braedan's warrior years. But Emma had been so kind to her, keeping her company whenever she could and giving her plenty of food and a safe place to stay so she obliged her host and described the way in which Braedan had fallen in love with his new bride. Emma nodded and exclaimed in all the right places.

'And now my sister and I are going to live with them.' Linota ended the story with a smile, hoping it didn't look as strained as she felt.

Emma sighed. 'It's so romantic.'

Linota frowned. Her sister-in-law had nearly died several times as a maniac had chased her across the country, trying to force her into wedlock so that he could get hold of her land. The chase had only ended when Braedan had killed the man. It was hardly a romantic tale.

But she wanted to keep Emma happy. 'Yes, it's very romantic. How did you meet Clayborne? Was it as... exciting?'

Emma snorted. 'No. I had to marry him. The old Earl insisted on it.'

'Oh?'

'I was widowed young. He chose my second husband for me. I got lucky with Clayborne. He's a good man. I know women who have not been so fortunate.'

Emma stared into the fire, her eyes sad. Linota shifted to her knees—should she go to Emma and offer some sort of sympathy? But Clayborne and Emma seemed so well matched that surely pity was the wrong emotion.

She settled back down. She'd known lords arranged the marriages of unwed women, but she'd never spoken to anyone who'd experienced it before. She'd imagined peasants having more choice in their potential spouses than noble-born women, but it appeared they had even less.

Emma turned away from the fire and smiled, her melancholy moment apparently over. 'I think the old Earl didn't like me getting close to Erik. He was a mean old coot. He didn't like anyone being happy.'

All the air whooshed from Linota's lungs. She'd thought there was a familiarity with the way Erik had referred to Emma. She should have known they used to be lovers. Perhaps they still were. She was so naive.

She stood quickly. 'I need to leave.'

'What? No!' Emma stood up in front of her, holding her hands aloft as if to catch her. 'You can't go. We've already discussed this. I'm sure Erik will return soon. He—'

Fury pumped through her veins. 'I am not Erik's chattel. If I want to leave, then I can.'

A fine trembling started up in Linota's fingers and began to spread through her body.

'I know, pet. I know he doesn't own you, but he wants you to be safe. He cares for you.'

Linota folded her arms across her chest. Yes, he cared about her so much he had left her in the home of his mistress. She was a fool. A young, besotted fool, who needed to take a hold of her own destiny and find out what was going on.

Emma dropped her arms. 'Are you upset because of what I said about Erik?'

Linota turned her head towards the stairs. She refused to see the look of pity on Emma's face. She didn't need sympathy from Erik's ladylove.

'I'm sorry, pet. I wasn't thinking. All I shared with Eric was some clumsy kisses, years and years ago, when he was a young lad. It was never anything more than that.'

Linota could feel heat slowly creeping up her neck. *Why had she made it so obvious that she cared either way what Erik got up to with his women?*

'Pet?' Emma reached out and gently touched the sleeve of Linota's robes. 'I don't think you have anything to worry about on that score. I saw the way he looked at you yesterday. I've never seen him look like that before. I don't think he'll as much as glance at another woman if you're in his life.'

Linota closed her eyes. It was all that she wanted to hear, but it did nothing to alleviate the pain in her chest. In the end, it didn't matter if Emma was his lover, or all the women in Borwyn's town and fortress. Nor did it matter if he did only look at her the way she looked at him. It didn't change anything. She would still have to marry Borwyn, or some other nobleman, and Erik would still continue to have lovers that weren't her.

Linota sank back down to the floor, all the anger leaving her in a rush. She picked up the bowl again and bit into a chunk of mutton. The meat was melt-in-the-mouth-tender, but when she tried to swallow it got stuck in her throat. She coughed.

'Are you all right?' asked Emma.

Linota sipped her wine. 'Yes, I—'

Whatever she'd been about to say died on her lips as she looked up. Erik was standing in the doorway, a faint smile touching his lips.

She leapt to her feet, her heart pounding in her throat. He opened his arms and she ran to him, everything else forgotten.

Without stopping to think she flung her arms around his waist and burrowed her head against his chest. His arms came around her and he held her tightly against him.

She was vaguely aware of Emma slipping past her and then they were alone.

'Where've you been?' she asked, her voice muffled by his tunic.

'I'm sorry, my love. I have been at the fortress, trying to…' He cleared his throat. 'It's been difficult. Nobody has any answers for me.'

'Has Katherine arrived?'

His muscles tensed beneath her cheek.

'What's happened?' She pushed herself slightly away from him so that she could look at his face.

He hesitated and her knees weakened. Up until this

moment she'd imagined that Katherine was safe and well at the fortress, or at least nearly there, but Erik's frown suggested otherwise.

'Is she…?'

'She had a small accident,' he said gently. 'She fell off her horse as she was chasing after you.'

'No…'

Linota's legs buckled beneath her. Erik's arms tightened around her, keeping her from falling.

'She is well.' He brushed a strand of hair away from her face. 'But the accident delayed her and Borwyn's arrival.'

'Oh, Katherine.' Linota shook her head. 'She is such a terrible rider. It's not surprising she fell off. I know Borwyn gave her some advice on how to improve, but she wouldn't listen. She's so stubborn.' Linota laid a hand on his chest and looked up into his eyes. 'You'd tell me if she was really hurt, wouldn't you?'

His long fingers curled around hers. 'Of course I would. I believe she was briefly knocked unconscious, but there is no lasting damage. I'm sure she is very worried about you, but hopefully you will be reunited shortly.'

He gazed down at her and the moment stretched between them. His head lowered and she held her breath, waiting for his lips to touch hers. A log fell in the grate and Erik jumped. A look crossed his eyes that she couldn't interpret. He dropped his hands and stood back.

His gaze flickered over the top of her head, towards the fire. 'I see I am interrupting your meal. Please carry on with your food.'

He moved past her towards the flames, holding out his hands as if to warm them. She knew, from the feel of him, that he wasn't cold. He was avoiding holding her, but he'd called her his love and held her tightly. Whatever was holding him back from kissing her she was sure it wasn't a lack of desire to do so. Her heart didn't sink even as he kept his back to her.

She settled back down next to the trencher and this time when the smell of the meat hit her she realised she was ravenously hungry. She bit into a huge chunk and almost moaned as the meat melted on her tongue.

'Would you like some?' She held a cut of meat out to him.

'Thank you, but I ate at the fortress.'

He smiled down at her, his eyes twinkling in the candlelight.

'Can you tell me what's going on?' she asked as she scraped the bowl clean. She tore off a hunk of bread and began to chew on it.

The amusement in his gaze faded.

'It's…complicated,' he said slowly.

She patted the floor beside her. 'Come and tell me.'

For a moment she thought he would refuse. She studied the trencher in front of her, hoping that, in the dim candlelight, he wouldn't be able to see the blush she could feel flooding across her face.

She heard him release a long breath and then move across the room. She darted a quick glance across at him as he lowered himself to the ground, his long legs stretched out in front of him. He didn't look comfortable and her heart twisted. Something was wrong and he didn't trust her enough to tell her.

'Linota.'

She looked up in surprise. He sounded pained. Their gazes met and held.

Her pulse pounded in her throat.

'I...' he said.

She waited, but it seemed as if his words had failed him. His gaze flickered from her eyes and down over the rest of her body. Even without experience she could read the intent in his look. Her stomach fluttered with a very different kind of hunger.

He leaned towards her, then stopped. Her fingers itched with the need to reach up and touch the fine wrinkles at the corners of his eyes and the curve of his sharp cheekbone.

He remained still, no longer in his space but not quite in hers either.

She nodded.

She felt his soft groan against her lips.

The touch, as soft and gentle as a breeze, lit a fire within her. It rushed over her skin, burning her nervousness away. She wanted him. Not just this chaste kiss, but more.

The space between them seemed cavernous; it would not do.

She felt his grunt of surprise as she pulled him against her. She didn't want to give him time to think. She pressed her mouth against his and hoped he would take charge.

She didn't know what happened next between a man and a woman, didn't know how to make him lose control. She only knew that she wanted to continue, to see whether the flames licking along her veins would burn brighter or fade away.

For an agonising moment he held still and then he moved, sliding his fingers into her hair at the base of her neck and tilting her head. She gasped as his tongue swept along the seam of her lips and then into her mouth as she opened to him.

His tongue touched hers and fire inside her burned brighter. She pulled on his tunic and he half fell on her. The delicious weight of him pressed her to the floor. His kiss deepened. She heard the soft thud of her wine glass tipping over, but she didn't care. This moment was all about him and how he made her body burn.

His mouth left hers and his lips ran along the edge of her jaw and down the skin of her neck, his stubble scraping exquisitely against her skin.

She ran her fingers over his soft, silky hair and lightly traced her nails over the skin on the back of his neck.

His fingers were at the ties of her tunic and she copied him by tugging at his.

'Linota,' he whispered before claiming her mouth again.

This time their kisses were wilder, nearly frantic. She moved her tongue in rhythm with his and he groaned, pulling her tunic off and throwing it to the side.

She tried to do the same with his, but she couldn't get it past his shoulder. She felt his smile against her mouth, but he didn't lift his head as he shrugged out of it.

She heard it drop to the floor and then his hands returned to her body.

She arched into him as one strong hand skimmed the

length of her back. She was desperate to feel the skin of his chest. She realised she was pulling at him when she heard him grunt.

He lifted his head slightly and gazed down at her. His pupils were almost completely black.

'We shouldn't,' he whispered.

She didn't want to hear that. She didn't want his conscience intruding on this moment. All she wanted was to feel his skin against hers. To know that he was as insensible as she was in this moment.

She lifted her head and pressed her lips to his, her tongue flicking over the softness of them.

It had the desired effect. He opened to her and within moments the frantic desire returned.

He didn't stop her as she finally pushed the fabric of his clothes to one side and ran her fingers over his chest. A soft smattering of hair covered his chorded muscles. She ran her fingers across and down over his stomach. Here the skin was taut. Under her soft exploration she could feel small scars crisscrossing his skin.

She wanted to look, to drink in the sight of him, but she knew that if she stopped this kiss he would come to his senses and stop.

A cold rush of air brushed against her nipples. She realised that while she had been exploring him he had made short work of the ties on her dress.

A fine tremor ran through her as his warm hand encircled her breast, his thumb brushing over her nipple. She shifted beneath him. A restless sensation was building within her. She wanted more, to satisfy this unfulfilled desperate craving.

He smiled against her mouth and then his lips began

to work their back down the length of the sensitive skin of her neck and to the hollow at the base of her throat.

She moaned deeply as his mouth settled over her other nipple, biting and licking until she was squirming underneath him. She wanted…she didn't know what she wanted, only for this to continue and never end. More of this wonderful awareness of her body and the way Erik was making it come alive.

He pushed the remains of her dress away. From deep inside her, she heard her mother's shrill voice preaching about a woman's virtue, but all thoughts fled as Erik moved over her, brushing his tongue over her centre.

What…? Was this…? Should she…?

There was another swirl and she bucked off the floor. This had never…

Erik began to move quicker, increasing his pressure until all that existed was his tongue and her body.

Her hands fell from him as she lost herself in the acute sensations rushing through her, unfurling in her veins and reaching every point of her body. She was building towards something, each pass of his tongue bringing her closer. The fire was coiling in her now, travelling towards her centre, waiting.

His hands spread her thighs wider, before his fingers joined his tongue, gliding over her flesh. She cried out as her body erupted in sensation, the fire rushing through her, flooding her veins and sending her spiralling.

Erik stayed with her as she trembled, his tongue gentle now, almost soothing. The new sensations still ran through her but it was quieter, more subdued, but no less delicious.

Gradually they faded altogether and she slumped on to the floor, boneless.

Erik lifted his head and rested it against her stomach.

Her fingers stole into his hair and he sighed, the soft air from his exhalation brushing against her skin. She had no idea how long they stayed like that. She would have been content to be there for ever, the fire crackling to their left, its flickering light turning Erik's hair golden, his stubble tickling her belly.

Far beneath them, in another world, she heard Emma say something to Clayborne and Erik stirred.

He pulled away from her and propped himself up on one arm.

Linota's feeling of bone-deep contentment fled when she saw the anguish in his eyes.

'I'm sorry, Linota. I shouldn't have done that.'

She propped herself up so that their faces were close together.

'Don't do this,' she whispered. 'Don't pull away from me now.'

'I've taken advantage of your innocence and your—'

'No,' she said, reaching out and lightly touching the skin of his cheek. 'I wanted this as much as you did, if not more so.'

Erik laughed silently. 'I don't think it is possible to want you any more than I do. It is practically killing me not to sweep you into my arms and make you mine in every way that is possible.'

She stilled.

'Then why don't you?' she whispered, tracing his lips with the tips of her fingers.

He closed his eyes. 'Ah, Linota, don't make this harder than it already is.'

'But…don't you want to? I know I'm not experienced, but I can learn. I—'

'Linota,' he said, his eyes snapping open, his gaze locking with hers. 'You are beautiful and perfect in every way. I am the luckiest man alive to have spent these last few days with you, but you and I are not meant to be.'

His gaze flickered over her naked body and she saw the ripple of desire as it washed through him. She held still, hoping his resolve would crumble once again and that he would take her as he clearly wanted to do. She almost howled when his trembling fingers tugged her dress on to her and began to tie it back up. She didn't move to help him. If this was to be the last time he touched her then she wanted to make it last.

'Why aren't we meant to be?' she whispered.

He tugged sharply on one of her ties. 'You are going to make a fabulous marriage to some lucky nobleman. You will live a life of luxury and you will be grateful that you didn't throw away that chance on an unwanted bastard.'

'But you aren't unwanted, Erik. I want you.'

'Linota, I can't,' he said, his gaze meeting hers once more. She was shocked by the misery in the depths of his eyes. Why did he have to be so anguished? If he cared for her at all, then why couldn't they fight to be together? They could marry this evening and her siblings could do nothing about it.

'Why can't you?' she asked softly.

'You deserve better.' He placed a gentle kiss against

her forehead. 'There are things you don't know about me. Things which make me unsuitable for you. You would very quickly regret tying your life to mine and that would destroy me.'

'I wouldn't regret it,' she whispered. 'I love you.'

Erik's hands stilled briefly and then he began to fasten the ties, moving quicker than before.

Linota pressed her lips tightly together.

Erik stood abruptly and pulled his tunic on.

'It's late,' he said. 'You need to get some sleep. Tomorrow will be a long day, but hopefully you will be reunited with your sister at the end of it.'

Linota pushed herself to her feet. 'Aren't you going to say anything?'

Erik pushed an impatient hand through his hair. 'You don't love me, Linota. You might think that you do after what we've just shared, but I promise you that feeling will fade.'

'It won't,' she said, barely restraining herself from stamping her feet.

He might not say that he loved her, but she was beginning to think that he did. She could see a strong emotion shining in his eyes when he laughed with her and she'd felt the tenderness in his touch as he'd explored her body. It was only his loyalty to Borwyn that kept him from making her his own. She was sure of it.

He thought his brother deserved her because of her dowry, but he was wrong. Borwyn would only make her miserable, just as she would him. They were not meant for each other.

'You're very sweet,' said Erik, fixing his cloak over his shoulder. 'And I'm sure—'

Linota held up her hand. 'Don't treat me like a child. I may be younger than you, but I'm old enough to know my own mind. I love you and I think you love me.'

He took two steps towards her and she almost stumbled backwards as he loomed over her.

'You don't know me and what I've done,' he said. 'When you do, you will change your mind.'

She straightened her spine. 'Never.'

He smiled sadly. 'We shall see.' He dropped a brief kiss against her lips. 'Sleep well, Linota. Tomorrow will be a long day.'

He turned from her and strode out of the room without looking back.

Chapter Eleven

Linota ran her hands over her dress, trying to remove some of the wrinkles. Fortunately, the wine glass had been nearly empty when Erik and she had knocked it over. She crouched down and mopped up the remnants with her sleeve.

She'd had enough food and so she pushed the glass and the trencher to one side and tried to get her braid into some semblance of order.

She'd thought she'd done a good job, but she still caught Emma smirking at her when she came back into the room.

'Is everything all right, pet?' asked Emma as she bustled around, lighting a couple of extra candles.

'Yes, I—'

A loud pounding sounded at the door.

'Who's that?' Linota edged closer to Emma. The sound had a frantic edge to it, as if the person on the other side would bash through the thick wood if they couldn't get through.

'I don't know.' Emma bundled Linota into a tight hug, turning slightly so that she was in front of Linota.

The sound of something banging against the metal lock reached them. Linota's legs weakened and she clung to Emma, her only thought, *Please don't let it be Gamel.*

Clayborne ran into the room just as the front door crashed open. He placed himself in front of the women and Linota was grateful for his solid bulk between her and whatever was heading their way.

Pounding footsteps raced up the staircase and the intruder burst into the room.

Linota gasped.

The Earl of Borwyn stood in front of her, his lips drawn so tightly they were almost white. His fists were curled tightly and he advanced on Clayborne, who backed up quickly, clearly startled to be confronted by the furious Earl.

Lighter footsteps followed and then stepping into the room was the last person Linota expected to see.

'Katherine,' she cried.

She broke free of Emma's grip and ran to her sister, flinging her arms around her and holding on to her tightly.

'There you are.' Linota breathed heavily against her sister's hair. 'I've been so worried about you.'

Katherine stiffened in her embrace and Linota held out her arms so she could look at her sister. A large, purple bruise was visible near her hairline, but otherwise she looked well. 'Erik told me you'd been hurt. Are you all right?'

'Erik,' said Katherine blankly.

'Yes, Erik, he's been looking after me since those horrid men grabbed me. He said we couldn't trust anyone apart from Emma and her husband. Oh, I've been so worried about you.'

Linota wanted to shake her sister. Katherine wasn't smiling. She didn't seem overjoyed to see her. What could possibly be wrong? They were reunited and they weren't hurt. Katherine should be beaming from ear to ear.

'What's going on?' she asked, turning to glance at the rest of the occupants of the room. Nobody was moving and every line in Borwyn's body was rigid.

'Emma?' she said, hoping that the woman who'd spent the day mothering her would have an explanation for the tension that crackled in the small room.

'I'm sorry, pet,' said Emma, dropping her gaze to the wooden floor.

Linota's heart pounded. 'Sorry...?' What did Emma have to be sorry about? She'd been nothing but lovely to her since the first moment they'd met. She turned back to her sister. 'Katherine, what's happening here?'

'Katherine—' Borwyn's austere voice sent a sharp shiver down Linota's spine '—take your sister to the bottom of the stairs. I'll join you both shortly.'

'What's he going to do?' demanded Linota as Katherine tried to tug her from the room. 'He's not going to hurt them, is he? They've been so kind to me over the last two days. Don't let him hurt them, Katherine.'

'Nobody's going to get hurt,' said Katherine, as she began to tug Linota harder. 'The Earl just wants to talk to them.'

Borwyn grunted and Linota twisted to look at the scene behind them. Neither Emma nor Clayborne were putting up any sort of fight. Both of them were looking

at the floor, their shoulders slumped. They looked...
they looked *guilty*. But that couldn't be right. They had
done nothing wrong. They had taken her in and kept
her safe and fed.

'I'll explain outside,' said Katherine gently. 'Please,
trust me.'

Linota didn't want to leave her two new friends to the
mercy of the stern Earl, but it seemed she didn't have
a choice. She couldn't defend them if she didn't know
what the problem was.

On trembling legs she followed Katherine downstairs
and out into the street below.

She hadn't been outside for over a day and she'd
forgotten how cold it was. The frigid air hit her lungs,
making her gasp in shock.

'Are you truly all right?' Katherine asked.

She turned to her sister. 'I'm fine, but I've been so
worried about you. Erik said you fell off your horse
while riding and that you were knocked unconscious.'

'That is true,' said Katherine, lightly touching her
bruised skin. 'It was only a small accident. What I don't
understand is how you came to be in a room above a
baker's shop. You were carried off by a group of men,
Linota. I was so scared!'

Linota's shoulders relaxed slightly. So that was the
problem. They thought Emma and Clayborne were
somehow mixed up with her abductors. It would be
easy to explain and hopefully they could laugh off the
last few awkward moments. 'I wasn't with those men
long enough to be very frightened. By the time I started
to panic, Erik had caught up with us and he dealt with
the men.'

Even in the darkness Linota couldn't miss the contempt that swept across Katherine's face at the mention of Erik.

'Erik Ward has betrayed you,' Katherine said flatly. 'He is ransoming you in order to get money out of Jarin.'

Linota inhaled sharply. Katherine was mistaken or lying. There was no way Erik had betrayed her. He might not have told her that he loved her, but he definitely cared about her, on that she was certain. 'No, he wouldn't do that. He cares—'

'He would and he has,' said Katherine bluntly.

Linota stepped back, unable to bear being near her sister.

It wasn't true. It couldn't be.

'Erik is behind a plot to completely ruin the Earl of Borwyn,' stated Katherine. 'He has arranged for you to be kidnapped and for a ransom to be paid for your safe return.'

Linota shook her head. Erik would not do such a thing, not to her and not to Borwyn. There was no mistaking the affectionate tones in which Erik spoke about his half-brother.

'He has been at the fortress all day,' Katherine continued. 'I have spoken to him and not once did he mention that you were safe and well. He let me believe for a *whole day* longer than was necessary that you were with those vile abductors. He lied to my face, Linota. Repeatedly!'

Ice spread through Linota's veins. 'No...'

'Did Erik tell you I was at the fortress?'

Linota thought back over the conversation they'd had before...before her whole world had become lost to sensation. Had he mentioned Katherine? Yes, he had. She frowned as she tried to recall his words. She'd asked whether Katherine had returned and he had said...

'Were you delayed in getting back to the fortress?' she asked.

'Yes. I fell off my horse and then...well, quite a bit happened, but it has probably taken an extra day or two more to get here than it should have done. Why?'

Linota nodded. Erik hadn't answered her question directly. He hadn't said whether Katherine was back or not, only that she'd been delayed in returning to the fortress. He hadn't lied to her, but he hadn't told her the truth either. That suggested something was wrong, but not that he was guilty of everything.

'How are you so sure?'

Katherine hesitated and Linota's heart stuttered. Did she really want to know?

'Aside from keeping you from me, which is not the action of an innocent man, Linota, there are several reasons both Borwyn and I are sure.'

'Such as?' Linota pressed.

'He's caused unrest on Borwyn's borders.' Linota shook her head, there was no way Erik would do that. He cared for his half-brother; she knew he did, it was in the way he spoke. Surely that wasn't something you could fake. But Katherine ignored Linota's silent denial and carried on. 'He told Borwyn all about the ransom for you, he even specified the amount and—'

'And...?'

Katherine lowered her voice. 'You must keep this next bit to yourself. Do you swear it?'

Linota nodded. 'I swear.'

'The sum Erik asked for is the exact amount Borwyn has left. Only Erik knows that detail.'

Linota let that statement coil around her for a moment, the words sinking into her like a thousand pricks of a needle.

'Borwyn and I followed Erik here this evening. Only a short while earlier Erik sat with Borwyn. They discussed getting you back from your abductors. Borwyn told Erik to capture the men holding you regardless of whether you got caught in the process. Erik agreed.'

Linota forced herself to remain standing as Katherine's words turned her knees to liquid.

Katherine went on, blaming Erik for everything, saying that he had been plotting against Borwyn for some time, that he was after Borwyn's wealth. Linota thought of Erik's humble dwelling, the beautiful furniture he'd carved himself. There was not one moment she could think of over the last few days that indicated Erik was focused on enlarging his fortune.

'What about his family?' she asked. Surely not everything Erik had said to her over the last two days had been a lie.

'Erik doesn't have any family,' said Katherine gently, perhaps realising that Linota was on the verge of tears.

Linota nodded and gazed down at the floor. Had he really not told her the truth about anything? Had the man she had fallen for ever even existed? If she could only speak to him, then she would know.

'I'm sorry, Linota. I—'

But whatever Katherine was about to say disappeared into the night air because at that moment Borwyn appeared with Emma and Clayborne.

Clayborne had his arms tied behind his back. Emma was unbound, but her wide, anxious eyes broke Linota's heart.

'I'm sorry, my lady,' said Emma as she walked past and the tears Linota had fought hard to keep inside welled up. She turned away from Katherine so that her sister couldn't see her response.

Emma's apology had hit her harder than any slap for it confirmed the motherly woman had been hiding something from her all day. And if Emma was guilty, then Erik… She couldn't even bring herself to form the thought. The man she loved couldn't have done such terrible things. He was kind and thoughtful and he'd made her feel so precious and cared for.

He could have taken her innocence earlier. She'd been more than willing, but he hadn't. Surely that showed the goodness of his character.

But as he'd been leaving he'd said she didn't know him. Was that true? Was he really the traitor her sister seemed to believe he was?

Her mind went completely blank as she trudged through the streets of the town and up to the huge fortress that dominated the surrounding skyline. This internal blankness was something she'd learned how to do whenever her mother went into one of her violent rages. Awful things might be happening outside her body, but if she retreated into herself they couldn't hurt the centre of her being.

If asked again, she could not describe the journey she took from Emma's bakery to Borwyn's guest chamber, high up in the fortress's keep.

Katherine buzzed around her on the periphery of

her consciousness. When Katherine began tugging at her clothes Linota understood she wanted her to have a bath. She climbed in without thinking, but as the warm water swilled over her she felt as if she was washing Erik off her, as if his mouth had never trailed over her skin awakening blissfully intense sensations.

Silent tears dripped into the water as Katherine bustled around the chamber, keeping up a steady stream of words. Linota could hear her, but she could make no sense of what her sister was saying. Katherine didn't seem to expect a response, though, so perhaps she was just talking to fill the silence. It was what her sister always did after one of their mother's violent outbursts.

Katherine wrapped her in some clean clothes, which were far too big, and tucked her into a large bed. Katherine curled up next to her and began to sing softly. Linota closed her eyes and wished herself very far away.

Slowly, mercifully, the world turned black and she slept.

Chapter Twelve

Erik leaned against the wall to the left of the keep's entrance. The night had long since fallen and he needed to get inside and see Jarin, to look at his friend and continue to lie to his face.

He swallowed, but that did nothing to relieve the hard lump in his throat.

He closed his eyes and rested his head against the rough stone of the wall. He hoped, beyond anything, that Katherine wasn't with Jarin. It would be beyond painful to look at Katherine and see the worry in her eyes about her beloved sister and know that he was partly responsible for putting that haunted look there.

Erik had the power to tell her that Linota was alive and safe, but if he did then he put the life of his young niece at risk and he couldn't do that to an innocent child.

It was only for one more night and day. Jarin would hand over the ransom and Erik would make a show of returning Linota. Only when Erik had Isabel safely in his custody would he confess all to Jarin.

But at some point this evening he had come to a revelation. He was going to have to reveal to Linota his part in her supposed abduction. It was going to be the hardest thing he had ever done, harder even than facing trained knights on a battlefield, but he knew that he needed to. She said that she loved him. He pressed a hand to his aching chest. He'd wanted to tell her he loved her, too, but he couldn't. Not when he was lying to her, not when she abhorred liars so greatly.

He would tell her the whole truth tomorrow, as soon as he saw her. He had to have faith that enough had passed between them that she would forgive him or, if that was too much to hope for, she might understand *why* he had acted in such a way.

His body tightened as memories from earlier crept into his mind.

For the rest of his life he would remember the feel of her skin beneath his lips and the way her fingers had gripped his hair as he'd kissed her. He was sure that was her first experience of pleasure. She had been so unguarded in her response to him, such a joy to be with. His lips twitched—amused even now when he was otherwise feeling so desperate—at the memory of her gasp of surprise as his lips had travelled over her body and brought her to a satisfying climax.

To go from her body to meet de Bevoir had made him sick to his stomach. He'd finalised the details of the exchange, then got away from the vile man as quickly as he could.

Erik stepped away from the wall. It was time to face Jarin, to tell him the next part of the plan to get Linota back. Once this was over he hoped to God that

his brother would forgive him for all that he had done,
even though he knew that was an improbable dream.

He pushed his hair back from his face. He'd had time
today to ponder Jarin's reaction and his thoughts were
doing him no good. Jarin was the first person to treat
him as if he had any worth and knowing he would lose
that good opinion hurt him more than he'd imagined.

He had to keep focusing on Isabel. She was what
mattered right now.

A young guard stood just inside the entrance to the
keep. He stood up to his full height as Erik approached.
'Master Ward, the Earl has asked that you attend to him
in the Great Hall as soon as you arrive.'

Erik nodded, forcing himself to show no surprise.
Jarin had never requested his presence before. Erik was
free to come and go as he pleased, although he always
did make a point of reporting to Jarin whenever he arrived. The summons only added to the heavy weight
settling in his stomach.

He turned to his right and strode into the Great Hall,
forcing himself to release the tight grip he had on his
sword handle. He nodded to men and women of his ac-
quaintance as he neared the dais at the far end of the
room. Jarin was sitting upon a great chair, looking down
at those gathering around him, a small frown between
his fair eyebrows.

In the early days of Jarin's ascension to the earldom
they had laughed about Jarin's position high above everyone else. It had seemed like a grand joke that Jarin,
his childhood friend, should be in such a position with
all these people looking up to him. Now, with his fine
clothes and broad shoulders, it appeared Jarin belonged

there. Erik had never felt so far removed from the man who sat directly in front of him.

Erik bowed to his friend. 'My lord.'

Jarin's gaze snapped to him, the look in his eyes unreadable. 'Erik, I'm glad you have arrived. I have some details I need to discuss with you. Mistress Leofric will join us in a moment as this concerns her as well.'

'Of course.' Erik's heartbeat pounded in his throat.

Having to lie to Jarin was bad enough, but having to pretend that Linota was lost to her sister was something else entirely. The girls looked nothing alike and yet he knew how close they were. To hurt Katherine was to hurt Linota and that was something his soul rebelled against.

'Ah, here she is.' Jarin stood. 'Good evening, my Lady Katherine.'

Erik noticed how Katherine's eyes shone as she approached Jarin and smiled despite the snakes writhing in his stomach. Women always seemed to fall in love with Jarin and it appeared Katherine was no exception. It wasn't all down to Jarin's lofty position, he was also a charming man when he wanted to be. It had never occurred to him that Jarin might prefer Katherine over Linota. If Jarin returned those affections...but no. He mustn't go down that route. He couldn't hope for something that could never be. If she didn't marry Jarin it would be some other lucky nobleman. He would have to say goodbye to Linota and learn to live without her.

'Shall we retire to my private rooms?' Jarin seemed only to be talking to Katherine, as if the rest of the room didn't exist. 'I think we would be more comfortable if we spoke there rather than in front of an audience.'

Erik nodded, although a quick glance around the Hall revealed that no one was looking at him. If privacy was what Jarin wanted, Erik would show willing even if he didn't want to wait a moment longer than necessary to deliver his news and be gone.

Jarin's private room was only a few steps away from the Great Hall. It was small, but far cosier than the cavernous Hall where most of Jarin's business took place. The two of them had spent many an evening in here discussing fortress matters or laughing over something ridiculous that had happened that day. It was as much Erik's sanctuary as Jarin's. Tonight, the walls felt as if they were closing in on him, as if they knew of his betrayal and were already condemning him to a wretched end of days in the fortress's foul dungeons.

Erik waited; a heavy silence weighted the air. Erik was reluctant to break it. Whatever he said would only be lies and these two people deserved better.

Jarin turned to him and met his gaze. 'We found Linota.'

Erik's heart stopped.

For a moment his brain could form no thoughts.

His worst fear had come true. Linota had been found and now that she had she must know that he had lied to her. She might already hate him.

He tried to swallow past the lump in his throat. He needed to get away from here, to think and to plan. There was not only Linota to consider, but also Isabel. She was in grave danger and only he could save her.

His mind raced. He had only just left de Bevoir. De Bevoir couldn't know about Linota's discovery, not yet. Erik needed to get to him before de Bevoir found out.

That was the only way he had a chance of getting his niece into his custody.

'Why did you do it, Erik? I don't understand.' Jarin's eyes were full of hurt and Erik's heart crushed. The look cut him even deeper than he'd imagined. But he didn't have time for Jarin right now. His brother was a grown man. He would get over this disappointment. Isabel needed him.

Jarin had everything while Isabel had nothing.

As soon as he had his niece safely in his arms he would return to Linota and beg her forgiveness on his knees.

He moved towards the door.

Jarin moved to block it.

Anger swept through Erik, the rage a welcome relief to the guilt. It was better, stronger and more familiar.

Jarin, with his pig-headed ignorance, was stopping Erik getting to where he needed to be. He took another step and Jarin blocked him, righteous indignation sweeping across his features. 'I need to know, Erik. I thought we were friends.'

Erik's anger bubbled over. 'You don't know anything. We're not friends. We're brothers.'

White-hot rage ripped through Erik at Jarin's surprised look of disbelief.

'Brothers?' said Jarin dully.

It was so good to finally tell him, to see the look of surprise on Jarin's face as he realised they were not so different after all. 'Brothers,' he confirmed. 'Only you're too wrapped up in yourself to realise it.'

The anger was becoming a living thing within him, pulsing with the desire to tear through the world. To rage in the face of everything that had conspired against him.

'How long have you known?' Jarin asked.

Erik snorted in disbelief. *This* was what Jarin wanted to focus on! Not why Erik had hidden Linota from him, but on their relationship, such an insignificant detail. 'That I'm Borwyn's bastard? All my miserable life.'

Jarin looked stunned. Surely it wasn't so much of a surprise. The two of them looked alike. It was not like this mattered. Only Linota and Isabel did.

'Why have you never said anything?' asked Jarin, seemingly still bewildered.

'Our ever-loving father threatened me with dire consequences if I breathed a word to anyone.'

That wasn't the whole truth. He'd also always feared Jarin would want nothing more to do with him once he'd learned the truth. Jarin had hated his other brothers and Erik hadn't wanted his only friend to see him like that. From the look on Jarin's face now, he'd been right to be circumspect.

'Why did you take Linota?' asked Katherine.

Erik flinched. He'd forgotten she was still in the room. How she must despise him, too.

Jarin moved to stand between himself and Katherine and Erik's anger hardened. How could his brother believe he was a danger to Katherine? He would rather die than hurt a woman. Jarin might not have realised they were brothers, but he surely must know this fundamental aspect of him.

He was wasting time, he needed to get to Isabel.

'Does it matter why I've done it?' he asked.

Neither Katherine nor Jarin moved. There was no

time to explain about his niece. The longer he stayed here the more chance de Bevoir would discover their plot to ransom Linota had failed. Erik knew he would take Isabel away from him as punishment. De Bevoir was not a man who would take failure well.

'I did it for the fortune,' he said at last. It was the simplest explanation, although it was quite untrue.

'You've done this for the few pitiful coins I have left? That doesn't seem like you,' said Jarin.

'You don't know me.' Jarin had shown that in words and deeds in this very room.

'Yes, I do. You're the boy who stole bread from the kitchen so that I could eat after our father had locked me in my room. You're the person who carried me when I couldn't walk because he'd beaten me so badly. I've seen you nurse hedgehogs back from the brink of death because you care about people and animals that can't take care of themselves. I know you.'

Erik was torn. All this was true and yet... Jarin had moved to protect Katherine. Erik couldn't bear another moment of this mental torture. When there was more time he would explain. He would tell his half-brother everything. It might be too late, but it was a risk he would have to take.

'People change.' He shrugged, edging again towards the door.

'But why? Please help me to understand this, Erik.'

'Now you want to know about me? You've had years, Jarin. Years in which you could have asked me if I needed you. It's too late now.'

Far too late. Their relationship might never recover. He couldn't mourn that right now, though. He would have time to go over what he could have done better over the last few days, but he could do that away from Jarin, as long as he managed to get Isabel to safety.

'Did our father turn you against me?' Jarin asked, still trying to understand.

Jarin's bewilderment only served to anger Erik further. 'No! I'm my own man. I make my own decisions.'

Jarin shook his head. 'Our father hated me. He couldn't bear it that I was the son who was going to inherit the earldom, so he took the only thing that really meant something to me—your friendship—and he destroyed it. He manipulated you like he manipulated everyone.'

Erik snorted. Trust Jarin to think the world revolved around him. 'Once again you think you have it all worked out. Believe what you want. I'm leaving.'

He advanced on Jarin, who stood unmoving before him. Erik did not want to hit his brother—hurting him went against every fibre of his being—but he would if Jarin wouldn't let him go.

'Let me pass,' he growled.

'I don't want—'

Erik had reached the end of his patience.

He tried to push past Jarin, but his brother held firm, reaching out and grabbing hold of his shoulder. He tried to twist out of his grip, but Jarin only held on tighter.

Without thinking, he ploughed his fist into his brother's stomach.

Jarin grunted, but remained upright.

'Let me go,' roared Erik.

For the first time it occurred to him that Jarin probably had no intention of letting him go anywhere. Erik would have to pay for his crimes. For all Jarin knew, Erik had abducted a young woman for material gain. He deserved to hang and perhaps that's what was in store for him.

Erik didn't have time to care. If that was his fate, then he would have to deal with it. It was probably better to dance at the end of the hangman's noose than watch his brother marry Linota. Right now, though, his focus had to be on getting Isabel to safety.

He shoved against Jarin, not wanting to hit him again, but knowing that he would if Jarin didn't let him go soon.

'Calm down,' yelled Jarin, shaking him.

If Jarin wouldn't let him go, Erik was going to have to make him.

He raised his fist, prepared to punch his brother again to get him to move. Time seemed to slow as Katherine called, 'No!' and moved in between the brothers.

As Jarin moved slightly, Erik's punch landed on the side of Katherine's head. There was a horrible crunch as the tiny woman lurched sideways and crumpled to the floor.

Erik felt the blood draining from his face.

He'd hit a woman.

A woman so small and vulnerable she looked like a broken bird sprawled across the stone floor.

Beside him Jarin stirred.

'I'm so sorry,' Erik began. 'I didn't mean—'

But he didn't get any further.

Jarin turned to him with a murderous glint in his eye.

His brother, who never fought unless it was the last

resort, punched Erik so hard it drove the breath from his lungs.

Erik didn't raise his fists to defend himself. Although he could, he knew he deserved this. He had committed the ultimate crime and hurt someone far more vulnerable than himself.

It didn't surprise him when Jarin raised his fists once more.

He welcomed the pummelling he received and when Jarin's fist connected with his head in a punch so strong it resounded through his body, he sunk willingly into oblivion as unconsciousness took him.

Linota blinked. A tall, severe-looking lady stood warming her fingers by the fire. Linota had never met her before. She looked around the room, but Katherine was nowhere to be seen. She blinked again.

'Ah, you're awake,' said the mystery lady. 'I'm Mistress Ann Sutton. Your sister has gone to speak with the Earl and has asked me to look after you in her absence.'

Linota gave a small nod. She was awake, but she was heavy with weariness. She supposed she should care that Katherine had left her to sleep while she had gone off to speak to Borwyn. Only a few days ago she would have been incensed to be left out, as if she was the child. Right now all she wanted was to lie back down and sink into oblivion once more.

There was a gentle knock on the chamber door. Mistress Sutton whisked over and opened it slightly. There was the sound of muffled voices and then the door closed softly.

Mistress Sutton moved over to the bed and looked down at her.

There was a kindness in her eyes that Linota hadn't expected.

'I'm afraid I'm needed elsewhere in the fortress,' said the woman softly.

'Will Katherine be returning?' Linota asked.

Mistress Sutton's hesitation was brief, but it was enough.

'What's happened?' she asked, raising herself on to her elbow.

'Nothing for you to concern yourself with.'

Linota frowned. Why did everyone always say that? 'It does concern me. Where is my sister?'

Mistress Sutton glanced towards the door.

Linota flung back her bed sheets and made as if to stand. She was so tired, but she was damned if she wasn't going to find out what was going on.

'You need to get back into bed,' said Mistress Sutton, trying to bundle her back into the covers.

'Not until I know what's going on,' said Linota, breaking free and getting to her feet.

Mistress Sutton sighed. 'Very well. I will tell you, but you are under strict instructions not to leave the room. There are guards outside who will make sure that happens.'

Linota nodded and gratefully slipped back into the bed. She didn't want to leave anyway. Being up and about was too exhausting.

'Katherine has been knocked unconscious.'

'What!' Linota sat bold upright, her exhaustion

briefly forgotten. There must be some mistake. 'How did that happen?'

'Erik Ward hit her.'

Linota's world spun. 'No…that's…that's not possible. He wouldn't…he couldn't…'

Mistress Sutton pursed her lips. 'I don't know the details. I'm only repeating what I have been told. The Earl has sent for me and I must go to him. Try to rest. As soon as I have more information I will return and inform you.'

Linota nodded numbly.

The older woman reached down and stroked Linota's hair. The touch was so gentle that Linota closed her eyes.

She heard Mistress Sutton turn and make her way to the door. She opened her eyes as the lady reached out to open the door.

'Mistress Sutton,' she whispered.

'Yes?' said the lady, turning slightly to look at her.

'Does Erik Ward have a sister?'

Mistress Sutton frowned and shook her head. 'No. Erik Ward does not have a sister. Is that what he told you, child?'

Linota nodded slightly. Her words stuck in her throat.

'Erik Ward is a rogue,' said Mistress Sutton.

Linota waited for her to expand, but she said nothing more. A moment later she nodded at Linota and left the room.

Linota lay back on the bed and stared at the ceiling.

She wanted to turn her mind off and sleep until the pain in her chest had subsided, but a voice kept pelting her with unpalatable facts.

Erik had abducted her and held her for ransom.

He'd touched her all over and made her come apart, all the time keeping the truth from her.

Erik didn't have a sister.

Erik had hit Katherine so hard he had knocked her unconscious.

Everything Erik had told her had been a lie.

He was as much of a traitor as the men who had betrayed her father. He was worse because he had taken her innocent trust in him and used it against her.

She would never forgive him.

Chapter Thirteen

Everything hurt.

The whole world was pain.

Erik rolled on to his side, searching for relief, but something stopped him. His left arm was pulled taut above him, his muscles straining in agony.

He tugged, trying to release the pain; metal clunked heavily and his head swam.

He blinked, forcing his eyes open.

He was in his own chamber, but… He raised his gaze to his arm. A thick manacle encircled his wrist and was secured at the other end to the wall by a thick chain.

He closed his eyes, remembering Jarin's look of bewildered hurt and Katherine, so small and defenceless, lying on the ground, knocked down by a punch he should never have wielded.

What he'd done was unforgivable. No wonder Jarin had him chained up. He was lucky Jarin hadn't had him locked into the dungeons; it was no less than he deserved.

He slumped back on the bed, wincing as his bruised

muscles protested. Jarin had hit him hard and, because Erik knew he deserved it, he'd let Jarin do his worst.

Hell, he'd have beaten himself over what he'd done to Katherine if that were physically possible. He remembered the sound of Katherine's tiny body hitting the floor with a thud and he doubled over, retching.

When the spasms subsided he tried to settle his body. He had to get out of here and go to Linota. He needed to explain what had happened before she heard it from someone else and hated him. Of course, she might already know everything, but if he could just explain. If he could show her that he hadn't had a choice. If she truly loved him like she said she did, then she would at least listen to him. Surely!

He closed his eyes tightly. He was an unfeeling bastard. How could he even think about Linota forgiving him when he had failed to rescue Isabel? He was the worst sort of man, thinking only of himself and his own pleasure.

He would search out Isabel first and then go to Linota. He would make sure his niece was safe and then see to his wants and desires. But first he needed to get out of these chains.

A key sounded in his chamber door. He slumped back on to the bed and tried to even out his breathing. Perhaps whoever it was would leave him alone if they thought he was sleeping.

Heavy footsteps sounded across the room and Erik sighed quietly—he'd recognise that tread anywhere. Jarin had come to question him and there was no way he would believe Erik was asleep. They knew each other too well. He opened his eyes as Jarin neared the bed, bracing himself to see hatred on his brother's face.

He didn't move as Jarin loomed over him.

Jarin's face was oddly blank. No emotion shone in his eyes and Erik swallowed. Somehow, seeing the blank look, the one Jarin used whenever he was being the Earl and not his friend, was worse than anger.

Erik licked his lips. 'How is Katherine?'

'Still unconscious,' said Jarin flatly.

Erik closed his eyes. He would not be able to live with himself if Katherine died. 'I'm sorry.'

Jarin nodded brusquely. 'I'm sure you are. Tell me why you did it.'

'I wanted to get out of the room and you were holding me. I never intended—'

Jarin tusked in annoyance. 'I don't mean why you hit Katherine. I could have killed you last night for punching her, but I've calmed down. I know you never intended to hurt her, only me. You've succeeded, by the way. I am hurt, only the wound is not visible.'

Erik turned his head. He couldn't look at Jarin. He couldn't bear the look of disgust on his face.

The silence stretched between them.

Erik could tell him the truth, but he still held back. There was still a slim chance de Bevoir hadn't heard about Linota's rescue and Erik's capture. If Erik could slip unseen out of the fortress, there was still a possibility he could get to his niece.

If Erik told Jarin everything, Jarin would want to help because that was the sort of man he was. But Erik could not risk Jarin going after de Bevoir. Jarin couldn't leave the castle without everyone knowing, meaning word would reach de Bevoir quickly and he would take evasive action. Worse, Isabel might get hurt in a skirmish and his soul rebelled against the idea.

Jarin continued to question him, but Erik refused to be drawn. Even as his heart broke at the disappointment in Jarin's voice he continued to stare at a middle distance somewhere above Jarin's head.

Even without looking directly at him he could sense Jarin's frustration, but he knew his friend well. Jarin had hit him last night in a blaze of anger, but he would not do so now. Jarin was a rational man who believed in talking through a situation. He would believe he could wear Erik down with his constant questioning, perhaps not today, but some time in the near future. And he was right. Erik would tell Jarin everything, just not right now.

'You're not going to tell me the truth, are you?' said Jarin eventually.

Erik didn't answer.

'Did you cut Katherine's saddle, causing her to have that fall?'

Erik's hand jerked against the chain. 'Katherine's saddle was deliberately damaged?'

'Yes. She could have died.'

Erik's heart pounded in his chest. He would kill de Bevoir if he ever got his hands on him. 'No. I did not cut the saddle. I would never do something like that. I don't know who did either. Are you sure it wasn't an accident?'

'Quite sure.'

Erik slumped back on to the bed. De Bevoir had made his plan seem bloodless. Keep Jarin away from the fortress while he stole some of Jarin's wealth. The land that had historically belonged to Garbodo's family would be returned to Garbodo without any fighting. It had almost seemed noble.

Erik had been blinded by the thought of getting Isabel to safety.

Erik had been a fool to trust de Bevoir.

De Bevoir had almost killed one Leofric sister and abducted the other.

There would be hell to pay when Erik next set eyes on him.

'Was our father as vile to you as he was to me?' asked Jarin.

Erik's heart thudded painfully, his vision blinded by rage. For so long he had wanted Jarin to acknowledge their shared paternity. In all of his wild imaginings he had never pictured it like this. He'd half-hoped Jarin would be pleased to discover they were brothers, but that had been a child's fantasy.

Erik rubbed his forehead with his free hand; he could be truthful about this at least. 'In some ways our father was worse to me, but as I was merely a bastard it wasn't as relentless for me as it was for you.'

'I am sorry.'

Erik looked at his brother in surprise. Jarin sounded properly apologetic and Erik's insides squirmed. Jarin was a good man, he did not deserve Erik's disrespectful actions. He paused. 'It was not your fault.'

Jarin nodded and turned to leave.

'Jarin,' Erik called before Jarin could leave the chamber. 'Please could you undo the manacle?'

Jarin stilled, his hand resting on the door. 'Are you going to run away?'

'No.'

'I want you to swear an oath, Erik.'

Heat flooded Erik's face as shame at losing Jarin's trust flooded him. He'd known from the start that this was the price he would have to pay. He'd thought it worth it, but right now it seemed like a very high cost indeed.

'I swear on the honour that I have left that I will not run away.'

Jarin looked at him for a long moment. 'I will send a guard in to unlock the chain. They will remain stationed outside your door.'

Jarin stepped outside. Erik watched him go without comment. It seemed Jarin didn't trust his heartfelt oath after all.

Dusk was falling as Erik let himself back into the keep by a secret entrance. Bribing his guards had been disappointingly easy. No wonder de Bevoir had been able to find out so much about Jarin; his guards had virtually no loyalty at all.

Erik had already begun planning how to fix the problem when he realised it would be nothing to do with him. His actions meant he would no longer be Jarin's steward. He'd almost staggered under the weight of that realisation, but had forced himself to keep moving. He'd wanted to catch de Bevoir before the man realised what had happened.

In the end, his perseverance had counted for nothing. He'd returned to all the places he'd seen de Bevoir and those he'd guessed at while he'd been blindfolded, but there was no sign of him and his men. Not even the hint that they'd even been in Borwyn's township.

Erik had lost everything for nothing.

He climbed the steps inside the keep.

Jarin would have put the Leofric sisters in one of the best chambers the fortress had to offer.

After the frustrations of his day Erik longed to see Linota. Her smile was like a balm to the soul. And she loved him. Him, a worthless bastard. It was almost impossible to imagine, but he'd seen the look in her eyes when she'd sworn to him it was true. It had to be. Clinging to that knowledge was the only thing that had got him through the long, horrible day of searching for Isabel, only for every place to be a dead end.

He'd wanted to chase after de Bevoir and head to Garbodo's lands, but he had to see Linota first. To tell her the truth behind everything that had happened.

Besides, de Bevoir might not have returned home. Perhaps he was regrouping and, if so, it was up to Erik to tell Jarin. He owed that to his brother, as his friend and as his liege.

Up ahead there was the brief sound of someone knocking on a door, followed by the noise of it opening.

'Mistress Leofric.'

Erik stilled as Jarin's voice floated down to him.

'My lord.'

Erik's heart clenched at the flat sound of Linota's response. It sounded so unlike her. There was no trace of her normal, gentle laughter.

'I am sorry for the ordeal you have suffered.'

Erik couldn't make out Linota's response. He hoped

she was saying something in defence of him. Yes, she had spent a short while with her abductors, but for the most part she had been safe and protected with him.

Jarin coughed.

'Mistress Leofric…'

The hairs on the back of Erik's neck stood up. Time seemed to slow down as he waited to hear what his brother would say next.

'Mistress Leofric…'

Erik's heart began to pound. Jarin sounded nervous! Why would he be nervous unless he was going to ask her something momentous?

After all that had happened Jarin couldn't be about to…surely it was too soon. They'd only just arrived at Borwyn. Jarin hadn't met Linota's older brother; he'd barely spent any time with Linota herself.

'As you are probably aware,' Jarin went on, 'the Earl of Ogmore has settled large dowries on you and Katherine.'

What was Jarin going on about? Surely this wasn't a marriage proposal? Jarin wasn't crass enough to discuss such a thing as dowries with a young woman.

'There is also your situation to consider.'

Erik leaned against the wall, his legs suddenly unable to support him.

'Your family has been through a difficult time over the last few years. An alliance with the Borwyn name will put an end to that.'

If Jarin had been talking to anyone other than Linota, Erik would have laughed. This offer of marriage, for that was what it was despite there being no mention of a wedding, was all wrong.

Hell, there was no way Jarin could love Linota. Jarin couldn't know about the little frown that appeared between her eyebrows whenever she was thinking about something intently. Or the way she laughed so easily or freely. Nor could he know about the soft gasps she made when she was being thoroughly kissed or that she was afraid of the dark and loved roasted meat above all food.

Jarin didn't know all that, but he could still see that Linota was the most beautiful woman who had ever walked across the face of the earth. He should be begging Linota to become his wife, not discussing dowries and family alliances.

In what felt like a world away Jarin continued. 'I have discussed a marriage between your good self and me with the Earl of Ogmore and I feel it will be an advantageous match for both of us.'

Erik held his breath.

Surely Linota would tell Jarin no. She had told Erik she loved him only yesterday.

There was a long silence.

Sweat beaded across Erik's brow. She couldn't be contemplating the union.

'I...' Linota began.

Erik straightened, straining to hear her response.

'I know this must be difficult for you. We don't know each other well, but I promise that you will want for nothing, that I shall keep you safe and that no one will be able to harm you.'

'Thank you for your kind words,' said Linota, in that strange, flat voice. 'I would be honoured to be your wife.'

Erik doubled over as if he had been punched in the

stomach, a loud ringing sounding in his ears. He tried to suck in a breath, but his lungs weren't working properly.

He stumbled away, back down the stairs towards his chamber.

He'd lost her.

And he couldn't blame her. He'd lied to her, knowing how much she despised those who did so.

He'd risked everything and failed.

Chapter Fourteen

Castle Swein—spring 1332

Linota concentrated on the needle, on the steady rhythm of passing it through the material on one side and then the other and the faint whoosh of the thread as she pulled it tight.

Next to her, Katherine was talking to their sister-in-law, Ellena. The soft murmur of their voices was soothing.

The three of them had fallen into the routine of sewing together every afternoon in a quiet corner of the Great Hall at Swein, Ellena's home. It was a time for them to get together and talk, although they never discussed anything difficult or unpleasant.

Ellena would laughingly tell them something amusing that had happened around the castle that day and Katherine would talk about how she was learning to ride a horse properly.

They never discussed the Earl of Borwyn or his half-brother, Erik Ward. And for that Linota was grateful.

Winter had finally given up its hold on the country and buds were quickly unfurling in the woodland around Swein. For the first time in many months Linota had woken up this morning without numb fingers and toes.

Her heart, though, that was still frozen.

Katherine said something and Ellena laughed. It was such a beautiful sound made by someone who was truly happy. Ellena's marriage to Linota's brother was a joyful experience. It made Linota glad to see her brother so content and, in getting to know Ellena, Linota had discovered a friend.

Watching the small, secret smiles the married couple gave to one another when they thought no one else was watching made her thank her own judgement that she had not gone through with her marriage to Borwyn. She'd come so close to making that mistake. It was only on the eve of the wedding that she'd come to her senses.

A union between her and Borwyn would have been a miserable disaster for the both of them.

For days after discovering Erik's betrayal and lies she'd been so wrapped up in her own misery that she had thought little about the world around her. On the eve of the wedding she realised Borwyn had only offered to marry her out a misplaced sense of obligation.

She had been under his protection when she had been snatched by de Bevoir and his men and Borwyn's honour had led him to offer her marriage. Numb from the shock of discovering she'd fallen in love with a man who didn't really exist, she'd accepted. What did it matter whom she married?

It had taken a few days, most of which had been

spent travelling from Borwyn to her brother's new home at Swein's Castle, but she'd eventually realised tying her life to a man she didn't love wasn't the answer to the pain she was feeling.

The girlish hopes and dreams she'd had since she'd first set eyes on Erik had gone and a new, darker world had emerged, but that didn't mean she should make it worse by involving Borwyn in her misery.

Once she'd made that decision, life had appeared clearer to her, as if she'd spent a week living under a thick blanket of fog only for it to suddenly disappear.

She'd noticed, then, how often Borwyn looked at Katherine. She'd watched as Katherine's eyes would linger on Borwyn in return, how polite and formal they were with each other while their bodies leaned towards one another.

They were in love, but for some reason not betrothed.

Linota imagined that when she released Borwyn from his obligation towards her he would rush straight into Katherine's arms and beg her to marry him. Once again she had been wrong.

Whatever had happened between the two of them during their last meeting had resulted in Borwyn leaving the castle and not returning.

Katherine had been a force to be reckoned with ever since. She always had a bright smile across her face and was determinably learning new skills, but the smile never quite reached her eyes. Linota was desperate to know what had happened between Katherine and Borwyn, but after being rebuffed on the subject more than once she'd learned not to pry.

Just as she'd learned not to speak about Erik.

As much as Katherine obviously loved Borwyn, she passionately hated his half-brother. This was the man who had abducted Linota and kept them apart for two, long days. Katherine would never forgive him and she couldn't understand why Linota did not feel the same.

Linota couldn't understand it either. She should hate him. He had taken her innocent heart and lied to her, repeatedly, all for his personal gain.

But she couldn't. No matter how many times she told herself to stop loving him, her heart refused to listen. She hoped one day the feelings would subside and she would be content with her lot. Maybe she would marry eventually and have children with another man.

For now, she would have to be content with being someone's doting aunt. From the way Ellena kept touching her stomach and smiling into the middle distance, Linota didn't think she would have to wait that long.

Linota glanced over at Katherine, who was concentrating fiercely on her stitching. Linota hid a smile. Sewing was the one thing her sister still couldn't master, no matter how hard she tried.

Linota looked across at Ellena who winked at her; she, too, had noticed just how dreadful Katherine's stitches were. Linota had to swallow a bubble of laughter and relief nearly made her giddy. Her heart was healing if she could laugh at the ridiculous.

Ellena returned her attention to her own stitching. 'Braedan and I have been planning a celebration at Easter,' she said, as her fingers flew over her intricate design. 'And we are planning on inviting the Earl of Borwyn. It would be good to extend the hand of friendship to him, don't you think?'

Linota froze, her fingers suspended in mid-air, her needle clutched painfully tightly against her skin. If Borwyn came, would Erik come, too? No, of course he wouldn't. She was being foolish. Erik had probably been banished from Borwyn or else he was locked up in the fortress's dungeon. He would not be travelling anywhere with his half-brother and, even if he was, he would not be welcome at Swein. Braedan would make sure of it.

It shouldn't matter. She needed to forget about Erik. She would likely never see him again and she wouldn't trust him even if she did. She concentrated on her needle once more, trying to ignore the pain blooming in her chest.

'I don't think Borwyn will come,' said Katherine quietly, her head still bowed.

Linota's heart constricted painfully. It hurt her to see Katherine so sad. 'I think he will,' she said.

And if he didn't, Linota would ride to Borwyn herself and drag him back to Swein.

Katherine paled. 'What makes you think so?'

Whatever her sister was thinking, it wasn't the truth. Borwyn had loved her, Linota was sure of it.

'I don't understand why he left in the first place,' Linota said in a rush. 'What did you say to him that last evening? Did you tell him you thought he was the best of men like I told you to? Because I don't think you can have done. The attraction between you was so intense it was like standing next to a fire whenever you were together. I felt as though I would burn from it sometimes.'

Ellena nodded. 'I noticed it on my wedding day. Neither of you were able to take your eyes off each other, even then.'

Their words didn't soothe Katherine. Mumbling some excuse, she ditched her sewing and fled from the room.

'Oh, dear,' said Ellena sadly. 'I thought we were doing the right thing in telling her of Borwyn's attraction, but we've obviously upset her.'

'I know.' Linota dropped her sewing to her lap. 'I don't know what to do for the best. I thought they would be together by now. Do you think he has forgotten her? I hate to see her looking so miserable. I was so sure he felt the same way about her. She can be so prickly sometimes and I do wonder what she said to him to make him stay away. I thought he was a stronger man than this, but to be scared off for so long...'

'Only time will tell if repairs to that relationship can be made.' Ellena made as if to take up her sewing again, but then laid her needle down. 'Seeing as I've upset one of you I may as well press on with my unwanted comments. I can see that you are miserable, too, Linota, and I think I know the cause. If we put our heads together, we may be able to come up with a solution.'

Linota pressed her hand to her stomach where an army of sea serpents had suddenly taken up residence.

'There is nothing the matter with me,' she said firmly.

'That's not true,' said Ellena kindly but firmly. 'I see the pain in your eyes whenever your sister denigrates Erik just as easily as I can see you wistfully gazing into the distance when your mind is elsewhere. I think you fell for this Erik Ward when you were with him. Is that true?'

Linota played with the edge of the sheet she was working on. She had kept her feelings for Erik buried deep inside her for months now. Katherine wouldn't talk about him apart from when she was carving chunks out of his personality. Linota wanted—no, she needed—to talk about him with someone who would listen rather than rant.

'Yes, it's true.' She picked at her embroidery. 'I did fall for him, deeply.' Her heart fluttered, it was so good to finally say the words. To admit she'd done something so foolish as to love a man who had betrayed her in every way. 'I wish I hadn't,' she added. 'I don't want to care for him. He lied to me. I may have feelings for him, but even if he wanted my forgiveness I couldn't give it to him.'

Ellena nodded slowly. 'Your sister certainly thinks he lied and deceived you all and yet you seem like a sensible woman. He must have done something to win your admiration. Tell me what happened to make you see the best in him.'

Linota tilted her head and thought about what had attracted her to him in the first place.

'He's very handsome,' she blurted out.

Ellena flung back her head and laughed. Heat swept up Linota's neck. She touched her cheeks only to find them burning, too.

'Yes, he is handsome,' Ellena agreed. 'Even I noticed that and I was already in love with your strapping brother.'

Linota pulled a face. She wasn't blind to the overwhelming attraction between her brother and his new wife. It was lovely, but also left her feeling a little sick; he was her older brother after all.

Ellena shook her head. 'Enough about Braedan. We were talking about you. There must be more to Erik than his pleasing physique.'

'He makes…made me laugh.'

'Laughter's good. There is nothing worse than being married to a man who makes you miserable; I should know.' Ellena paled a little and her eyes took on a haunted look. Linota reached out to touch the back of her sister-in-law's hand. It was no secret that Ellena's first marriage had been horrific and although Linota didn't know the details she knew enough to be glad the man was dead and buried. Ellena shook her head and smiled. 'Don't think I am going to change the subject. I want to know more about Erik Ward. I want to know if he's worthy of my new sister.'

Linota's chest constricted. She squeezed Ellena's hand, trying to communicate without words how wonderful it felt to be part of Ellena's family.

'I'm not sure I want to talk about him.'

'It might help.'

Linota shook her head. 'I'm not sure about that. Nothing can change what happened. Erik lied to me about everything. I even told him how much the truth meant to me and he still went ahead and did it. He used me for his own gain.'

'On the surface it does seem as if he has done the worst. But the truth is not always black and white. Perhaps he had a compelling reason for acting as he did. Did you ever ask him?'

The tips of Linota's fingers turned cold. 'No. I never spoke to him after...'

Ellena smiled gently. 'So you never gave him a chance to explain?'

'Would you have done?'

Ellena glanced down at her sewing and sighed. 'No, I wouldn't have done. In fact, your brother did something similar to me.'

'He did?'

Linota had a hard time imagining that. Braedan adored Ellena and would do anything for her. He did try to disguise the fact he was wrapped around her little finger—he was a hardened warrior, after all—but most people knew exactly how devoted he was.

'Yes, he did. And afterwards I realised that his actions had been to protect his sisters and as I've come to know and love you, I understand why he did what he did.'

Linota turned her attention back to her pattern, trying to pick up where she'd left off. 'But I loathe people who lie. It was lies that condemned my father, lies which meant my sister and I spent years confined to our chambers.'

'Sometimes people lie and betray for their own gain. That is unforgivable. Other times the reasons are more complex. You need to find out what motivated Erik. Only then will you find peace.'

Linota concentrated fiercely on her pattern as she pondered Ellena's words. Could it be true that Erik had acted with the best of intentions? Was there a way for her to understand what he had done? Her heart fluttered at the possibility and then dropped once more. 'Even if I could forgive him, there can be no future for us.'

Ellena frowned. Linota continued her explanation. 'I am expected to marry well. Erik Ward is a bastard.'

'I'm sure Braedan can be persuaded—'

'Braedan is possible, especially if it was you who were to persuade him, but not Katherine. It has been her particular ambition throughout our childhood that I marry well and bring honour to our family.'

Ellena's frown deepened. 'Katherine would not be so cruel as to expect you to marry someone you didn't love. She only wants your happiness.'

Linota ran her fingers over her braid—once more it felt too tight against her scalp. 'Katherine hates Erik. She would never believe that Erik could make me happy. Even if she accepted his low birth she couldn't accept Erik himself.'

Ellena nodded. 'That certainly is an obstacle. Braedan isn't keen on him either.' She dropped her sheet on to her lap, abandoning all pretence of sewing. 'You must find out the truth.'

'What truth?'

'You told us that Erik had a sister. You need to find out if that is true.'

'Mistress Sutton—' Linota began.

'—doesn't know everything,' Ellena finished for her.

The room stilled. Linota's pulse pounded wildly in her throat. She allowed herself, for a moment, to believe that everything Erik told her had been true. The pain in her heart lessened briefly only to return with a hard punch to the chest. There was no way for her to ever find out. 'How can I discover the truth?' she whispered.

'I believe things are about to be made easier on that front,' said Ellena, a small smile playing at the corners of her lips.

Heavy boots strode across the Great Hall and came to a stop beside their seats. Linota froze; surely it couldn't be. Linota looked up and for a moment her heart tumbled wildly in her chest. The man who stood before her had Erik's wide shoulders and curling blond hair. For the first time in months her body breathed easily.

She blinked and her heart fell to her feet when she realised the man before her was not Erik, but his brother, Jarin Ashdown, the Earl of Borwyn. Ellena got to her feet to welcome him; Linota stayed rooted to her chair. She couldn't have moved even if she'd wanted to, so heavy was her disappointment.

'My good ladies,' Borwyn said formally, his shoulders stiff and unyielding. 'I hope that you are both keeping well.'

'Thank you, kind sir,' answered Ellena. 'We are both well. I trust you are, too?'

Linota's heart began to race while Ellena and Borwyn exchanged polite remarks with one another. There was only one reason the Earl could be here—at least there was only one she could think of that made sense.

Borwyn had come for Katherine.

She clasped her hands tightly in her lap and began to pray fervently.

She wanted her sister to be happy, of course she did. But she couldn't lie to herself that she wanted this match so very badly, not just for her sister but for herself. Because if Katherine came to her senses and accepted Jarin as her husband then there was a link, no matter how tenuous, with Erik.

Chapter Fifteen

Borwyn's fortress—spring 1332

'Are you sure you won't come down and eat?' asked Katherine, swirling round their guest chamber, her permanent smile dazzling.

'Yes, I'm feeling rather tired after our journey,' said Linota, flopping back on to her bed and doing her best to look as if the two-day journey from Castle Swein to Borwyn's fortress had completely exhausted her when the exact opposite was true.

Luckily Katherine was too preoccupied with her impending marriage to Borwyn to pay too much attention to her.

'I'll bring some food up for you,' Katherine said as she floated towards the door.

It really was very…warming to see how happy Katherine was now that she had agreed to marry Borwyn. On the few instances that Linota had seen Borwyn he had been equally delirious with happiness.

'Mmm,' Linota mumbled, pretending that she was almost dropping off.

The door opened, but instead of stepping through it Katherine came back into the room.

'You're not hiding from Erik Ward, are you?'

'No, of course not. I'm tired, that's all.'

Katherine wasn't convinced by Linota's pretended innocence. 'Borwyn has reassured me that Erik Ward is not in the fortress at the moment, so there is no need for you to stay up here if that's what you're doing.'

A sharp pain wedged itself in Linota's chest. She'd promised herself that all she wanted was to know the truth about Erik, but deep down she knew that wasn't true. She wanted to see him again.

Katherine hadn't moved from her position by the edge of the bed as she waited for a reply.

'I'm not worried about seeing E—Master Ward again,' she said, hoping that Katherine wouldn't question her too deeply. It was true she wasn't worried about seeing him, she was instead filled with a desperate longing and a deep-seated anxiety that her investigations would prove he was a liar rather than the other way around. Until she knew for sure, she wanted to keep her thoughts and feelings to herself.

Katherine reached out and gently touched her arm. 'I don't have to go.'

'Yes, you do.' Linota rolled on to her side and smiled up at her sister. 'This is a feast in your honour, Katherine. Go and enjoy it.'

'I will. But please send someone if you need me. I will come straight away.' Katherine leaned over and dropped a kiss on Linota's forehead. 'And when you feel up to seeing Erik Ward again, I can be with you. It might make you feel better if you heard the story from his point of view. Not that I forgive him for keeping you hidden from me.' Katherine frowned. 'But I'm inclined to be a little more sympathetic now I know more of the story.'

Linota nodded. 'Thank you, Katherine, that's kind of you. But right now I think I'd just like to sleep.' There was no way Katherine was going to be there when Linota next spoke to Erik. There were things she wanted to say to him that didn't require a witness.

Linota wanted to find out the truth for herself, not from someone else who might get the story wrong.

She settled back on to the bed and closed her eyes. She could feel Katherine's eyes on her and she worried she was overdoing it, but eventually Katherine's footsteps sounded across the room. Linota heard the door open and finally close behind Katherine. She let out a long breath she hadn't realised she'd been holding.

She stayed lying down and told herself one of her father's stories. She normally loved remembering the soothing tales, but today she had to force herself to slow the recitation down. It wouldn't do for Katherine to return to the chamber to find her leaping from the bed like a spring lamb.

When Linota was sure enough time had passed for Katherine to reach the Great Hall to join the feast put on in honour of her betrothal to Borwyn, she climbed down from the bed.

Creeping over to the door, she peeked into the corridor outside, half expecting to see guards stationed outside, but thankfully all was quiet.

She quickly tugged on her boots and slipped out of the room, pulling the door shut behind her.

She ran down the stone corridors, stopping every time she reached a corner to peer around it. The fortress was eerily empty, but she kept going despite the chills creeping down her spine.

She stopped outside what she had discovered was Erik's chamber.

While he'd been at Castle Swein, Borwyn had told them all that he and his half-brother were reconciled. He'd tried to talk about Erik but, frustratingly, Katherine wouldn't let him do so in front of Linota, obviously believing anything to do with Erik would only upset her. All she knew was that his actions during the days they'd spent together had nothing to do with Erik securing his own fortune. Jarin had accepted his betrothed's wishes and Linota hadn't wanted to draw attention to how much talking about Erik mattered to her.

She knocked lightly on the door, her heart pounding as she both dreaded and longed for the sound of Erik's voice.

Her heart fell when there was only silence in response.

Slowly she pushed open the door and stepped inside. A shard of light pierced through the shutters illuminating the stone floor. She took another step into the room, dust dancing around her feet. She stood on the spot and turned around, taking in the room.

It was very sparsely furnished. A large bed stood against one wall, blankets arranged neatly on top. A beautifully made chest was positioned at the bottom of it. She walked over and ran her fingers over the intricate pattern carved into the top of the wood. It was so similar to the one in his cottage that she had no doubt Erik had made it himself.

There was not much on the one table in the room. Some strange-looking tools were arranged at one end. Linota guessed he used these to work with wood because she'd never seen anything like them before.

There was nothing else on the table.

She didn't know what she'd been expecting. Perhaps evidence that he'd found what had happened to his sister, although what this would have looked like she wasn't sure.

She eyed the chest. She'd crossed some sort of moral code walking into this room. Could she cross another one by opening the box?

She took a step towards it, her fingers trembling.

She touched the latch and then snatched her hand back.

It was too much, an invasion of his privacy he probably couldn't forgive if he found out. But she'd come so far. To return to her room now would be a failure and who knew when she'd get a chance to come here again. There were many feasts over the next few days to celebrate Katherine and Borwyn's nuptials. She wouldn't be able to plead tiredness again and Katherine was unlikely to let her wander off by herself.

When the festivities were all over she was returning to Swein with Ellena and Braedan, to live with them rather than Katherine and her new husband.

Katherine was disappointed. She'd thought Linota would live with her, but Linota knew it would be too hard. She couldn't see Erik on a daily basis and pretend nothing had happened between them, not when the memory of his lips on her body still hadn't faded from her memory. The physical closeness would slowly kill her. Visiting her sister would be hard enough, but perhaps if she knew Erik hadn't lied to her about his sister, if that one thing was true, then she would be able to meet and interact with him with some degree of calmness.

Her mind made up, she reached for the latch once more.

Before she could open the lid she heard the unmistakable sound of the chamber door opening.

Time seemed to slow as she looked around the room, searching for somewhere to hide.

There was nowhere.

She stepped away from the chest and clasped her hands together so whoever was coming would not see how violently her fingers were trembling.

Erik wiped the back of his hand across his mouth and paused in the entrance to his chamber. He was thirsty, but he'd nothing to drink.

He'd headed to the Great Hall before remembering tonight was the feast in celebration of Jarin's upcoming marriage to Katherine. Jarin had sworn Erik would be welcome but he'd seen the strain in his brother's eyes and known his newly betrothed did not really want Erik anywhere near herself or her beloved sister.

Linota's brother was also down there. Sir Braeden might play the civilised man sometimes, but Erik had no doubt Leofric would rip him apart if he knew what had transpired between Erik and Linota in the room above Emma's bakery.

Erik wouldn't defend himself even though he'd be able to. He was guilty. He had touched Linota's beautiful body even knowing he was a worthless bastard who was lying to a woman who trusted him explicitly.

Hell, he shouldn't wait for Sir Braedan to do it. He should rip himself apart. He might yet. The only thing keeping him going, that stopped him going completely insane during the long, endless days that stretched on and on without Linota, was his search for his niece.

Erik closed his eyes. To think that Linota was within the same walls as him. It would only take moments for him to slip down to the Hall and cast his eyes on her once more.

He let out a long breath.

He wouldn't do it.

Not tonight. But he knew he didn't have the resolve not to set eyes on her before she left. He needed to see her again just as he needed to breathe.

Now he was going to rest. Another day of fruitlessly searching for Isabel had drained him more than a hundred battles.

He stepped into his chamber and froze as the door closed behind him.

As if he'd conjured her from his imagination, Linota stood in front of him, her back straight and her head held high. Her hands clasped tightly in front of her.

He swallowed.

She didn't move.

Perhaps he had gone insane. The longing that nagged at him every day, that didn't disappear even when he slept, had finally tipped him over the edge and now he was seeing things.

He closed his eyes and shook his head to dispel the image.

He opened them again.

She was still there.

He took two steps towards her. Closer, he could see her pulse pounding in her neck. His gaze flickered over her. Her knuckles were white, her skin pale.

She was real.

'Why are you here?' He winced when she flinched at his harsh words.

He cleared his throat, speaking softly this time. 'I mean, why aren't you at the feast?'

She opened her mouth as if to respond and then closed it again.

'Well?' he asked.

'I should go,' she whispered.

He nodded slowly. Yes, that was probably for the best. She shouldn't be alone with him, in his chamber. Not that she would come to any harm, but the longer she stayed here the harder it would be for him to let her go again.

She made no move to leave.

He took another step forward.

His gaze locked with hers and the rest of the room fell away. There was only Linota, nothing else.

He reached for her and she didn't step away as his fingers traced the backs of her hands and up the length of her arms to her shoulders, bringing them to rest along the soft skin of her neck.

Her lips parted and her pupils darkened.

Gently he lowered his mouth to hers. She lifted her head as if welcoming his touch and he deepened the kiss, pouring all the months of longing and despair into his actions. Her tongue met his and he grunted, pulling her flush against his body.

Her hand stole into his hair and she gripped it tightly, almost painfully, as she held him in place.

His hands found the ties of her tunic and he began to pull on them, loosening the garment and pushing it to the floor. It hit the ground with a soft thud.

His hands ran down her back, feeling her soft curves through her dress. She whimpered as his hands skimmed the curves of her bottom. His body roared in satisfaction at the sound. He began to pull at the ties on her dress, his only thought to get her beneath him, to give them both a release from this raging desire.

One tie came undone and his fingers drifted to the next one.

His mind was almost totally lost.

But he wasn't so far gone that he didn't feel the press of hands against his chest.

He lifted his head and gazed down. The palms of Linota's hands were pressed against him, pushing him away. He glanced at her face. Her cheeks were flushed, her pupils wide and her lips swollen. She looked like a woman swept away with desire, but the stance of her body said otherwise.

'Please stop,' she whispered.

He heard the pain in her voice and he stepped back as if scalded. She stumbled and he reached out a hand to catch her.

Once she was steady he removed his hand once more.

His body clamoured to take her back into his arms. Instead he strode over to his worktable and began to arrange his already ordered tools.

He concentrated on his breathing, in and out. He was a man, not a beast. He would not touch a woman unless she was willing.

'Why are you here, Linota?' he asked again.

There was a long pause and he turned to check she was still in the room.

She was where he'd left her, her embroidered tunic still at her feet.

A flush of shame washed over him, but he didn't move to pick it up. He didn't trust himself to be near her again.

'I'm here to celebrate my sister's marriage to Borwyn.'

'Aye, I know why you are in Borwyn's fortress but why are you in this chamber, *my chamber* to be exact?'

Her fingers twisted into the folds of her dress, her gaze darting towards his storage chest and away again.

'Would you believe me if I said I was lost?' she asked in a quiet voice.

'No.' It wasn't possible. His chamber was in the opposite direction to the Great Hall.

She smiled sadly and bent to pick up her tunic, her braid falling over her shoulder as she did so.

He tore his gaze away from her and focused on a point on the wall behind her.

'Linota, please tell me the truth as to why you are in here.'

Even though he wasn't looking directly at her, he could sense her entire body stiffening at his words.

'The truth! Do you really think I owe you that?'

He reared back as her words hit him harder than any punch he'd ever received.

'As you're in my chamber uninvited, yes, I think you do.'

'And did you not think I deserved the truth the last time we were together, or do you believe me too feeble-minded?' She thrust her arms angrily into her tunic. Even as her body vibrated with anger he still wanted to cross the room and pull her into his arms.

'I never lied to you,' he said. It was true. He hadn't lied. He'd been very careful about that. It was the only way he could justify his actions to himself.

She snorted, folding her arms beneath her chest. Placid, gentle Linota was beautiful; angry Linota was magnificent.

He scratched his jaw. Stubble was beginning to poke its way through and it scraped along his fingers. 'I didn't lie to you. I'll admit I didn't tell you the whole truth, but I didn't know you well enough to know if you were trustworthy or not.'

'You knew me well enough to put your mouth...' Words seemed to fail her and she waved her hand over her body to indicate what he'd done.

Not that he needed reminding. That last afternoon with her was seared into his brain. The memory of the taste and feel of her stayed with him wherever he went. At night he would dream of her moving beneath him. He would wake, hard and wanting with desire, and nothing he did slaked his thirst for her.

Not that he had been with another woman. He'd had offers, but he'd not even been tempted. He wanted

Linota or no one. From the look on her face right now, it would be no one for ever.

'Aren't you going to say anything?' she demanded and he realised he'd been staring at her body.

He cleared his throat. 'I didn't see you complaining when I kissed you all over.'

She made a noise in the back of her throat, which sounded something between a growl and a snarl of rage. He couldn't help but smile at the noise.

'You are unbelievable,' she hissed.

She stormed over to the chest at the end of his bed. She threw open the lid and began to pull the items out, tossing them on to the mattress as she did so.

'What are you doing?' He strode over and grasped her wrist, not hard but enough to stop her.

'Let me go.' Her nostrils flared and she glared at him.

He dropped her arm, but didn't move away.

'Have you gone insane?' he asked as she delved back into the chest. 'What are you hoping to achieve by throwing my belongings around?'

He knew he should march her out of his room and forbid her from returning, but even though she was incandescent with rage against him he still preferred to have her in his chamber than not. He was pathetic.

'I want to see some proof, even if it's something tiny, that your sister actually existed.'

'What good will that do?'

'You lied to me about everything else, but I keep asking myself what was the point of inventing a sister. If I know at least one thing was true, I might...'

He waited for her to finish her sentence but she carried on with her single-minded search.

'Might what?' he prompted.

She shrugged. 'It doesn't matter.'

It obviously did matter a great deal, but he didn't push her. If she wanted to search his belongings, she could. He had nothing to hide. Not any more.

'Mary did exist. She doesn't now,' he said simply.

The pain over her death had dulled, but not the loss of his niece; he still found that hard to accept. And he wasn't going to give up trying to find her until she was in his custody.

Linota shook her head. 'Mistress Sutton said you don't have a sister.'

'Who's Mistress Sutton? Oh, I know. The tall, severe lady who looks permanently disappointed. Why would she know whether or not I have a sister? She doesn't know me. I told you, I hid Mary as best I could. A small bastard child in a large fortress is hardly significant.'

Linota paused for a moment, her hand hovering over the chest, but then she shook her head and carried on.

Stepping away from her, he leaned against the nearest wall and folded his arms as if he didn't have a care in the world. He didn't have many belongings and she could hunt through them all she liked. She would find no proof his sister had ever lived among his paltry effects.

'Careful with that,' he said when she got to the bottom of the chest.

She bent down and with both hands lifted the ornate sword that normally lay beneath his other belongings.

'This doesn't look like a steward's sword,' she said, holding it aloft.

'That's because it isn't. I'm not a steward any more.'

He inhaled sharply. Jarin had forgiven him and Erik was grateful. Jarin had even offered to keep him on in the role of his steward, but Erik had declined. Jarin needed a more experienced man to guide him. Linota was still holding the sword, the expression on her face accusing. 'It belonged to my father.'

'Did you steal it?'

He pushed himself away from the wall and took the unwieldy sword from her. 'I think you've said enough. You should go now.'

She didn't move as he began to fold his winter clothing and place it back in the chest.

'I'm serious, Linota. If you've only come here to insult me then you need to leave. Go and join your sister in celebrating her forthcoming wedding.'

'I want to believe you, Erik.'

He glanced sideways at her. Her eyes were wide and glistening with unshed tears.

'I can tell you my story, Linota, but that doesn't mean you will believe it.'

'Please tell me anyway.'

He paused. Hadn't he wanted to do this from the very beginning? And now she was here and wanted to hear what he had to say. 'Very well.'

Linota perched on the end of his bed, her hands folded in her lap, as he told her what had happened to him from the moment de Bevoir approached him. He told her all about his young niece and how he was still searching for Isabel, how he wouldn't stop until he'd found her.

He didn't tell her he had been outside her room when she had accepted Borwyn's proposal. Or how that acceptance had sent him to his knees. Or the overwhelming relief he'd experienced when he'd found out she hadn't gone through with the marriage. He didn't think he would have been able to see her married to his brother and not go insane.

He knew she would have to marry someone else, but that faceless nobleman would live far from Borwyn's lands. He would not have to see her grow round with someone else's child. The knowledge that she was sharing another man's bed would be painful, but not as excruciating as witnessing the proof of it.

'You could have trusted me with the truth,' she said when he'd finished his tale.

He shook his head. 'I couldn't take that risk, don't you see? Isabel's life depended on it.'

Linota stood abruptly. 'I would have helped you find Isabel.'

Erik rubbed his forehead. 'All I needed from you was to stay hidden. I—'

She interrupted him. 'You didn't want my help.'

'I didn't need it,' he bit out.

Why couldn't she see what he was saying? He'd always had to look after himself. These last few months not withstanding, he'd been pretty good at it for most of his life. He didn't need the help of the one woman he wanted to keep safe above all others.

She didn't respond to his outburst. Instead she nodded and made towards the chamber door.

'Shall I escort you to the feast?' he asked, not quite ready for his time with her to be over.

'I'm not going to the feast.'

'I'll walk you back to your chamber, then.'

'I'm not going there either.'

He huffed out a breath. 'I'll take you to wherever you are going. You shouldn't be alone, not even in the depths of Borwyn's keep.'

'I'm not staying in the keep.' She pulled open the door and stepped into the corridor.

'Where are you going?'

'To look for your niece.'

Chapter Sixteen

Linota strode out into the corridor, not waiting to see Erik's response to her statement.

She wasn't even sure she was going to go through with searching for this mysterious Isabel, but she was determined to show Erik that she was eminently capable of helping him. How she was going to achieve that she wasn't sure.

She had rounded one corner when heavy footsteps followed her.

'What in God's name are you thinking?' thundered Erik as he caught up with her. 'Do you honestly believe you're going to walk into the town and find a girl I've spent months and months searching for?'

She swung round to face him and almost hit her head on his leather tunic. She glared up at him. 'As you haven't found her, you're obviously not looking in the right places.'

A red flush washed across Erik's face as his eyebrows came down in a deep frown. It was the first time Linota had ever seen his anger directed at her. She could see why he had a reputation for being a fierce warrior. Fire blazed in his blue eyes and the obvious rage pounding through him caused her body to tighten as she took a step backwards, not because she was scared of him—quite the opposite. She wanted to pull him to her, to finish what they had started in his chamber. But she would not give in to that temptation.

His eyes narrowed and she knew she should be scared—no sane person could look into that face and not see the restrained violence burning there—but for some reason she wasn't. Perhaps she trusted him after all.

'I have searched everywhere,' he bit out, his voice tightly controlled.

'Then show me.'

He stared down at her.

'Fine,' he growled. 'I will take you around Borwyn and show you every building I have searched so you can see for yourself what a pointless endeavour it is.'

He turned on his heel and strode towards the entrance of the keep, not looking to see if she was following. She scurried after him.

The sky was a dusky pink as they stepped into Borwyn's walled town.

She couldn't quite believe her luck at getting this far. 'Where do we start?'

'We'll start where I saw Isabel.'

Linota had to run slightly to keep up with his long strides. 'Which was where exactly?'

'In a building down a small side street.'

She recognised the path they were taking as the one that led to Emma's bakery. 'Is Emma all right after…?'

Erik grunted. 'She is fine. Borwyn realised she was only doing what I asked. She and her husband were released from the dungeons that same day.'

Linota was glad. She didn't like to think of the motherly Emma being locked up in that foul place.

Something that had played on her mind ever since Borwyn's proposal to Katherine was how the brothers had reconciled. Linota was sure Borwyn would have told Katherine everything when he came to visit them in Swein, but if he had, Katherine had not repeated the information to Linota. It was frustrating that, even after everything, Katherine still thought Linota needed protecting.

Erik still lived at the fortress He still slept in the same quarters he had before. Borwyn must have forgiven Erik for what had happened between them, but until now Linota had not been able to bring herself to ask Katherine what had happened. Oh, she'd tried once. But Katherine had fixed her with such a sympathetic smile that Linota hadn't been able to continue. She didn't want anyone's pity, even Katherine's, or perhaps especially Katherine's because she really wanted her sister to treat her as an equal and not a child to be cosseted.

'How did you and Borwyn restore your relationship?' she asked as they turned down another street.

'How much do you know?' He pulled her into a shadow as a group of drunken revellers staggered past.

'The last I knew you were imprisoned in your chamber and then you weren't. I don't know anything in between.'

'Ah, well…' His chin dipped. 'Quite a lot has happened since.'

'Tell me,' she said, nudging his side.

The drunken men stopped outside a house opposite and began a bawdy tune. Erik's grip tightened on her arm, but Linota couldn't stop the smile spreading across her face.

Linota couldn't suppress her giggles as the men continued to sing about cocks and hens, the double meaning funny even in the unusual situation.

Next to her Erik's body was still and tense.

He turned his glare from the men and looked down at her. Her breath caught in her throat; his eyes were nearly completely black. Her lips parted and his gaze dropped to them.

All her humour died. Everything centred on his mouth, so close to hers. She wanted to feel it move against hers once more. It would take only the smallest stretch to reach him. But they were outside, so close to Borwyn. Anyone could see them. Bad enough that she was out here with Erik, it would be so much worse if she was seen kissing him. Braedan would kill him on the spot.

Erik tore his gaze away from hers and back to the singing men. 'Let's keep going.'

He led her down the narrow street and into a smaller one where the walls of the opposite houses nearly touched.

'This is where I saw Isabel,' he said, stopping in front of a dilapidated building. The remains of a door hung open. Erik stepped through the gap and Linota followed.

'I've been here many times. There is nothing to see.'

He strode to the centre of the room. 'Please don't let me stop you searching, though.'

She stepped a little further into the room. It was largely empty. She walked over to a stack of abandoned wood, which looked like it might once have been part of some sort of furniture. She turned over the top piece with her foot.

Erik folded his arms across his chest and watched.

'You were going to tell me what happened between you and Borwyn.' Linota turned over the next piece.

'What do you want to know?'

'I want to know why he forgave you for lying to him.' Perhaps if she could understand this she could make sense of why he had lied to her also.

'I explained everything to Jarin.'

Linota upturned the last of the pile. She shuddered as woodlice scuttled in every direction.

'Find anything?'

She turned to Erik. A slight smile tugged at the corners of his lips. He was laughing at her.

Before she knew what she was doing, she strode across the room and prodded a finger in the centre of his chest. 'Don't you dare laugh at me! I want to know! I deserve to know. I trusted you with my...life. I believed you were a good man.'

His smile disappeared in an instant. 'What is it you want to *know*, Linota? Does it really make a difference? You're safe, your sister is safe. Everyone lives happily ever after, don't they?' He swung away from her. 'When I saw Isabel she was upstairs.'

Her heart pounding, Linota followed Erik as he raced

up the creaking staircase, avoiding the steps that looked so worn they might fall through at a moment's notice.

The solitary room upstairs was devoid of anything.

'She was lying right here, my little niece.' Erik's eyes were wide, his jaw rigid. 'She looked so like her mother, her brown eyes were wide with fear. Fear, Linota! Absolute total and utter terror.' He shoved his hand through his hair, turning away from her to stare at a spot above her shoulder. 'I could do nothing. I couldn't get her away from the men who held her captive. You want the truth, I'll tell you the truth. I failed that little girl, just like I failed her mother.' His voice quietened. 'So I'm sorry, Linota. Sorry if I hurt your feelings by keeping you hidden for a couple of days. I'm sorry that I made your sister suffer by your absence. But by doing that I was trying to keep my niece safe.'

Linota stepped closer to him. He was breathing heavily. She reached up and lightly touched his chest.

'Maybe that was wrong of me.' He was quieter now, almost whispering. 'Maybe I could have trusted you with the truth and, if it had been just me, I would have risked it, Linota. But I couldn't, not for Isabel. I'm the only person she has in the world.'

Linota dropped her hand and moved away. She believed him. Believed that Isabel existed and that Mary had been his sister; she believed it all. She wished he had trusted her with the truth, but she was beginning to understand why he hadn't.

'Where else did you see her?' she asked softly.

His shoulders slumped slightly, the movement so small she wouldn't have noticed if she hadn't been studying him intently. He'd been expecting a different reaction from her, but she didn't know how to play this game, didn't know whether he deserved to know of her forgiveness.

'I didn't see her anywhere else.' He sounded tired and her heart twisted. 'Let's return to the fortress.' He made to move out of the room. 'There is still time for you to enjoy the last of the feast. I believe they have some of the same entertainment you so enjoyed the night I met you.'

That night at Ogmore's seemed so far away now, the girl she'd been there so completely different from the one she was now.

'You must have other places to explore,' she said, refusing to budge. She would not return to the fortress until she had some answers.

He paused. 'I have had no further success. Every avenue ends like this. A complete and utter waste of time.'

'Show me…' She walked over and lightly touched his sleeve.

His gaze locked on to her hand where it rested against him. She could feel the hard muscles of him underneath the fabric.

'Lin, I…'

Her heart stuttered. No one had called her Lin since he'd last uttered that name.

He cleared his throat. 'This could be dangerous, Lin. I don't want you getting hurt.'

His gaze moved up to her eyes. She saw the vulnerability lurking in the shadows, behind the confident man he showed to the world.

'I'll be safe with you to protect me.'

He half smiled at that. 'I haven't done a great job

of that in the past. You have been hurt on my watch many a time.'

'That's not true.'

He raised an eyebrow.

'You've always come to my rescue. Come on.' She began to tug on his arm, guiding him down the steps.

'Where now?' she asked as they stepped outside.

Night was falling now. Bats were appearing, their little bodies swooping and looping across the darkening sky.

Erik sighed. 'Are you sure I can't persuade you to return to the fortress?'

She didn't respond.

Erik sighed again. 'I traced him to an abandoned building on the east side of the town. He's long since left. I'll take you there if you swear to me that after you've seen for yourself that the place is deserted we will return to the fortress.'

Linota didn't want the evening to end, but she knew she would have to return to her chamber before Katherine. She didn't want Katherine to find out what she'd been doing when she'd assured her she was going to stay in their shared chamber and sleep.

'I promise I will return to the fortress after we have been to this building.'

That stopped him in his tracks. 'You do?'

'Yes.'

He gazed at her for a long moment. She held his intense stare. She could drown in his blue eyes. The look in their depths was obvious even with her lack of experience. He wasn't even trying to hide the desire that shone from them. She longed to reach up and brush her lips against his, to feel the thrill of excitement that raced through her whenever she touched him. But she didn't. He had never given her reason to hope that his feelings ran any deeper than intense attraction, never indicated that he would like to spend the rest of his life with her. He'd promoted the match between her and Borwyn right until the end. If this evening was all she had left of her time with him, then she wanted it to be about discovering the truth, not about being blinded by desire.

'Erik, please tell me what happened between you and Borwyn.'

'Why?'

They began to walk along the now mostly silent streets, her arm bumping into his as they moved.

'I want to know. I think I deserve it, don't you?'

Linota counted fifteen steps before he spoke again. 'I told him about my childhood. About our shared father and how he treated me, which wasn't great, in case you are wondering. I told him about Mary and Isabel. Jarin only has a vague memory of Mary. The fortress is a big place and I didn't get to know Jarin well until after Mary had left. Jarin has a kind heart and it pains him that he had a sister he knew nothing about.'

'It wasn't his fault.'

'No, it wasn't.' Erik took a deep breath. 'After he'd learned about the threat from Garbodo, Borwyn sent spies into his land.'

'Did they find anything?'

'Not much. Garbodo has disavowed de Bevoir, saying that the man acted alone and that he knew nothing of his intentions. Borwyn has strengthened the border between him and Garbodo's land and the threat appears to have died down for now.' Erik lightly touched her elbow, turning her down another side street. 'Of Mary, we found out very little. We understand that she married a soldier who moved to Garbodo's lands some time ago, taking his wife with him. I don't know if the marriage was happy or not. I like to think it was. Her husband was killed in a skirmish and Mary died not long afterwards. Isabel was their only child.'

'What about de Bevoir? Can't he be captured and questioned?'

Erik smiled down at her. 'I can't imagine anything I would like better. Actually, that's not true. There *are* a couple of things I would prefer to do...'

Linota's heart fluttered. Was he suggesting...? But, no, he didn't appear to be.

Erik continued. 'Having him at my mercy would be enjoyable. Unfortunately, he is no longer Garbodo's right-hand man and not one of our forays into Garbodo's lands or any of the surrounding ones has produced any answers.'

'He can't have disappeared.'

Erik grimaced. 'Garbodo isn't forgiving of mistakes. It's most likely de Bevoir is dead for having failed to bring Borwyn to his knees.'

'Oh.' Linota's heart skipped a beat.

'Here we are.' Erik drew to a stop. 'I never saw de Bevoir and Isabel here, but I believe this is where they stayed when they were in Borwyn.'

Linota stepped into a small square building. 'What is this place?'

'It was a trading post, but it flooded a few times and so we abandoned it and moved the operation to the centre of the town. The building has been deserted for some time, but locals saw a man who fits de Bevoir's description coming and going a few times. Another person heard a child crying on two occasions.'

Erik grimaced and Linota reached up to smooth out the lines that creased his forehead. She slowly rubbed the skin and then dropped her hand. It wasn't right to touch him when he wasn't hers.

Erik blinked. 'There were some blankets upstairs. They looked like they had been recently slept in when I found them. We can take a look, but there really isn't anything to see.'

Linota climbed up the staircase at the back of the room. Now that the sun had set there was very little light left to see anything. She walked around the edges anyway. There were a few blankets dumped in the corner, but otherwise the space was empty.

'Linota.'

She stilled at the sound of her name on his lips.

'There is nothing to see. I cannot produce evidence to prove that I was telling the truth about Mary and I may never be able to. I'm sorry that I hurt you. Sorrier than you will ever know. But this has to end now. Please let me escort you back to the fortress.'

'I believe you,' she whispered.

'What?'

'I believe you about Mary. I believe that Isabel exists and I believe that you thought you were doing the right thing by me, even though it wasn't.'

'Linota.' He breathed heavily, stepping towards her in the darkness. 'You don't have to—'

'I know,' she said, closing the distance between them.

She stood on her tiptoes. She was going to kiss him. She'd longed for the taste of him for so long before today and now he was here and she was going to damn the consequences.

Her lips lightly brushed his. It wasn't enough. She moved forward to kiss him again, but he leaned away.

He frowned down at her. 'Why didn't you go through with the marriage to Borwyn?'

'I...' she said, but her words got stuck in her throat.

By returning to Borwyn she'd hoped to understand Erik's motives, but she'd never given any thought to what might happen afterwards. Hadn't dared to believe that what had occurred between them had been any more than him using her for his own needs. But now the look in his eyes, the hope and light that shone in their depths, had her heart racing.

Erik swallowed. 'I thought maybe...'

His gaze locked with hers and she couldn't look away.

'What did you think?' she whispered.

'I thought, maybe... I hoped that...you didn't go through with it because of what you said to me.'

'I...' She inhaled deeply, trying to find the words.

There was a sickening thud and Linota screamed as Erik's solid body pitched forward into hers.

Linota tried to save them both, but Erik was a wall of muscle and there was little she could do to stop them crashing to the ground. Her head hit the floor with a resounding crack. Her stomach roiled with nausea. She tried to move to her side, but Erik's weight pinned her down.

The world swam around her. She tried to suck in a breath, but she couldn't get enough air to her lungs.

Above her loomed a dark shape. She squinted, but the world was still spinning.

There was a grunt and muffled cursing. Erik stirred above her and then his weight disappeared. There was another sickening crunch of something hitting bone and Erik stopped moving completely. She reached out to touch him, but he was pulled away from her.

'No,' she shouted, scrambling to hold on to him.

Another curse and then pain exploded in her head as she was backhanded across the face. While she gasped she heard the sound of his body being pulled across the floor and then dumped to the ground with a solid thud.

She tried to push herself to her knees, but her body wasn't co-operating. The room was swirling alarmingly.

Her breath came in hurried pants as footsteps moved towards her.

She was powerless to stop the meaty hands that grabbed her arms and bound them behind her back. She tried to resist, but she was dragged, on her knees, across the floor and dumped next to Erik's body. The footsteps moved away again.

'Please don't be dead,' she muttered as she tried to turn towards Erik's body.

Without her arms and with the world spinning violently it was difficult to move. After several long moments she managed to face him, her head twisted at an awkward angle to her body.

He did not look good. Blood rushed down the side of his face from a deep cut in his forehead and his skin was an alarming shade of white, but…she squinted to make sure and…yes, he was breathing.

Tears pricked her eyes and she blinked rapidly to stop them falling. She couldn't afford to be blinded right now.

'Erik, wake up,' she hissed.

Her heart leapt as he moaned deeply.

'Wake up,' she said, louder this time.

'It won't do either of you any good if he does wake, Mistress Leofric.' Linota closed her eyes. Surely it couldn't be de Bevoir? Not after all this time. What did he hope to gain by this madness? 'It's no use trying to get closer to him either.'

Linota cried out as de Bevoir's fingers bit into her arm. Worse still, Erik didn't stir at the sound. How badly had de Bevoir hit him? Without Erik's strength, how could she stop de Bevoir from doing whatever he wanted with her?

Chapter Seventeen

Erik's head pounded. His eyelids were so heavy. He tried to crack them open, but he only managed a tiny slit. Wherever he was there wasn't much light. He tried to search his memory as to how he had ended up with his head pounding but he couldn't remember drinking too much ale. He licked his top lip and tasted blood.

There was a rustling to his left and a slight whimper. His heart stilled as the sound registered: Linota.

He fought the instinct to call out her name. Something bad had happened and he'd been knocked out cold, but he couldn't quite recall what had caused him to be lying in a heap.

He closed his eyes. The last thing he remembered clearly was… Linota, a shaft of light illuminating her face. She was telling him something, something important, but the images slipped from his mind like wisps of smoke on an evening breeze.

He wanted to call out to her to find out if she was all right, but he clenched his jaw, fighting the impulse. Staying silent would give him an advantage.

'You put your faith in the wrong person, Mistress Leofric.' Erik's heart stilled. He'd recognise that voice anywhere. De Bevoir was here in the room with them; Erik should have known. All his bad moments had been because of this man. He clenched his fists; it was time to end him once and for all. He forced himself to breathe evenly as de Bevoir continued. 'Perhaps if you'd stayed in the castle like the lady you are supposed to be then you wouldn't be in this mess. But you had to follow this piece of vermin around.' De Bevoir kicked Erik in the ribs and he bit down to stop himself from grunting as the air left his lungs.

'What do you want from me?'

Erik cringed. Linota's words were brave, but the wobble in her voice betrayed her; he would get her out of here. He would continue that kiss and then...

'What do I want from you? That's an interesting question, Mistress Leofric. What I really want is to have my life back. It was comfortable living as Garbodo's steward. But thanks to your imbecilic lover I no longer have that option.'

Erik tugged on the ropes that bound him. They were crudely knotted, but still tight. He pulled on them again, harder this time. The bindings burned against his skin, but he didn't care; he needed to be quick. He wanted Linota out of here and away from this madman.

He cracked open his eyes, wider this time. He was lying in the corner of the room; Linota was some way over, slumped at an unnatural angle.

He fought the rage back down and tried to think through the cloud of pain fogging his brain.

'I'll tell you what I want,' continued de Bevoir. 'I

want your ransom. Borwyn was prepared to pay it once before, I'm sure he will agree to it again, perhaps more now he is marrying your sister. He might even give me something for his bastard half-brother.'

'He'll think you're lying.' Linota's voice was hoarse, as if she were holding back tears. Erik's rage built. De Bevoir would pay for causing Linota even a moment of pain. Erik would make sure of it.

De Bevoir snorted. 'If he doubts me, I'll send him your lengthy plait and something more personal of Erik's. I'm sure the Earl will come round quick enough.'

How was it that de Bevoir managed to sound as if he were discussing something pleasant at the feasting table while all the time spouting such insanity? Because the man was clearly insane. Erik had been distracted by Linota's sweet mouth earlier and de Bevoir had been able to sneak up on him. That would not happen again.

It seemed Linota agreed. 'Erik won't let you hurt me.'

'Oh, I wouldn't worry about being harmed, my dear lady. You'll both be dead soon enough. I'm not so much of a fool as to leave you both alive when this is over. You weren't supposed to live anyway. Borwyn couldn't make the alliance with Ogmore if both Leofric sisters were dead, could he?' De Bevoir laughed and Erik suppressed a shudder. De Bevoir really was insane. 'Erik won't rest until he comes after me. He's already been relentless in his pursuit. I've had to change my hiding places so many times because of him. No, I have no intention of letting either of you live after this is over.'

Linota's small whimper tore at Erik's heart. Erik had to stop listening to de Bevoir's ravings and concentrate on a plan to get them both out of there. A plan that involved Linota leaving without getting wounded in any way.

A small movement, barely perceptible, drew Erik's attention to the corner of the room. He blinked, trying to make out what had changed.

Nothing…and then the flicker again. He held his breath, listening.

The faint press of a footstep and the slight brush of something fabric was all he could make out. De Bevoir continued with his rant, oblivious to the fact that someone else lurked in the shadows.

Or maybe he wasn't.

As the other person stepped into a patch of light, Erik's heart sank and swelled in equal measure. Isabel stood, her back pressed to the wall, her tiny hands clutched in front of her.

Erik had been searching for her for so long it was almost impossible to believe that she was in front of him right now at the worst possible moment. Now he had another person to get out of this situation. But he would save them both, even if he died trying.

Isabel's gaze was fixed on de Bevoir, her eyes so wide Erik could make out the whites surrounding her pupils. Her dress was shabby and torn and she was so thin it looked painful, but he couldn't make out any cuts or abrasions on her; perhaps de Bevoir had left her physically unharmed.

'And…' de Bevoir's rant cut through Erik's thoughts as he got louder, for the first time displaying his agitation '… I've been saddled with Erik's runt of a niece. But I heard an interesting bit of gossip recently. Do you want to know what it is?'

Linota didn't answer.

'It seems the ever-noble Earl of Borwyn is going to claim her as family. Come forward, Isabel.' De Bevoir gestured with his hands and Isabel took a small step forward. 'Closer now.'

Erik watched as Isabel took several trembling steps towards the madman.

De Bevoir grabbed Isabel's face in his hand and turned it to the light. 'She doesn't look anything like the Earl, does she?' He shrugged. 'But if he's willing to publicly claim her as a relative than I'm sure she'll be worth a bit of gold to him. I stand to make enough to live comfortably from all of you. I may travel to France. I've had enough of this poxy country.'

He shoved Isabel away from him. She stumbled and hit the floor with a small thud.

De Bevoir stalked over to Linota and grabbed her by the hair. 'You're coming with me.'

Linota cried out as he pulled her upright. She kicked out at him, connecting with his knees.

De Bevoir stumbled and then righted himself, hitting Linota across the cheek as he stood.

Erik had seen enough.

He powered to his feet and rushed towards de Bevoir, barging into him and knocking him to the floor.

'Get back,' he growled to Linota.

Instead of moving back towards the wall, Linota stepped forward and took Isabel into her arms.

On his back, de Bevoir struggled to push himself away. Erik pressed his foot firmly against de Bevoir's squirming stomach. Even with his hands tied behind his back Erik was far stronger than de Bevoir. De Bevoir's fingers scrabbled against Erik's boot, trying to remove him, but Erik only increased the pressure, pinning the man to the ground.

'Linota, take Isabel and wait for me downstairs.'

'What are you going to do?' Linota's voice trembled, but Erik didn't look up. He wasn't taking his eyes off his slippery adversary.

'I'm going to end this.' De Bevoir's eyes widened. Good, he should be frightened. 'Take Isabel please, Linota.'

He didn't turn to watch as he heard Linota mutter something softly to his niece or even when he heard their soft footsteps descending the stairs.

De Bevoir's bravado returned with their departure. 'You half-baked fool. You're not going to be able to do anything with your hands tied behind your back.'

Erik smiled. 'I wouldn't stake your life on it, if I were you.'

Chapter Eighteen

A cool breeze had picked up while they'd been inside. The small girl shivered and Linota wrapped her arms tightly around Isabel's too-small shoulders.

'We'll be before a warm fire before you know it,' Linota said brightly.

The girl said nothing, only pressing her back into Linota's body.

No sound came from the building behind them. Linota was torn between the urge to take Isabel to the safety of the fortress and the urge to storm back inside to help Erik. He'd powered across the room strongly enough, but his hands had been tied behind his back and blood had seeped from the wound on his forehead.

Bats swooped and whirled above them as time passed without any sign of Erik. Linota's nerves stretched so tightly she was sure they would snap at any moment.

'What's happening?' whispered Isabel. 'Will I have to go back to Master de Bevoir?'

The girl's involuntary shudder told Linota everything she needed to know.

'No! You will never have to go back to that man. We're going to wait until Erik comes back out. If he doesn't, I want you to run to the fortress you can see, high up on the hill, and ask for Mistress Katherine Leofric. That's my sister. You will be safe with her.'

Isabel turned to look up at her. 'What about you?'

Linota smiled. 'I'll be right behind you.'

That seemed to settle the child and one of Isabel's thin arms slipped around Linota's waist. Linota inhaled deeply. Heavy boots sounded from inside the building and she dragged Isabel deeper into the shadows, her heart pounding wildly. She would make sure that Isabel ran, but she wasn't going anywhere unless the person she could hear heading towards them was Erik.

She didn't realise she was holding her breath until Erik appeared in the doorway. Air rushed out of her lungs and her knees weakened. She clutched Isabel's shoulder for support.

Erik scanned the area, his eyes passing over their hiding place.

Linota slipped her hand around Isabel's shoulders and stepped towards him. 'We're here.'

Erik started towards her, raising his arms and then stopping when he caught sight of Isabel.

Linota's heart fell. It looked as if he was about to hold her, but then he'd stopped. Had she missed her last opportunity to be in his arms?

Erik dropped to his haunches. 'Hello, Isabel.'

The little girl clung closer to Linota and she realised just how selfish she was being. Here she was, bemoaning the lack of Erik's body next to hers while this small child's life was in turmoil. Erik hardly looked like a

knight errant either. He was covered in his own blood
and grime streaked down the side of his face.

Linota crouched down slightly to look Isabel in the
eye. 'It's all right, there's nothing to be afraid of. This
is your mama's brother, Erik. He is going to take care
of you.'

Erik tugged at something around his neck and then
he held his hand out. Resting on his palm was the little
horse Linota had seen him with on the night they had
spoken for the first time. 'Do you recognise this, Isabel? It belonged to your mama,' he said softly. 'I made
it for her when she was a little older than you are now.'

Erik continued to hold his arm outstretched. The
horse was so tiny in his huge, calloused hand. After
several long moments Isabel took a step towards him
and took the carving from him. She stared at it for a
long moment and then her tiny fist closed over it. She
didn't say anything, but neither did she cower back into
Linota.

'What happened to de Bevoir?' asked Linota.

Erik's gaze flickered up to her, his jaw tightening.
'There is nothing to fear any more. He won't be coming after us.'

Linota shuddered, but didn't press for details. It was
probably for the best if she and Isabel were left in ignorance about what had happened in the darkness of the
dilapidated building.

Erik cleared his throat and stood to his full height.
'We had best return to the keep.'

Erik didn't speak as they returned to the fortress.

Before de Bevoir's untimely arrival she had been so
sure he'd been about to discuss his feelings for her, but

now he said nothing. Perhaps she had been wrong. She'd told him she loved him, but he'd never said that back to her. He'd never given her reason to hope.

In their months apart, she'd thought her feelings were perhaps just a young girl's dream. A girl who had longed for adventure had fallen in love with a man who had shown her exactly that. She'd hoped that, when she saw him again, he wouldn't loom so large in her mind and that the image she had built up of him in her heart could be dismissed as romantic idealisation.

She'd been wrong.

He was every bit as she'd remembered: strong, amusing and abundantly kind.

Everything he had done, everything he had sacrificed, was for the little girl who now walked between them.

Had any of it been for Linota?

Part of her believed he had kept her safe during their ordeal together because he cared for her. But the other part, the part that was whispering to her now, wondered how much her safety was necessary as part of his plan to save his niece. Oh, she had no doubt he was a good, honourable man, but had she ever been anything special to him? Or would another woman have received exactly the same level of care?

Linota's stomach tightened as they reached the fortress without her having the courage to ask him.

The guards let them pass without comment, but Linota knew it was too much to hope that news of her slightly bedraggled state would not reach her siblings. She didn't care.

'Mistress Leofric.'

Linota's heart sank as Erik addressed her formally. She looked across at him, but she couldn't read the expression in his eyes. She didn't know what he was thinking, or even if he was thinking of her right now.

'Yes,' she said quietly.

'I'm going to take Isabel to the kitchens to get her some food. Will you be all right to return to your chamber from here?'

'Oh, yes,' she said, her heart twisting. 'Thank you for taking me with you this evening.'

Erik smiled sadly. 'Once again you were harmed on my watch, Mistress Leofric.'

'It was worth it.' Linota nodded down at Isabel and tried to smile. It was hard when her heart hurt so much.

'Thank you,' he said quietly and then he slipped his arm around Isabel's shoulders and led her away.

Linota watched until they had disappeared from sight.

She started to head to her chamber and then stopped. That room held no appeal. Instead she turned and walked quickly towards the chapel.

Her footsteps echoed in the empty room; the air was still and silent.

She slipped into the last pew and rested her head in her hands, fighting the tears which threatened to spill.

She'd done what she'd once thought was impossible. She'd found out what had motivated Erik to keep her hidden from Katherine. She'd forgiven him, or rather, she'd come to the realisation that there was nothing to forgive. Everything he'd done had been to protect an innocent life. He was the honourable and brave man with whom she had fallen in love. There had been no betrayal, only a man forced to act in an impossible situation.

She should be celebrating and yet a rock had settled between her ribs.

She loved him just as much as she ever had. Perhaps more, now that she knew about the lengths he'd undertaken to save his niece.

She clenched her fingers together tightly.

She'd told him she loved him and he hadn't said it back.

They'd been together for most of the evening and he still hadn't said it.

Had she just lost him for a second time?

Chapter Nineteen

'There you are.'

Linota didn't know how much time had passed since she'd stepped into the chapel, but from the look on Katherine's face it had been a while.

'I'm sorry. I didn't mean to worry you. I just needed...'

'I wasn't worried. I know in the past I have been over-protective, but you've proven time and again that you can take care of yourself. I only...wait, have you been crying?' Katherine slipped on to the pew next to her and rested a hand on her arm.

'A little,' Linota confessed.

'Do you want to talk to me about what's upset you?'

Linota took a deep breath and exhaled slowly. 'I love Erik.'

'Ah,' said Katherine, squeezing her arm gently. 'I see.'

'Do you?'

'I suspected as much, but I wasn't sure. You haven't spoken about your time with him. I thought at first you were too hurt by his betrayal, but now I know I was wrong.'

'Are you angry?'

Katherine laughed gently. 'If you had told me that when I first found out he was deliberately keeping you away from me, I would have killed him with my bare hands. Now... I understand him a little better so I would like to know if he feels the same way about you.'

'I don't think he does.'

Katherine tilted her head to one side. 'Why do you think that?'

'He's had plenty of time to tell me so, but he hasn't.'

'Perhaps he doesn't feel that he's worthy of your love.'

Linota straightened. 'He is worthy.'

Katherine smiled. 'I'm not saying that he isn't, only that perhaps that's how he feels. Jarin has told me things about their shared father. He was a hideously vile man. I've no doubt he took great delight in making Erik feel he was worth less than dirt.'

The evening had been such a maelstrom of emotions that Linota didn't know what to think, but if he still believed, after everything that had passed between them, that he wasn't worthy of her love then she needed to tell him. She had to risk her own humiliation just to make sure he knew.

She stood abruptly. 'I need to see Erik.'

'Yes, that's probably for the best. Only Braedan's looking for you right now. Can we go and see him first? You know what he's like. If we don't go and see him, he's bound to think we've been abducted and he'll have the entire fortress searching for us.'

The two women shared an eye-roll over their over-vigilant brother.

'Fine, but I hope it won't take long.' Now she'd made a decision she wanted to act on it before it was too late.

'If he goes on, I promise to try to stop him.'

'Thank you. I'm lucky to have you as my sister.'

'I know.'

Despite her anguish Linota laughed softly.

Linota looked out for Erik as the two of them made their way through the fortress towards Jarin's private chambers. The place was busier than normal, as guests enjoyed the entertainment put on for the feast. She couldn't spot Erik's dark blond head in the crowd and guessed he was still with his niece. She told her foolish heart not to be disappointed.

Linota hadn't been in Jarin's private rooms before and was curious as to what they would look like. That fell away when she stepped inside.

Braedan was standing next to the fireplace, his arms crossed in front of him, a deep scowl furrowing his forehead. Behind him, wearing an uncharacteristic grin, was the Earl of Borwyn, but they could have been standing there wearing nothing but their bare skin for all Linota took notice of them.

Instead, she found herself transfixed by the sight of Erik. He'd wiped the blood from his face, but he was still in his rumpled clothes from earlier, his hair just as unruly.

His gaze locked on to hers as soon as she was through the threshold.

She took a step towards him before stopping.

'I think that gives us our answer,' said Borwyn, slapping Braedan on the shoulders.

Braedan grunted.

'Answer for what?' Linota asked, not taking her eyes off Erik's face. As she stared, the amused twinkle she so adored began to shine once more in the depths of his eyes.

Braedan pushed his hair away from his face. 'Erik has come to me to request a betrothal between yourself and him.' Linota's heart began to pound painfully as heat rushed over her face. 'He has recently taken on the role of master builder...'

Braedan carried on talking, but Linota stopped listening. She could only stare at Erik, getting caught in his blue gaze. His lips tilted slightly and she smiled in response.

'I'm not sure Linota is interested in how she is going to live once she is married right now,' said Borwyn, slapping Braedan on the shoulder once more.

Borwyn appeared to be enjoying himself immensely.

'She hasn't given her consent yet,' growled Braedan. 'You know I said both my sisters could choose whom they marry. I won't have them be miserable in wedlock. Think carefully as to whether you want to accept, Linota. I don't want you to marry a man you don't trust.'

Erik winced and Linota's heart squeezed.

'I trust Erik with my life, my soul and my happiness.'

Erik's smile widened, the lines around his eyes deepening, and Linota's heart thrilled.

'I think we should leave the two of them alone,' said Katherine from behind her. She'd been silent throughout the exchange and Linota had forgotten she was in the room.

Braedan grumbled, not keen to leave them alone together, but Katherine cajoled him out, with Jarin grinning all the while in obvious delight.

It seemed to take an age but eventually the door closed behind them all. She and Erik were finally alone.

Chapter Twenty

Linota stood before Erik, her hands tightly folded in her dress.

Erik wanted to cross the room and pull her into his arms, but first he wanted to be sure that marriage to him was what she wanted. He'd thought so, but she'd not said yes yet.

'Why is Borwyn so amused?' she asked.

'As much as Jarin respects your brother, I think he enjoys it when he is suffering a little. I don't think Sir Braedan made things easy for Jarin when he wanted to marry Katherine.'

'Oh, I didn't—'

'Linota, I may look like I'm calm, but I'm slowly dying over here. Will you give me your answer?'

He nearly laughed at the look on her face, but he didn't. This was too important.

'Answer to what?'

He stepped closer, coming to within a hair's breadth but not actually closing the gap between them. He gazed down into her wide, blue eyes.

'Will you marry me?' he asked softly.

'Are you sure *you* want to marry *me?*' The uncertainty in her voice nearly killed him.

Unable to suppress it any longer, he barked out a laugh. 'I am not worthy of you.'

She muttered darkly and he laughed again. She was a feisty one, his Linota. She would stand her ground and challenge him. He was looking forward to finding out exactly how in the many years to come.

'I don't mean I'm not worthy of you by birth. Only that no one is worthy to be married to you.'

His fingers reached out and lifted a length of her glorious hair. He watched as the candlelight lit up the different shades of gold within the strands. He was going to spend hours exploring her body, learning all the many ways he could bring her pleasure, but for now he was going to make sure she knew there was nothing he wanted more than to be joined with her in marriage.

He dropped to his knees before her, taking her hands in his. 'I love you and want to be married to you more than I have ever wanted anything. Please will you consent to be my wife?'

For a long tortuous minute, she said nothing. His heart began to pound painfully in his chest as the moment stretched. Surely he hadn't been mistaken in her feelings? Surely she still loved him?

'Oh, Erik,' she said eventually, sinking to her knees in front of him. 'I love you so much. Yes, I will be your wife. I thought—'

'What did you think, my love?' he whispered against her lips.

'That—' His tongue flickered against the seam of her

mouth and she opened for him. The first taste was more intoxicating than wine. The second weakened his knees.

'Tell me.' His lips trailed down the length of her neck, his fingers loosening the ties of her tunic.

'I—'

His soul roared in triumph as he slipped her tunic from her body. She was incapable of forming a sentence and he loved it.

He returned to her mouth, his tongue more insistent now. He wanted to consume her. His hands roamed over her body. He wanted to see all of her, but she was kneeling on her dress, pinning it to the floor.

Instead, he pulled her dress down over her shoulders, his hand moving across her skin to trace the small, perfect breasts he had revealed.

She moaned as his fingers skimmed over her nipples and his cock strained towards her, desperate to be inside her, desperate to make her his once and for all.

But he didn't want to rush. He hadn't waited for so long and desired her this much for it to be over in a few short moments. He wanted their first time to last all night, if possible. Hell, he didn't want to move from his chamber for a week.

He moved back slightly to look at her, his resolve nearly breaking as he took in her heavily dilated pupils, her swollen lips and those achingly beautiful breasts peeking over the top of her dress.

'I love you so much. Being married to you is going to be perfect.'

She reached over and gently pushed a strand of hair away from his face. 'You are perfect,' she whispered. 'I love you so much it hurts. Being married to you is going to be…' Her lips quirked. 'Being married to you is going to be an adventure.'

He laughed and pulled her to him. 'We will have an adventure.' He picked her up and carried her over to the bed in the corner. 'Preferably one that doesn't involve risking your life.'

He perched her on the edge of the bed and then knelt between her legs once more. 'I think the first adventure we should undertake is my exploration of your body. Don't you?'

He didn't give her time to answer before he placed his mouth over a nipple, drawing it into his mouth, licking and pulling until her fingers stole into his hair.

He turned his attention to the other breast. His hands, which had been tracing the length of her spine, drifted down her body to the hem of her dress. Slowly he began to trace the delicate shape of her ankle, up over the curve of her calf and around the soft skin of her thigh.

His fingers skimmed over her undergarments, pressing gently against her core. She bucked off the bed and he almost lost control.

He smiled against her breast. She was so close to completion and he'd barely even touched her. He leaned back on his heels to see his handiwork.

Her expression was dazed, her eyes almost completely black, her nipples glistening from his attentions. He pressed another kiss to her mouth while his hands divested her of her clothes.

He lifted his head as her small hand pressed against his shoulder.

'Erik…is this…?'

His fingers slipped over her core and her legs parted

invitingly. He grinned. Right now, with this woman, was where he belonged.

He nipped at the soft flesh behind her ear. 'Is this what, love?'

'This feeling...' she panted '...is it normal?'

His fingers stroked and coaxed, her long low moan his reward.

'Very normal, my love. It will only get better.'

'That's not...that's not possible.'

He laughed and moved down her body, stopping to pay more attention to her breasts. His body was clamouring now, desperate to be inside her, but this was her first time. He was determined to give her everything. He expected nothing in return and the thought humbled him. She was his, now and for evermore, to love and to please.

He moved lower.

'Oh, Erik. I don't think... It's lovely, but... I...'

Erik ran his tongue over her core once more. He wished he could see her face, to watch as she experienced these waves of pleasure, but for now he was focused entirely on her core. He would bring her to completion and next time, next time he brought her to this point, he would watch as she came apart for him.

His fingers joined his tongue and the noises she made ceased to make sense.

His world narrowed until it was only Linota and the way she was moving. Even his own needs fell away as Linota's climax began.

She called out his name as her fingers tugged at his hair. He stayed with her, licking and stroking as she bucked beneath him. Even as the contractions tailed off, he continued to lick her, his touch gradually becoming softer as her breathing slowly returned to normal.

When her muscles finally went limp, he kissed the insides of her thighs, trailing his lips to her knees and then leaning back to look at her.

She was slumped on the bed now, an arm thrown over her eyes.

'That was...' she began, and then she shook her head. 'I can't even describe...'

He stood, adjusting his cockstand as he did so, which was straining against the wool of his braies.

'It was my pleasure to serve you, Mistress Leofric.'

A faint smile crossed her lips. 'Thank you, Rik.'

He growled and peeled her dress from her body. 'I thought we agreed you would never call me Rik.'

'Ah, yes that's right,' she said, a wicked glint in her eyes. 'We agreed on Rikky, didn't we?'

'We absolutely did not,' he said, placing a gentle bite against her collarbone.

She giggled and he grinned. He loved that sound. He would never grow tired of hearing her laughter.

'Erik?' She pushed herself up on to her elbows.

'Yes, love.'

'Can I make you feel like that?'

He swallowed, his throat dry. 'Yes, love.'

She ran her hands over his chest, stopping at the edge of a large bruise. 'Does it hurt?'

'Not any more.'

She smiled her wide, beautiful smile. 'You don't have to be brave for me.'

He brushed his lips over the hollow of her throat.

'I'm not. It hurt like the devil himself had burned me earlier, but now that we're together...'

His mouth closed over hers and he revelled in her delicious moan.

He shrugged out of the rest of his clothes and bought his body flush with hers.

Her hands skimmed over his shoulders and down his back. He hissed as they traced the curve of his buttocks, the gentle touch causing him more pleasure than he'd ever experienced. Her gentle exploration continued over his hip and round to his cock. She hesitated for a moment and then she lightly brushed against it.

He fisted the blanket into his hands as she ran her fingers along its length, not wanting to frighten her with the violence of his response. But, hell...her touch was exquisite.

'Is this...?' she murmured against the skin of his neck.

He could feel the heat of her blush against his jaw.

'If you...' He reached between them and showed her how to wrap her hand around him. He groaned as she moved up and down his length, cautiously at first, but with increasing confidence as his groans filled the air.

He moved his mouth back over hers, his tongue dancing with hers as he became increasingly desperate. 'I want... I want you so badly.'

'Yes,' she whispered.

He groaned in relief. He couldn't take much more of her touch before he spent in her hand like a young lad with no control over his body.

He wanted her with him, to finally make her his.

He moved over her, settling between her thighs and

pushed himself up on to his elbows so he could look into her eyes. 'I love you, Linota.'

'I love you, too.'

He eased into her slowly, kissing the soft skin of her neck, her lush lips and the hard pebbles of her nipples.

She gasped as he filled her to the hilt and he paused, waiting for her to adjust to him. 'Stop me if—'

But she began to move and all words were lost.

The fire was burning low, its flickering glow casting shadows on Erik's sleeping face. Linota curled into his side and ran her fingers over the soft hair on his chest.

His hand moved over her hip, his fingers so warm and sure against her skin.

He was hers now and she was his.

His eyes flickered open.

He smiled as their eyes met. He pressed a kiss to her forehead and pleasure shot through her as potent as the strongest glass of wine.

The heat of his gaze sent flickers of desire racing through her. Her face obviously betrayed her hunger because she felt him hardening against her stomach.

She moaned as his tongue met hers, his kiss like molten fire. For a long moment she lost herself as his hands travelled over her, awakening the sensations that had only recently subsided.

She moved a hand to his chest and gently pressed against him. He lifted his head and looked down at her. 'Before we get carried away again, I want to know what happened after I left you and Isabel.'

His lips grazed her forehead. 'I realised that if I planned to wed you it would be easier to have Sir Braedan agree to the match. I went to see him after I'd fed Isabel. At first he wouldn't listen, but Ellena persuaded him to hear me out. She's looking after Isabel for me now.'

His lips moved further down her body. She sighed in pleasure as they closed over a nipple, licking and sucking until she was almost insensible—almost. 'What did you say to him?' She was embarrassed by her breathy and fluttery voice, so very unlike her normal one.

'I—I told him that I love you and that I will spend the rest of my life making sure you are happier than any other woman in the kingdom.' Erik sounded annoyingly composed as his hands took over from his mouth. 'He felt his sister could do better than a master builder.' Linota growled and Erik grinned. 'Jarin stepped in and pointed out that as his brother I was entitled to a living.'

He bent his head and began lavishing attention on her other nipple.

'What…?' She moaned, sliding her fingers into his soft hair. 'What living?'

Erik sighed and rested his forehead against her chest, his warm breath brushing over her sensitive skin. 'Jarin wants to give me a stronghold to live in and oversee. It's only an afternoon's ride along the estuary from here. It's a comfortable living. Or I can stay in my position as master builder and we can live here. There's also Ogmore's dowry to consider. I told them you and I would decide on our future together. Now, can I carry on?'

He bent his head once more and moved over her breasts, his fingers slipping between the curls at the top of her thighs.

'I want to live in your cottage,' she said in a rush.

'Me, too, love, but I suppose we may have to make do with living in luxury.' He smiled against her skin. 'Now, I can't be doing this properly if you are still able to think. Perhaps if I…'

His fingers danced over the sensitive flesh between her thighs. Her legs fell open as her grip on his hair tightened. He continued to worship her body until the only sounds she could make were desperate, pleading gasps.

'That's better, my love,' he whispered against her skin.

She shook her head against the mattress. She might be incoherent, but he was still able to speak. This would not do. She pushed against his chest. He lifted his head, a slight frown between his eyebrows.

'You want me to stop?'

She nodded.

His fingers brushed her core. 'Are you sure?'

She closed her eyes as pleasure shot through her again. She bit her lips and pushed him, harder this time. He rolled on to his back and she ran her gaze down the length of his body. His muscled chest was scarred and bruised. She had never seen anything as magnificent.

She lowered her mouth to the base of his throat and began to move her lips over his body. Very shortly, he lost his ability to speak in full sentences, too.

Epilogue

Erik fisted his hands behind his back, hiding them from Jarin. He didn't want his brother to know how badly they were shaking.

The grin Jarin shot him suggested he knew. Wisely, though, he kept his mouth shut.

Erik tightened his fists, battling with himself to remain calm. His body was acting as if it was sure Linota was in the process of fleeing the fortress and yet he was absolutely sure that she would come to him today.

After what felt like a thousand lifetimes the door to the chamber opened. The air whooshed out of his lungs as Linota stepped over the threshold.

The gold seams running through her ornate dress picked out the golden threads in her hair so that she appeared to shimmer. She paused, a wide smile crossing her face as she caught his gaze and his heart stuttered.

Her family filed in behind her, but he didn't spare them a second glance.

By the time she'd crossed the room he'd stopped shaking. He reached out and took her hands in his, her skin soft and delicate against his rough calluses.

'You're so beautiful,' he murmured.

'So are you.'

He laughed softly. 'Are you ready?'

'I've been ready for a long time.'

He brushed the backs of her hands with his thumbs. This was it; this was the moment he'd longed for ever since he'd first caught sight of her.

'Then let's begin.'

She laughed, the sound so joyous his heart soared.

'I love you,' he said, as the ceremony to bind them together for ever began.

* * * * *

If you enjoyed this book, why not check out these other great reads by Ella Matthews

The Warrior Knight and the Widow
Under the Warrior's Protection